# From *A Hive of Suspects*

The superstitious natives of some primitive places believe in making all the noise they can outside a house of mourning to scare away demons coming for the soul of the dead. Anyone might have thought this was what was going on in the garden, though Jason Prendergast's religion had been Presbyterian, and his soul, if still in any way linked with his body, would be at the County Hospital by now, so that any demons in the offing would have come to the wrong address.

Penrose, the dour chauffeur, was there drumming with a spanner on an empty petrol tin. Vera Byrne was beating the dinner gong, while Mickser thumped a watering can with his fist. Mrs. Teely was calling out instructions, and Mollie Gildea was laughing helplessly on the garden seat.

Mickser had been the first to notice the bees, when he made for the open after his interrogation. Now they filled the air, thirty or forty thousand of them, moving very fast and buzzing very loud. At present they were not going anywhere in particular, just whirling round and round like a dark snowstorm. The idea of the noise was to make them think thunder was coming and cause them to settle, but these bees did not seem easy to deceive.

Whatever feelings it may inspire, a swarm happening close at hand is something you cannot just ignore. Even police discipline gave way, and everybody hurried out on to the lawn.

# Books by Sheila Pim

## Crime Fiction

*Common or Garden Crime* (1945)
(reissued by Rue Morgue, 2001)
*Creeping Venom* (1946)
*A Brush with Death* (1950)
*A Hive of Suspects* (1952)
All of Pim's detective novels are
to be reprinted by
The Rue Morgue Press

## Novels of Irish life

*The Flowering Shamrock* (1949)
*Other People's Business* (1957)
*The Sheltered Garden* (1965)

## Nonfiction

*Getting Better* (1943)
*Bringing the Garden Indoors* (1949)
*The Wood and the Trees* (1966, 1984)

# A Hive of Suspects

An Irish Village Mystery by
## Sheila Pim

The Rue Morgue Press
Boulder, Colorado

Author's Acknowledgments

In writing this story I have depended greatly on the help of
beekeeping friends. I must particularly thank Mr. R.N. Tweedy
for putting me in touch with The Bee Research Association,
and Dr. Eva Crane, Direction of the Association. For help in
other directions, some better unspecified, I am much indebted
to my friend Mr. Murrough O'Brien.

I also take this opportunity of thanking the Detective Branch
and the Technical Bureau of the Civic Guard for their mag-
nanimous assistance with this and earlier books, in which, I
am very conscious, I have done them less than justice.

SHEILA PIM

Publishers' Acknowledgment

The publishers are indebted to The Historical Society of the
Religious Order of Friends in Dublin for their help in compil-
ing information on the life of Sheila Pim for the introduction
to *Common or Garden Crime* as well as the condensed ver-
sion found in the present volume.

*A Hive of Suspects*
Copyright © 1952
Copyright © 2001
ISBN: 0-915230-38-0

The Rue Morgue Press
P. O. Box 4119
Boulder, Colorado 80306

Printed by Johnson Printing
Boulder, Colorado

# About Sheila Pim

SHEILA PIM took to crime, as she put it in the dedication to her second mystery, *Creeping Venom*, for her father's sake. Frank Pim loved his thrillers but was unable to get as many as he would like in neutral Ireland during World War II. Her first effort, *Common or Garden Crime*, was set in 1943 and published in 1945, followed a year later by *Creeping Venom*. *A Brush with Death* appeared in 1950 and *A Hive of Suspects* was released in England in 1952 and the following year in the United States, the only book of hers to appear in the U.S. in her lifetime. Two other books, *Other People's Business* (1957) and *The Sheltered Garden* (1964) had some mystery elements but were primarily novels of Irish life, prompting some reviewers to describe her as the Irish Angela Thirkell. Gardening was a key element in all of her books.

She was born in Dublin on September 21, 1909, of a Quaker father and an English mother. Her twin brother Andrew survived only two weeks. She had a second brother, Tom, two years her senior, who was born developmentally disabled and would need constant supervision for most of his life. Sheila bore the brunt of this care, as well as the maintenance of her father's home, after her mother died in 1940. Prior to this, she was educated at the French School in Bray, County Wicklow, and "finished" at La Casita in Lausanne, Switzerland, where she perfected her French. In 1928, she went to Girton College, Cambridge, where she took a Tripos in French and Italian and passed some of the happiest days of her life. Shortly before finals, her mother took ill and Sheila returned to Ireland to look after her and to provide some diversion for brother Tom.

Although she was forced to abandon any thought of formal training in botany, she became an enthusiastic amateur and contributed many essays to the Irish magazine, *My Garden*. Several of these were collected and published in 1949 in a slender volume entitled *Bringing the Garden Indoors* (a selection from which can be found on page opposite the opening chapter). Her major work in this field, however, was the biography of another gifted horticultural amateur, Augustine Henry, an Irish doctor who was one of the foremost plant collectors of his age. *The Wood and the Trees* was published in 1966 and revised and reissued in 1988.

After her father's death in 1958 and Tom's in 1964, Sheila threw herself into her activities at the Historical Society of the Religious Order of Friends, researching and conserving archival embroideries and portraits. At about this same time, she began an involvement with the Irish Travellers which she would continue for the rest of her life. Ostracized by much of Irish society, the Travellers are a nomadic people native to Ireland who follow a gypsy-like life and speak their own language, Shelta, which is closer to English than to Irish. Travellers are sometimes known as Tinkers—now considered a derogatory term—partly because many of them worked as tinsmiths, as well as itinerant farm laborers and door-to-door salesmen. Pim took many Traveller children into her home and eventually adopted an entire family which had been abandoned to the care of their travelling grandfather.

In Sheila Pim's last years, her growing deafness forced her to move into a sheltered housing complex where she still managed to grow a few herbs by her door. She fell ill and died on December 16, 1995, at the age of 86. For more information on Pim and her books see Tom and Enid Schantz' lengthy introduction to *Common or Garden Crime* (Rue Morgue Press, 2001).

# A Hive of Suspects

# Garden tips from Sheila Pim's
## *Bringing the Garden Indoors*

### <u>June</u>

*For Weddings:*

In Japanese flower arrangment a combination of roses with a branch of old pine symbolizes eternal youth and is considered appropriate for festive occasions, especially weddings.

For wedding guests who must throw things, provide bowls of rose petals, or peony petals, anything rather than confetti. It is kinder to the happy couple and to the charwoman who sweeps up.

*Miniature Roses:*

Under this heading I count every kind of rose with a small flower, whether it grows on a full-sized bush, like the "Threepenny-bit" rose, or properly belongs, like *Rouletti* or *Peon*, to the dolls' house garden.

The "Threepenny-bit" rose is the briar type, single, white, with pink-tipped petals, and not much larger than a coin. It is delightfully free flowering, but hardly one to cut. More suitable for miniature vases is a kind of small rose the same shape as modern hybrid teas. I can give only one name, "Bouton d'or.' They are worth enquiring for from specialist nurserymen.

At a show recently I saw an exquisite small rose labeled "Maltese Rose." Now, if this was the true Maltese Rose, it is not supposed to be taken out of Malta and must have been smuggled away. Having seen it, I can understand the temptation and will not strike a moral attitude. Is it fair to forbid the spread of varieties if they can be propagated from slips without injury to the parent bush?

# CHAPTER ONE

ON A HOT JUNE afternoon Edward Gildea, solicitor,was sitting in his office in Drumclash wondering whether his bees had swarmed since morning, and whether he would be justified in getting home a little early for once. He had both windows and his door wide open, but the windows were small and the house was in the middle of the town, and more dust came in than fresh air. There were voices below, to which Edward listened with apprehension. Then his clerk came in with a letter. Edward's face fell; he knew the handwriting.

It was headed: "Coppermine House, Morna," and ran

"Dear Mr. Gildea,
I have some instructions to give you and should be glad if you could make it convenient to come at once. Penrose will drive you back. Please bring my will with you.
Yours sincerely,
JASON PRENDERGAST
P.S. You might also bring your bee veil."

The chance of escape was lost, and driving out to Coppermine House was only one degree better than staying in the office. Edward groaned in spirit, but he got the will out of his safe and his bee veil out of his cycle bag, told his clerk he would not be back again, and accompanied Penrose, the chauffeur, to the glossy saloon car he had in waiting.

Edward would have brought the bee veil in any case. He kept it handy in the swarming season, because as Hon. Secretary of the Drumclash and District Beekeepers' Association he was liable to receive sudden S.O.Ss. Old Jason Prendergast was not a member of the Association, but nevertheless he felt himself entitled to make use of Edward's beekeeping skill as an extension of his professional services. When he sent for the solicitor to come to his house it often turned out that the bees required some manipulation.

Drumclash is a small country town. The car soon left it behind and followed the main road through fields to where wooded hillsides closed in on a river gorge. This was the Vale of Morna, a celebrated beauty spot. It was just then almost at the annual peak of its loveliness. The woods, mainly of oak, were in fresh full leaf, and though the bluebells were over and the hawthorn hedges were shedding their flowers, there were still rhododendrons; they like the soil and climate of the valley, and every cottage garden had its white or rosy bush.

The one blot on the landscape was the copper mine. You came on it suddenly round a bend: heaps of yellow rubble with bare rocks above them; screes scarring the hillside; chimneys and other erections against the sky at the top. The chimneys were old and ruinous, some mantled with ivy. Edward knew ravens built in them. Indeed, some aspects of the mine had a Gothic charm, and to jaded tastes the colors of the screes and slag heaps might form an interesting foil to the more conventional attractions of Morna's woods and streams. Or so it had seemed before the war. Parts of the workings dated back to the Normans, but the mine had never been more than a small-scale undertaking. There had been a burst of activity in the eighteenth and nineteenth centuries, but it had all come to an end after making one family rich..

Then Jason Prendergast had met a mining engineer called Sheed, who had pointed out that, although the copper was all worked out, wartime prices and modern machinery would make it an economic proposition to mine for zinc and lead. They entered into partnership. Old shafts were reopened and new ones begun. Huts appeared in the valley and hoists and cages on the skyline. More of the green banks disappeared under yellow slag. Everyone who cared for the amenities of the Vale was scandalized. There were protests, letters to the paper, talk of a petition, though nothing came of it. The firm of Prendergast and Sheed remained unaffected, made money, and silenced opposition by some well-placed subscriptions to local charitable funds. After the war they closed down. Jason Prendergast retired and settled down to live in the old nineteenth-century mine manager's house, in the very middle of the desolation. His partner occasionally came down to spend a weekend with him but otherwise he had few visitors. He never did anything to reinstate himself with his neighbors, and people who approached him for subscriptions nowadays met with disappointment.

The car turned off the main road into a steep and narrow lane that wound its way right into the heart of the mine. This was a strange region. The lower slopes were old slag heaps covered with a growth of scrubby heath and a scattering of fir trees. A stream, bright yellow with iron oxides, gushed down from an opening through a deep channel artificially made to drain it off. Higher up, the road turned on the brink of a chasm, skirting precipices of sheer slate where a part of the mine had once fallen in. There was no through way, the end was at the old chimneys at the very top.

Coppermine House was rather more than halfway up and formed an unexpected oasis. It stood on a flat terrace of its own, a green rectangle of lawn in front and a kitchen garden behind. One tall, solitary copper beech spread its branches over the lawn. Beyond the terrace the ground dropped away, shelving steeply, and a magnificent view opened up across the valley, over the tops of the oak woods and the cottages and gardens along the road to Morna. Behind the beech tree, to the left, stood out one huge bluff of rock called the Bell Rock. Its sides sheered straight down to the main road two hundred feet below.

The house itself was a Victorian villa with some romantic Victorian features. The walls were slated right to the ground. A glass porch was stuck on sideways in front. But what gave the façade a touch of distinction and a pleasing individuality were five weathered green canopies, shaped like cockleshells, hooding the tops of the five upper story windows. Other houses in the Vale had similar, though not identical, adornments, all made of copper from the mine.

Owing to the configuration of the ground, the yard and garage were out in front, near the garden gate, and there the car stopped. Walking into the garden, Edward Gildea was surprised to find people there, two young women and a man, sitting out near the base of the Bell Rock.

One of them was Jason Prendergast's niece, Phoebe. She had caused some excitement when she first came to keep house for him about two years ago. She was a beautiful, smartly dressed girl, and local gossips thought her position in the house ambiguous, until they found out who she was. There had been a Prendergast brother who cast off his family and married an actress, and this was their daughter. Phoebe was also an actress and said to have talent. She had already made quite a name in Dublin theatrical circles, but had given up her career to come and live with her uncle.

Phoebe Prendergast did not seem cut out for country life, and it was difficult to imagine what she and her uncle could have in common. Edward Gildea had felt sorry for the girl and had got his wife to invite her to tea once or twice to meet other neighbors, but they were afraid she had found them all very dull and were discouraged from trying again. Edward was pleased to see her with friends of her own, for he did not think she often had visitors. These looked like theatrical people. They stared at him as he passed and Edward, slightly embarrassed, lifted his hat to Phoebe. He thought she looked startled to see him, wondered why, and decided it must have been imagination.

A minute or two later he was shown into Mr. Prendergast's study, a room furnished exactly like an office. Old Mr. Prendergast was at his desk; it was his usual seat of operations and Edward would have been surprised to see him sitting anywhere else. He had a tray with the remains of tea in front of him. Without getting up he asked Edward to ring the bell for the maid to take it away. As an afterthought, he asked if Edward would have some, but Edward felt he was not meant to say "Yes," much as he would have liked a cup.

Jason Prendergast had faded but lively brown eyes in a face with nothing superfluous about it, no color, no hair, no eyelashes. He always wore a starched white collar, even in the country. His method of making conversation was to cross-question people. While waiting for the maid to remove the tray he ascertained how many hives of bees Edward Gildea had this year, how many pounds of sugar he had fed them in the winter, how many pounds of honey he expected to get from the early flow, which was just coming to an end with the hawthorn and fruit blossom, and how much of it would be in sections or frames for extraction. He turned each reply over in his mind before putting the next question, but made no comments.

When the maid had gone, he produced his own copy of the will, which he had been hiding under a newspaper, and came to business.

Edward Gildea had drawn up this will himself, not very long before. He approved of it. Apart from legacies to the servants it left everything to Phoebe Prendergast, in consideration of her devoting herself to her uncle in his old age. Though Jason Prendergast lived simply he was a rich man, and his niece, whether she knew it or not, was heiress to about fifty thousand pounds. Edward thought this was not bad compensation for the waste of a few years, and that even if the girl was having a dull time now she could look forward to the future.

It certainly could not be much of a life for her, alone with her uncle, for Jason Prendergast was out of sympathy with all her interests and ambitions. His tastes were for solitude and quiet. He did nothing much all day except potter round his bees. The theater was to him a world of extravagance and folly, his attitude to it was completely puritanical, and he was anxious to cut his niece off from the stage for ever.

The reason he had sent for Edward Gildea was to add a codicil to his will, making it a condition of Phoebe's inheritance that she must never act again.

Edward Gildea did not like this idea. He guessed the provision would be unwelcome to Phoebe. (He thought of the lively group in the garden, and wondered if Mr. Prendergast knew who they were and whether he approved of their being there.) Moreover, on principle, he was against tying up legacies that might lead to complications. He studied the draft wording which his client laid before him and asked, "What if she breaks her promise?"

"Then she forfeits the lot," said Jason Prendergast, disposing impatiently of a silly question.

"And then what becomes of it?"

"I don't care who gets it so long as she doesn't."

"Your other relations?"

The old gentleman paused to reflect. "No," he said: "Not Clementina Teely. I won't leave her a penny. I've already told her she's wasting her time enquiring after my health. There isn't anyone else, unless Hector's still alive in Canada. Don't suppose he is after fifty years. See what you mean, though. I hadn't taken the time to think it out. I'll send you on a list of charities."

"You could do that, of course," said Edward. "Then, who's to see that the condition is enforced? Are you going to appoint trustees?"

"Have to, shan't I?" replied the old man. "Appoint Sheed, and put down ten thousand to go into his pocket, if Phoebe runs off the rails."

"Henry Alexis Sheed, your executor and former partner?"

"That's the man."

"Isn't it putting him in an awkward position?"

"Not Henry," said Mr. Prendergast complacently. "I can rely on him to keep his eye on the main chance."

Edward Gildea did not think much of this as a testimonial to Mr. Sheed's character.

"Another thing," he said, continuing to argue, "what exactly would constitute a return to the stage? Your niece might take part in an amateur performance."

"Not if she wanted to live on my money."

"It would be unpaid work."

"It would be acting, and, contrary to the spirit of her promise. I want no room led for ambiguities. The lawyers aren't going to get anything to pick over in any will of mine."

He darted a look at Edward as if in hopes he might take exception to this remark. Edward disappointed him, however. He merely said, "You know, sir, there are a good many ins and outs to this. Hadn't you better take a few days to think it over?"

" No, I hadn't," snapped Mr. Prendergast. "You understand quite well what I want. I'm paying you to put it into legal jargon and make it watertight. If you can't, say so, and I'll go to somebody who can."

"Well, I'll, do my best," said Edward dubiously.

"Yes, you get on with it," said Mr. Prendergast. "I don't like any shilly-shallying over a will. Once you know what you want, get it down in black and white as soon as you can. 'We know not the day nor the hour.' "

There was no gainsaying this solemn reflection. Edward Gildea looked at his client thoughtfully, wondering how old he was. He looked as if he might live many years yet. If Phoebe had an overmastering vocation for the stage she might run away, but if she stuck it out, perhaps by the time she came into her fortune she would have lost touch with her old life—you soon dropped out of things in the theater—and the codicil would make no difference.

He knew Mr. Prendergast too well ever to argue with him, except on practical matters. If he was determined to blight his niece's ambitions, or, as he probably saw it, to save her from herself, he was not going to change his mind at the pleading of a country solicitor. There did not seem anything to be done, except take as long as one could drawing up the codicil, to give the testator time to relent of his own accord, unlikely as that might be.

Mr. Prendergast put his will away in a drawer, locked it up, and put the keys on a ring attached to one end of his watch chain. Summer and winter, he always wore a waistcoat and carried his watch on a silver chain in the pocket. He rose briskly to his feet, saying, "Brought your bee veil?"

Edward produced it, grinning. His client explained that he wanted help with putting a super-clearer on a hive. They moved out into the garden, where they found Phoebe alone.

She was sitting staring into space, in a moody attitude, though it was a graceful pose, enhanced by one of the fashionable frocks she always wore, whether there was anybody to appreciate them or not. The chief thing Edward Gildea remembered about her face was her large dark eyes, so different from her uncle's, though they might both have started out with the same kind in childhood, for dark eyes were a Prendergast family characteristic.

Jason Prendergast called across the lawn, making her start.

"Have they gone?"

She turned, rose, and came towards them, saying "How do you do," civilly to Edward, but looking past him at her uncle.

"Have they gone?" repeated Jason Prendergast.

"If you mean Mr. and Mrs. Claremorris," said Phoebe, "they didn't get much encouragement to stay."

As usual Jason Prendergast made no comment, words being among the things he never wasted. He lowered his bee veil and tucked it into his coat collar, and it is difficult to argue with anyone through a bee veil.

The tension made Edward Gildea nervous. He remarked unnecessarily, "Going to have a look at the hives."

"So I see," said Phoebe, turning her large dark eyes on him. "I shall remove myself to a safe distance."

At a previous meeting Edward had tried in vain to convince her that bees do not sting on sight. For some reason she had a horror of them. It was useless telling her that bees only sting in self-defense or defense of the hive and the queen or that a bee can only sting once and loses its life in the act. She believed egocentrically that every bee was out to leave its mark on her.

Edward, launched on a pet subject, defended bees and tried to reassure her, but she would not listen to him. She said, "Look what happened to poor Mr. Sheed last time he was staying here! He was badly stung, walking in the garden. His hands were all swelled up. It was terrible. And he never goes near the hives."

"How did it happen?" asked Edward, but he never got to the bottom of the story, for Jason Prendergast was showing signs of impatience. Phoebe, with a shrug of her shoulders, left them and went into the house.

A super-clearer is a device for clearing bees out of "supers," i.e., upper chambers of the hive. It is a board of just the right size to fit over the top of the brood box and has an opening in it fitted with a one-way device which allows the bees to go down but not up again. After it has been in place for about twenty-four hours the bees should all have gone down, leaving the space above clear for the beekeeper's operations. When honey has to be removed from a hive this is a great improvement on the old method of smoking the bees to death, but bees, unaware that it all comes of consideration for their comfort, are inclined to resent the intrusion of this barrier between them and their stores, and it is one of the jobs at which even good beekeepers may get stung.

Edward was not surprised to find that he had the worst end of it. It was he who had to hold up the crate of honey sections, weighing about twenty pounds and packed with bees. He held it over the hive while Mr. Prendergast slipped the super-clearer into place, taking his time over it and fussily adjusting its position to the last millimeter. Fortunately Edward was too well used to this sort of thing to be nervous, and as not being nervous is really the whole art of beekeeping, he came out of the operation unscathed.

Mr. Prendergast then indicated that that would be all for today and summoned the chauffeur to drive Edward Gildea home.

They went back to the Drumclash office as Edward had to collect his bicycle, and in the town he remembered something that had been puzzling him. " Claremorris," the name of Phoebe Prendergast's friends, had seemed familiar. Now he saw it on showcards in shop windows and bills stuck on telegraph poles:

THE HUMPHRY MADIGAN COMPANY
with
HUMPHRY MADIGAN
and
GRANIA CLAREMORRIS
present
A SEASON OF HIGH-CLASS DRAMA
etc., etc.

There was more of it than he had bothered to read. He had taken it for granted they could not be anything but the average motley crowd of barn-stormers. But if they were friends of Phoebe Prendergast's they might be some good, and those two had looked quite prosperous. He wished he had asked Phoebe what the show was like, for Mollie, his wife, enjoyed a good play and might like to go one night. Still it wouldn't have done to mention it in front of Jason Prendergast.


## CHAPTER TWO

EDWARD GILDEA was relieved to find that his own bees had not swarmed after all that hot afternoon, and as the fine weather seemed set to continue, he took steps to prevent them by splitting his strongest stock into two. A few days later he was looking to see if the old queen was laying, and if the other half of the colony were rearing a new one. He had the roof off a hive, tools scattered round, and a cloud of flying bees round his veiled head, when he became aware of Mrs. Gildea hovering in the distance.

He was in a strong position for ignoring interruptions, but Mollie Gildea's agitated signals, and the fact that she called him "Edward," whereas to her he was usually "Ned," suggested that something important demanded his attention. He steered clear of the bees and came near enough to ask what had happened.

Mollie said, "Old Mr. Prendergast's dead.'"

"To hell with him!" said Edward.

Then he explained that of course he had not meant to say anything of the sort, only a few minutes more or less would not make any difference to Mr. Prendergast, and he liked to do one thing at a time. Mollie Gildea said that was all very well, but Penrose, the chauffeur was waiting. He had brought a note from Phoebe Prendergast, who wanted Edward to go there at once, and there he was, sitting in the car in the road, where he might easily have overheard.

This man Penrose was an unprepossessing person. He had driven Edward to and fro on several occasions, but Edward had never known him to smile or speak unless he was spoken to. It was to be hoped he had not heard, but the Gildeas would never know from his face, the expression of which was always immovable and dour.

Phoebe's note, written in a very feminine and ornamental hand, said that her uncle had been taken ill mysteriously and died the night before. He had been found lying unconscious in the study by the maid when she went to take the tea tray away. At first they thought it was a stroke, but the doctor did not feel satisfied and there would have to be an inquest, so she would be very glad to have Mr. Gildea's advice.

Edward resignedly closed up his beehive and tidied up his impedimenta. When he went indoors to change he found Mollie changing too.

"I thought I'd come with you," she explained. "Don't you think you may need support?"

Edward thought he would. Mollie might certainly be more comfort to Phoebe. He did not much look forward to coping with a highly strung young woman suffering from bereavement and shock. Mollie knew how he felt, and she was always ready to do a kind thing when she could, but also she had a feminine grasp of the details of a situation and acted with a practical end in view.

She said, looking seriously at her own face in the mirror, "I wonder if this means Vera Byrne will be out of a job?"

"Who's Vera Byrne?" said Edward.

"The maid, of course. One of the railway station Byrnes who are most respectable, and she's such a capable all-round woman."

Edward saw the point. Their daily help was unreliable and Mollie had dreams of replacing her with a real maid who would live in. He said, "I shouldn't try and engage her today."

"Don't be silly," said Mollie. "All the same," she added, after placing a "Kirbigrip" thoughtfully in her shingle, "one might pave the way with tact. Because I'm sure Phoebe won't want her much longer. She's bound to return to the stage."

"She won't need to," said Edward.

"Then she does get the money all right?" said Mollie, for her husband never chattered about his clients. "I always wondered. It would have been just like him to go back on her in the end."

"I don't see why you should say that." Apart from not wanting to speak ill of the dead, Edward felt an impulse to defend his client. He suddenly realized that he had liked the old man. Jason Prendergast had had his faults. He had been grasping and antisocial and inconsiderate of other people's convenience, but now that he was dead these seemed to be merely features of a sturdy old character. Besides, Edward found it hard to think that anyone who kept bees could be bad at heart. Edward, it must be admitted, was a sentimentalist.

His wife, on the other hand, was preeminently practical and rather inclined to think she knew what was best for everybody. She said, "Phoebe ought to go back to the stage. Her heart is set on it."

"Lots of girls get stagestruck and grow out of it."

"That's a different matter. Anybody can see that girl is a born actress. He shouldn't have tried to keep her here. Oh, she may have been fond of him, in a way, but I do think it's all for the best."

"The stage is a hard life," said Edward.

"But she'd feel it was worth it."

"More fool she," said Edward.

"You have no soul," said Mollie.

Nevertheless, Edward was secretly glad that the codicil had not been signed.


The Gildeas' bungalow was on the slope of a hill above one of the two streams that mingled their waters in the river running through the Vale. From their door a narrow drive descended steeply to a secondary road, just wide enough for two cars to pass. They drove between a scrubby wood and fields hedged with a tangle of hawthorn, dog roses and honeysuckle, brambles and gorse. The fields were swimming gold with buttercups. In cottage gardens here and there grew more exotic plants. The climate of the Vale is such that yuccas, cordyllines and eucalyptuses as well as the rhododendrons and azaleas lend the already lovely scenery a foreign charm.

On the main road between the cliffs and the river a new color note was struck by green and magenta bills pasted up on the flat slabs of rock. They announced in bold black letters:


HUMPHRY MADIGAN

and

GRANIA CLAREMORRIS

A SEASON OF HIGH-CLASS DRAMA


The Gildeas could not read the rest from the car and did not like to ask Penrose to stop and let them look.

In the lane from Coppermine House they met the county ambulance and backed some distance to let it pass. It was taking the remains of Jason Prendergast away for a post mortem.

At the house there were other cars. One was a black Ford Ten which might have belonged to anybody, the other was a more out-of-the-ordinary vehicle and one which the Gildeas recognized. It was a prewar but spick-and-span Baby Austin belonging to a widow lady called Mrs. Clementina Teely. Mollie Gildea screwed up her face.

"What's she doing here?"

"She's a relation," said Edward. "First cousin or something quite close."

"Is she? I never knew that. I suppose she expects to be left something."

Edward was looking at the Ford Ten, and then at a uniformed Civic Guard who stepped out from behind it and saluted with gravity appropriate to the circumstances.

"Morning, Rice," said Edward, recognizing an old acquaintance of the Courts. "I suppose you've come about the inquest."

"Yes, Mr. Gildea," he replied. "The Superintendent's here, sir, and would like a word with you."

That was the first they heard of anything being seriously wrong.

Phoebe Prendergast came down to meet them in the hall, dressed in improvised mourning, a plain white blouse and black skirt, but otherwise looking very much her usual self. She was taking it better than Edward had feared she might, and showed no tendency to dramatize the situation. Perhaps, as Mollie had suspected, she had not been specially fond of her uncle. As she had lost both her parents this was not her first experience of death. At any rate, she was by no means prostrated, and quite able to talk business.

It looked as if there had not after all been much need for Mollie Gildea to come. Phoebe, however, seemed pleased to see her and asked her to go up to her own sitting room on the first floor where she would find Mrs. Teely. One kind of help that might be welcome would be someone to take Mrs. Teely on.

Phoebe took Edward into the study. It looked unfamiliar without Mr. Prendergast at the desk. Instinctively they left his place empty. Phoebe sat down in the windowsill, and Edward took the small chair he usually sat in.

"I'm sorry to have dragged you out in such a hurry," said Phoebe, "but I thought you ought to know what was happening. By the way, there's a Civic Guard Superintendent here who wants to talk to you, but he's busy round at the back."

"An inquest is always painful for the relatives," said Edward sympathetically, "but there's nothing to worry about in that, you know. It's a customary formality in cases of sudden death."

"Yes, I know," said Phoebe, "but in this case it may be rather more than a formality. Uncle's death really was mysterious. The doctor thinks it may have been poison."

Edward was startled. "You don't mean he took his own life!"

The girl shook her head. "Oh no, he'd be the last person in the world to do that. He was perfectly sound in his mind, and there wasn't anything wrong. But it looks as if it must have been something he had for tea. Luckily the remains hadn't been thrown out, so I suppose they'll be able to find out what it was, but he only seems to have had bread and honey."

"Honey?"

"Yes. He took a lot from that hive you were helping him with the other evening."

Sitting on the windowsill, Phoebe had her back to the light. Edward could see the silhouette of her head but not the expression of her face. Her voice told him more. She did sound worried.

"The Guards asked such a lot of questions," she said, "and they've made a rather unpleasant discovery. Apparently somebody got into the house from outside. There are scratches on the wall by the larder window. That's what they're all out looking at now."

"Did they take anything?"

Phoebe shook her head. "We haven't missed anything and nobody heard them, but the police seem to think there's no doubt about it."

Edward agreed that it was unpleasant, but inwardly he thought that if anybody had to be held responsible for what had happened it would be satisfactory to blame a passing tramp. If this poison business was not cleared up soon it would cause no end of talk. He wondered what the Superintendent wanted from him. Had he heard how he had been sent for by Mr. Prendergast, in which case might he not be inquisitive about that codicil?

"Well now, you know as much as I do, Mr. Gildea," said Phoebe, dismissing the subject with a little toss of hey head. "We shall have to wait for the police to tell us the rest. Meanwhile, what else have we got to talk about? Did you bring my uncle's will?"

Edward congratulated her on coming into a fortune. He saw she had been expecting it, but all the same he fancied he detected some slight relief at having the fact confirmed. Phoebe made no comment on the actual figures, as if they did not immediately convey to her the extent of her inheritance. She shed a few tears.

"Poor Uncle Jason," she said. "He meant so well."

A Civic Guard knocked at the door and asked if Mr. Gildea would see the Superintendent now.


## II


Meanwhile Mollie Gildea found her way up to Phoebe's room, resisting the temptation to peep through other doors which she knew could not be it. It was a temptation, for she felt the fascination of the queer old house. She had never been inside it before, but her imagination had worked on it as seen from the outside. The green rectangle of garden, the only level or fertile ground in that region of rocks and slag heaps, reminded her of pictures in children's books of magic carpets, or palaces transported with their gardens into the desert, a djinn holding up each corner. She had also heard stories of the place being haunted, but these her practical mind explained by the fact that the ground beneath the house was all tunneled with passages. You could actually descend into the mine from the garden itself through an opening covered by a heavy wooden trapdoor. Streams underground, or animals, would account for any strange noises.

The interior she found depressing. Old Mr. Prendergast had preferred dark stains and paint that would not show the dirt and such heavy mahogany furniture as you would hardly see outside a bank. The pictures were chiefly engravings in black wood frames. There were sets of Hogarth. "The Rake's Progress" hung round the hall, and "The Industrious Apprentice" accompanied you upstairs.

Phoebe, however, had achieved a different atmosphere in her own room, though the dark paint and paper were the same as the rest. The walls were covered with gaily colored playbills, a few framed programs, and a number of large glossy photographs signed across the corners. One inscrutable mask presided over the fireplace. There were quantities of flowers: rhododendrons, of course, and roses from the garden, and wild flowers for which someone had been farther afield. Mollie suddenly remembered the superstition that it is unlucky to bring gorse into the house.

It was the kind of room Phoebe might have had for a dressing-room in an old-established theater if she was a famous actress. It smelled of the flowers mingled with cigarette smoke.

Mrs. Teely got up from the window as Mollie came in, and greeted her with a vague, puzzled smile, as if not sure what she was doing there. Mrs. Teely was small, active and elderly, with wiry gray hair and eyes which had once been as large and dark as Phoebe's. For the first time, Mollie noticed the resemblance. Mrs. Teely was dressed in black jersey, she being the kind of woman who would always have something black in her wardrobe for emergencies, and she made Mollie, in flowered linen, feel several sizes too large.

"You are surprised to find *me* here," said Mrs. Teely, gazing up at Mollie as she slowly unclasped her hand. "Few people realized that Jason and I were related. My dear mother was his father's youngest sister, so that he and his brothers were my first cousins, all the same generation, in spite of differences in ages. It was not my fault that Jason and I saw so little of each other. He chose to live like a recluse, and what could one do? My heart ached for Phoebe, but one could not intrude. One could only hold oneself in readiness in case of need. The need has come, and here I am."

"I'm so glad," said Mollie. "I came over with Ned because I was afraid she might not have anybody to lean on. Men aren't the same, are they? Though she seems to be taking it very well."

"Ah yes, you came with Mr. Gildea," said Mrs. Teely, satisfied with the explanation. "So he acted for Jason. He will be a great help to Phoebe, for one does need a reliable business man. A lone woman is exposed to be taken advantage of, as none knows better than myself." She sighed. " I suppose

Jason has made Phoebe his heiress. He was very well off, more so than most people thought. All the money was in that branch of the family, and he did well for himself, too. You must not think that I have any expectations of being remembered in the will. No indeed. I am quite resigned to Jason's having forgotten my existence."

She gazed searchingly at Mollie, who hastily disclaimed any knowledge of Mr. Prendergast's affairs. "Ned never tells me anything about clients."

"No, no, of course not," said Mrs. Teely. "I was only trying to explain that my one object in coming was to take things off Phoebe's shoulders. The difficulty is to persuade her to let one help. You, Mrs. Gildea, may be able to induce her to relax. What are relations for? Poor girl, she has the family spirit of independence."

"I don't suppose there's much anyone can do at the moment," said Mollie. "Ned will make the funeral arrangements and all that."

"One could be a buffer," said Mrs. Teely. "Well do I know what it is to need a buffer."

Certainly for the time being there did not seem to be anything that the two would-be comforters of Phoebe Prendergast could do except talk to each other. So they sat down, and Mrs. Teely told Mrs. Gildea all about the household, on which she was well informed in spite of never having crossed the threshold in Jason Prendergast's lifetime. Her little daily maid was a sister of Mickser, the garden boy at Coppermine House, and that was how she had heard the news so early. She had come at once, wishing, she said, to save Phoebe the trouble of sending word to her.

"It would be no trouble to me to take over the running of the house for a week or two," said Mrs. Teely. "I know all the ins and outs. Vera Byrne is an excellent maid, but she needs someone over her. Just a head to do the planning, you know what servants are."

A dark suspicion formed itself in Mollie's mind that Mrs. Teely and she might be rivals for the future services of Vera, and that Mrs. Teely had stolen a march on her. Mrs. Teely, however, went on to say that Vera Byrne was unofficially engaged to Barney Penrose, and now they would probably make a match of it.

"That man!" said Mollie. "Whatever can she see in him?"

"Why, he's a most respectable man," said Mrs. Teely, "and a good Protestant, which Vera is too, though he's Church of Ireland and she's a Cooneyite. The Penroses were a Cornish family originally. They were brought over here by Jason's great- or great-greatgrandfather because they knew about mining, and there've always been some of them working for the family."

"Oh, English, were they?" said Mollie tolerantly. "That accounts for it. I expect he has a softer side when you get to know him."

Time passed, and presently Phoebe joined them. She came in and stood with her back to the door looking at the room with a blank expression as if she hardly knew what she meant to do there. Mrs. Teely immediately advised her to go and rest, at which she came to life. Looking Mrs. Teely in the eye she said, "He's left everything to me."

Mrs. Teely nodded bravely. "But of course, my dear. That was what Jason always intended. One always felt that at least it would still be in the family." She blinked a little, and hurried on. "Tell me, dear, have you thought of sending word to your Uncle Hector in Canada? *He* could not possibly have had any expectations from Jason after what happened, but still, I feel, he has the right to be told."

Phoebe stared at her. "I didn't know I had an uncle in Canada."

"Oh yes, dear. That is, if he is still there and still alive. Dear me, it must be fifty years since Hector went away. He may have married and founded a family. There may even be a whole branch of the Prendergasts out there. It would be only right to get in touch with them. I'm not surprised that Jason never mentioned Hector to you, for there was a little trouble, but surely bygones may be bygones after fifty years."

"But do we know his address?"

"It should be among your uncle's papers. I'll look for it for you," said Mrs. Teely.

Phoebe let the subject drop. She turned to Mollie to say she was afraid Edward Gildea would be some time yet.

"It's the Civic Guards," she explained. "There are so many things they want to know. I've told them everything I can about Uncle's death, but I believe I have to go over it all again and sign a statement. They're interviewing all the servants. There's no knowing how long it'll take. Do you think I ought to offer them anything? Drinks or anything? Or would that be a *faux pas*?"

"Not on any account," said Mrs. Teely. "It would be like tipping, and that you must never do to the police or they may arrest you for trying to bribe them."

"Ned will tell you if anything's expected," said Mollie, in a reassuring undertone.

"But what is all the fuss about?" demanded Mrs. Teely in tones of exasperation. "Why all these questions? What are the Civic Guards doing here at all? I cannot see what business it is of theirs. An inquest is one thing, and an inquisition is another."

Phoebe sat down, removing a sprawling long-legged doll from a chair and tossing it into a corner. "For one thing," she said, "the Superintendent tells me somebody must have broken into the house by the larder window."

"A burglar!" exclaimed both ladies.

Phoebe shrugged her shoulders. "At any rate they're looking for finger-prints."

"Ah yes, they would," said Mrs. Teely, as one with an inside knowledge of police work. "But hadn't you missed anything?"

Phoebe shook her head.

"As if you hadn't got enough to worry you," said Mrs. Teely in her most sympathetic strain. "So that's what the confabulation was about just now. I saw the Superintendent talking to Sergeant Rice at the front door. What a strange coincidence! For surely they can't think"—a new idea had struck her unpleasantly as she looked at Phoebe's face—"surely there can't be any connection between the larder window and Jason's death."

"How do I know what they think?" said Phoebe. The tension in her voice made Mollie Gildea uncomfortable. Even Mrs. Teely was silenced for a full minute, but her eyes moved from one to the other of her companions as if watching for an excuse to begin talking again.

Phoebe, however, spoke first, saying quietly, "I don't mean that the police aren't being considerate. Of course they have to do their job. The Superintendent has been most kind about sending messages for me by his telephone. He's sending a telegram for me to Henry Sheed, who's Uncle Jason's executor."

"Henry Sheed?" Mrs. Teely nodded approval. "A businessman and a friend. One of his few friends. He will be a help to us. I suppose he will be coming down for the funeral. I wonder now where he had better stay."

"Why, here of course," said Phoebe. "He often does."

"But things are a little altered now, dear. You would be alone together in the house."

"No we shouldn't. There's Vera."

"Even so, tongues might wag." Mrs. Teely's own head wagged. "Oh, I don't mean anything personal against Mr. Sheed. I am sure he's a gentleman in every way. But in circumstances like this, you know, it takes very little to start talk."

"I can't help that," said Phoebe. "It would be ridiculous for Henry Sheed to go and be uncomfortable in the village when there's a room here all ready for him."

"My dear, you may pride yourself on being unconventional. I know you won't mind my saying you have been brought up differently from other girls. But a single woman, an heiress, is in a delicate position. I daresay you think I am fussing, but I am sure Mrs. Gildea will agree with me."

Mollie Gildea wished she could have kept out of this. It would not have occurred to her spontaneously that there was any scandal in a sensible young woman like Phoebe being under one roof with an elderly friend of her uncle's, but then she was lacking in imagination. And she had to remember that as a responsible matron, married to a professional man, she ought to stand up for respectability.

"Mr. Sheed could come to us," she suggested.

Phoebe turned on her large reproachful eyes that declared she had let her down.

"He'd be dreadfully in your way and Mr. Gildea's. He had much better be here. He'll have work to do. He'll probably sit all evening over Uncle's papers, and I shan't see him except at meals."

"But I have a suggestion," said Mrs. Teely brightly. "Phoebe is quite right about the advantages of having Mr. Sheed here on the spot. In any case she should not be alone in the house. Now, to ease the situation, I can very well arrange to shut up my little house for a week or two and take up my abode here. There is a second spare room, and as I am quite accustomed to doing everything for myself I shall not be any extra trouble. In fact, I shall be able to give Vera a hand."

"Snake in the grass," thought Mollie, and Phoebe looked flabbergasted.

"No really," she said, "I shouldn't dream of putting you to all that trouble. There's no necessity—"

"I shan't listen to a word you say, my dear," said Mrs. Teely, not listening, and smiling at Phoebe with all her teeth. "You must allow an older woman to have her way. Don't think you will be inconveniencing me in the least. I shall enjoy a little change."

Phoebe glanced wildly at Mollie, who hated to neglect such an appeal, but could not decide which side to take. Her sympathies were with Phoebe, but she felt it was not the best thing for her to remain so isolated. Probably she had not yet realized how lonely she would be.

Mrs. Teely's attention, however, had been temporarily diverted. Sitting in the window, she was not allowing anything to escape her that happened outside, and she reported a new arrival. They all looked out and saw an important person marching solidly up the garden; they deduced his importance from the deferential attitude of two men who accompanied him, one in Civic Guard uniform, the other in plain clothes. The VIP was in plain clothes too but was unmistakably a military man.

A few minutes later Sergeant Rice came up to ask if Miss Prendergast would see the Chief District Superintendent.

As soon as Phoebe had gone Mrs. Teely stood up and remarked that now was her chance.

"It's no use trying to get poor Phoebe to concentrate on anything. One can't expect her to be clearheaded this morning. But Vera Byrne is a tower of strength. I shall have a little talk with Vera and get everything settled. She and I will get a room ready, and I shall just quietly move in and take on myself the task of organizing the household."

Mollie Gildea said nothing. If Mrs. Teely was determined to come and stay in the house she felt powerless to prevent her. It did seem to her rather high-handed behavior, and she did not at all like this intimacy with Vera Byrne. Was Vera really engaged to Penrose at all, or was Mrs. Teely only trying to put one off? Mollie Gildea had a suspicious mind.


## CHAPTER THREE


THE CHIEF DISTRICT SUPERINTENDENT'S name was Colonel Tunney, and nowadays he was a heavyweight, an armchair warrior whose campaigns were waged on paper against the Department of Finance. He was affable and only occasionally remembered his own importance.

The man more immediately responsible for what Mrs. Teely called the inquisition was Owen, or Eoghan, Menapia, the Superintendent from Drumclash. The District Headquarters were at Cranbay, some miles away on the coast, but the Chief District Superintendent felt it his duty to drive over and show an interest, seeing that the Prendergast family were part of the history of the county.

Superintendent Menapia had rung up headquarters early that morning. What caused him to do so was the doctor's refusal to give a certificate, coupled—in a policeman's mind—with the fact that the deceased had a lot to leave.

It happened that the doctor had only recently examined Jason Prendergast for purposes of car insurance. He had guaranteed him still fit to drive and thought he might have lived ten or fifteen years. He had no business to have a heart attack or a stroke. The symptoms, however, were stupor and paralysis of the heart. There was no vomiting, but the effect might nevertheless have been produced by poisoning. The patient might have eaten fungus or berries of some kind. It had been known for such cerebral collapse to be brought on by arsenic.

"I don't mean it was anything but an accident," said the doctor. "There was a cake there, with green icing, that I didn't like the look of. I locked up all the remains for you."

The Superintendent, accompanied by Sergeant Rice, went straight out to Coppermine House, arriving about midnight. He sealed up the cupboard which contained the remains of the deceased's last meal, and he took brief statements from Miss Prendergast and the maid. He also made arrangements for the ambulance to call for the body. He left the Sergeant at the house overnight, both for the protection of the two women and to keep an eye on things generally. Sergeant Rice was a keen man, ambitious to graduate into the plainclothes branch of the force. On the way over in the car the Superintendent suggested to him that he might look round for things like weed-killer or flypapers and also note any signs of tension or suspicious behavior on the part of the survivors.

There was nothing of that kind, but by the time Superintendent Menapia got back to the house next morning, Sergeant Rice had had a good gossip with Vera Byrne. Vera Byrne said she preferred working for gentlemen rather than ladies. Old Mr. Prendergast was never any trouble, but she would not have stayed on after Miss Prendergast came, only she did not think that would last for long. She wasn't saying anything against Miss Prendergast, but it was telling no lie to say she didn't hit it off with her uncle. They were always having words, generally about her being on the stage.

Through Vera the Sergeant had learned of Mr. Gildea's recent visit, and also of events leading up to it.

Two people had called that afternoon to see Miss Prendergast. They were Mr. and Mrs. Claremorris, old friends of hers and members of the theatrical company that was coming to Drumclash. When Mr. Prendergast found out who they were he was against letting them in at all, but Miss Prendergast brought them into the garden, and he and she had a stand-up argument in front of the visitors. Mr. Prendergast gave Vera orders not to take them out any tea, and when Miss Prendergast ordered it she didn't know what to do. You couldn't go on like that, with people giving you opposite orders. She wet the tea and let Miss Prendergast take it out herself, and she hoped Mr. Prendergast never knew, because he stayed indoors till Mr. Gildea came. Vera said this showed how the pair of them went on. She said, however, that they had appeared to be on friendly terms again next day.

So when Superintendent Menapia got Mr. Gildea to himself he asked him about his last interview with the deceased, and whether he had been contemplating changing his will, or anything of that kind.

Edward looked at him with an apologetic smile.

He and the Superintendent were old friends, neighbors too, for the Civic Guard barracks in Drumclash was just across the street from Edward's office. Menapia, like Edward Gildea himself, was a thorough countryman, though he looked an indoor man for he had a colorless face, with gray eyes and grizzled hair, and his eyes were tired behind steel-rimmed glasses. But long walks over the hills were his relaxation and he was a great enforcer of the Wild Birds Protection Act. If the Chief District Superintendent always looked a military man, Superintendent Menapia never looked anything but a civilian in uniform. He was quiet and generally easygoing but could be a stickler on small points.

Edward said, "I'm not bound to disclose my client's intentions."

"I'm not asking you to," said the Superintendent mendaciously. "I'm only trying to get an idea of the deceased's state of mind in the last few days before he died. I wondered if there'd been any change in him or if he was getting cranky in any way."

Edward was not taken in by this way of putting it. Suicide while of unsound mind was not what the police suspected. Jason Prendergast had left on his desk a half-finished order to a shop for wooden sections and wax foundation for his beehives, which he must have been in the middle of writing when he was taken ill. Hardly the kind of last document a man would leave who did not intend to live till morning.

The intended codicil itself was evidence against suicide. But if mentioned at this stage it might make a wrong impression on the official mind. Edward had a duty to his client as well as to the Law. Until the case was clearer he did not feel himself justified in disclosing information that might prejudice the police against Phoebe Prendergast.

He looked the Superintendent in the eye and said, "There was no change in the ultimate disposal of Mr. Prendergast's property."

"He still left everything to his niece?" said Menapia.

"He did."

"Do you think Miss Prendergast had any reason to suppose he was making such a change? Would she be afraid he was cutting her out?"

"Not that I know of."

"Do you know her well, Mr. Gildea?"

Edward shook his head. "Hardly at all."

"But you're acting for her now?"

"Yes, she wants me to carry on."

Menapia frowned. "You know me, Mr. Gildea. I'm not trying to trap you into a breach of professional confidence. All the same, you have an obligation to tell us anything that might have a bearing on the fact of Mr. Prendergast's sudden death. Our information is that he and his niece had a quarrel, and then he sent for you in a hurry."

Edward said truthfully that he knew nothing of any quarrel.

"He did have some business that seemed to him urgent"—the old man's words, " 'We know not the day nor the hour' " came back to the solicitor's mind with a prophetic ring—"but as well as that, he wanted me to give him a hand with his bees, putting on a super-clearer. He often sent for me on business in a case like that, killing two birds with one stone."

The Superintendent's face cleared. He knew Edward Gildea's reputation as a beekeeper, and though not one of the brotherhood himself, he knew bees required a lot of attention at this time of year. He felt this was a satisfactory explanation.

When Colonel Tunney arrived and Phoebe came downstairs again, they all went into the dining room, where the police had established a base. The remains of Jason Prendergast's last meal were spread out on the table. Anyone looking casually in at the window might have imagined the party were all sitting down to elevenses.

There were milk, sugar, tea and the unwashed cup, a small plate smeared with honey, a dish with the remains of a honey section, a plate with one buttered slice of soda bread, and a plate with the green iced cake. The cake had been suspect from the beginning, and immediately became the center of interest.

"Vera Byrne makes most of our cakes," said Phoebe, in answer to a question from the Superintendent, "but not this one. I bought it myself at the parish fête. I got there late, and there was nothing left to buy but the leftovers after the tea."

The cake was on a pasteboard foundation. It was divided all round in slices, and as arranged it made a complete circle, so that at first sight it looked as if none of it had been eaten, but on closer inspection one could tell that there should have been twelve slices instead of eleven. One had been taken out and the others pushed round to fill the gap.

"It was cut when I bought it," said Phoebe. "There may have been a piece missing then. I expect they pushed the others round so as to sell it as a whole cake."

"What, at the parish fête?" said Edward.

Her dark eyes turned seriously on him. "Don't you find that people who go in for doing good are capable of anything? They think it's all right for them."

A thin smile suggested that Superintendent Menapia agreed with her. In any case it hardly seemed likely that Jason Prendergast would have rearranged the pieces after taking one, though he might have done so in an idle frame of mind.

Colonel Tunney said, out of the depths of his experience, "It's a strange thing, but I've known any number of cases of people being upset by food bought at sales and fêtes. Looks as if people aren't very particular what they give to charity. I don't wonder at this cake being left over. Wouldn't touch anything with green coloring myself."

"I never thought about that," said Phoebe. "I've eaten green icing before now."

"Have you no idea where it came from, Miss Prendergast? Don't try to shield anyone. We have to find out, in the public interest."

"I'd tell you if I knew," said Phoebe. "I haven't the slightest idea. Most of these old ladies who run fêtes look vague enough to be a public danger."

Edward coughed. "My wife was on the teas," he said. "She's here now, sir. She might remember something about it."

"Oh, I didn't mean Mrs. Gildea," said Phoebe. "Mrs. Teely was there too. She was on the committee. You'd better ask her."

Mrs. Gildea came immediately when sent for. The Sergeant said Mrs. Teely would be down in a moment.

Mollie came in agog with curiosity, having had time to get tired of her own company upstairs. She was interested to note that the dining room had red wallpaper, as all dining rooms did at one period, and that the pictures looked like Prendergast ancestors, a typical Whiggish collection. They seemed to have stopped having themselves painted about the mid-nineteenth century. When her attention was drawn to the cake she knew all about it.

It had not been made by any vague old lady, but by a young married woman called Mrs. Cafferkey, wife of one of the Forestry officials. Mollie said, "I always think how sensible he was to marry such a good cook even if she is rather plain. She taught at a technical school before she was married, so she's quite a professional cake-maker. Her cakes are always beautifully decorated, and just as good inside. I never should have expected anything to be wrong with any cake that Mrs. Cafferkey baked."

"Can you be sure it's hers?" asked Colonel Tunney.

"Oh, yes. She always puts shamrocks and things on top because she's such a strong Nationalist. She must use an awful lot of green coloring. How dreadful if that was it! You must warn them at once, or the Cafferkeys may die too."

No need remained for Mrs. Teely's testimony, but at this point she arrived, and not only her, but Mickser the garden boy and Vera Byrne the cook. Mrs. Teely bustled in, pushing Mickser in front of her while Vera hovered anxiously behind. The desirable Vera was a small round woman in her thirties, with dark hair pushed under a cap and snapping black eyes that suggested temper, though at the moment she was looking frightened. Mickser was an undersized fifteen-year-old, who looked as if he had adenoids. Mrs. Teely thrust him forward as if he was a specimen on which she meant to lecture.

"Excuse my interfering," said Mrs. Teely, "but I have been doing a little detecting for you, and have found a culprit. Now, Mickser, own up, and you will feel much better."

Mickser stood with his mouth open, but no words came out, so Mrs. Teely had to supply them for him. In the course of the talk she had been having with Vera she had established confidential relations, and Vera had brought the subject of Mickser up.

Vera was sure Mickser had a good heart and meant no harm, but when she missed odd bits of cake or pieces of any kind out of the larder she knew well where they went. She would not have minded giving the boy a bit now and then, if he came and told her he was hungry, but the way it was with these boys, he'd rather climb in through the larder window and snitch them behind her back. Vera denied that she had winked at his goings on. She said she was always giving out to him about stealing. But she had never gone the length of telling Miss Prendergast, much less Mr. Prendergast.

When the police found out about the larder being entered, and started taking fingerprints off the shelves and all, Vera was in a state. Would they arrest Mickser, for whom she had a weak spot? If she told what she knew would it make it better or worse for him? Surely nobody could think Mickser would put anything in the Master's food.

Mrs. Teely had said that the police must be told, come what might. "Tell the truth and shame the devil," she adjured poor Mickser, who stood listening to the revelation of his iniquity with a hangdog expression that argued the worst. The utmost he could manage to say was that he was sorry, and he certainly looked it.

Colonel Tunney looked stern. He turned to Superintendent Menapia and asked if he knew the boy. The Superintendent did not, but Sergeant Rice knew his parents and testified that he came of respectable people and had nothing against him so far.

"When did you last climb in through the window, Mickser?" asked the Chief Superintendent.

"Friday afternoon, sir."

"He was hungry, being a fast day," interjected Vera Byrne.

"Friday afternoon," repeated the Chief Superintendent. This was Saturday. "And did you take anything then, Mickser?"

"A p-piece of the cake, sir."

The Chief Superintendent sat up, glared, turned round to look at Superintendent Menapia, who was looking quite as startled, and turned back to Mickser.

"A piece of what cake? Speak up, boy."

"That cake, sir," muttered Mickser, pointing to the creation of the patriotic Mrs. Cafferkey.

"Then," said the Chief Superintendent very severely, "what business have you to be alive now?"

Everybody stared at Mickser harder than ever, as if he was a human phenomenon.

Then Vera Byrne said: "Beg your pardon, sir, but I think there's only the one piece missing. It was cut in twelve, sir, and when Mickser took one he pushed the rest around a bit, hoping it wouldn't be noticed. Oh, I knew all right." She shook her head at Mickser, but combined it with an encouraging smile. " I don't think the Master had any of that cake at all, sir."

The Chief Superintendent made her say it all over again, asked her if she could swear to it, and even then did not seem thoroughly satisfied. But

Vera was a good witness, intelligent and clear. Her statements were the sort to be accepted. The facts were: Mickser had eaten the cake and survived; Mr. Prendergast had died, but had not eaten the cake. In spite of the green icing the cake seemed to be harmless, and the Cafferkeys might be considered as having a new lease of life.

Annoyed at having his preconceived ideas upset, Colonel Tunney took it out of Mickser. "You see the risks you run," he said, "taking food that's not intended for you. If you weren't poisoned yourself you might be arrested for murder, so let this be a lesson to you. I'll let you off with a caution. Unless Miss Prendergast wishes to bring a charge of stealing against you." He frowned meaningly at Phoebe, who hastily said she did not want to pursue the matter.

Mrs. Teely and Vera led out their captive again, and Mollie Gildea followed them. After they had gone the others sat staring at the tea tray as if they felt they ought to be able to tell from the look of the things on it which of them it was death to eat. Yet in itself the tray was a wholesome sight. It was a plain wooden tray covered with a linen cloth, the crockery had a rosebud pattern, the teapot was an honest brown teapot sitting on a colored tile. Apart from the green iced cake there was nothing to eat but buttered soda bread and honey in the comb. What could be more innocent?

That was what made it worse. It was not easy to see how the poison could have got into any of those things by accident.

A moment before, when sermonizing Mickser, the word "murder" had sprung to Colonel Tunney's lips. He hadn't given it an immediate application, but he had betrayed the fact that it was in his mind.

Phoebe's eyes were lowered. There was no knowing what she was thinking.

But Edward Gildea's mind could not admit the thought that Jason Prendergast had been murdered, an appalling thought, because if it were so, the only person who had the least motive that he could see was the beautiful young woman in front of him. Another idea had already occurred to him, an idea which he hesitated to put forward only because to the uninitiated it would look so farfetched. He did not want the police to think he was trying to waste their time, in the interests of his client. But if circumstances pointed to Phoebe Prendergast being accused of murder, then any alternative possibility ought to be investigated.

That was how Edward Gildea came to bring up the question of the honey. He thought it might have been contaminated in the course of nature. This subject of toxic honey crops up regularly in beekeeping journals. Some honey is said to be injurious to humans, though not to the bees that gather it. The first and most famous case dates back to ancient times. A passage in Xenophon tells how an army of soldiers were taken ill after eating honey from beehives along the shores of the Black Sea. In modern times cases have been reported from the same region, and also from New Zealand, South Africa, and parts of the United States. Such reports generally come from remote places, where the patients never came under scientific observation, leaving it open to doubt whether honey or something else was to blame. Altogether it is a splendid subject for controversy, and up to the present this had been its chief interest for Edward.

He was uncertain whether any reported case of honey poisoning had ended in death. Xenophon's soldiers recovered, but they may have been tougher subjects than old Mr. Prendergast. One thing Edward did remember that seemed distinctly relevant. The celebrated botanical explorer, Mr. Kingdon Ward, writes in one of his travel books of having had native bearers poisoned by wild honey on a rhododendron hunting expedition in Burma. If rhododendrons did it, then there were plenty round about. There was a bush in the garden, and there must be many more within the one and a half mile radius of the bees' flight. And up here in the mine area so little else grew that bees perhaps might be more inclined to concentrate on rhododendrons than go looking for variety.

Indeed, the more Edward thought about it, the more he felt there might be something in the idea, and as a beekeeper he longed to have some local research done by experts. He saw himself contributing an article to *The Bee World,* or perhaps reading a paper to the next summer school of the Federation of Beekeepers' Associations.

He was just getting the Chief Superintendent interested when they were interrupted. There were noises off: squeals, shouts and the beating of a gong. As if the bees resented imputations on their characters they were taking action. They were swarming.


## II


The superstitious natives of some primitive places believe in making all the noise they can outside a house of mourning, to scare away demons coming for the soul of the dead. Anyone might have thought this was what was going on in the garden, though Jason Prendergast's religion had been Presbyterian, and his soul, if still in any way linked with his body, would be at the County Hospital by now, so that any demons in the offing would have come to the wrong address.

Penrose, the dour chauffeur, was there drumming with a spanner on an empty petrol tin. Vera Byrne was beating the dinner gong, while Mickser thumped a watering can with his fist. Mrs. Teely was calling out instructions, and Mollie Gildea was laughing helplessly on the garden seat.

Mickser had been the first to notice the bees when he made for the open after his interrogation. Now they filled the air, thirty or forty thousand of them, moving very fast and buzzing very loud. At present they were not going anywhere in particular, just whirling round and round like a dark snowstorm. The idea of the noise was to make them think thunder was coming and cause them to settle, but these bees did not seem easy to deceive. It was not in a fact a very good imitation of thunder, for two of the effects producers, Mickser and Vera Byrne, had got carried away with excitement and were indulging in noise for its own sake. This annoyed Penrose, who was putting up a much better performance, making his petrol can rumble now loud now softly as if something in his soul found expression in the instrument.

Modern beekeeping aims at the prevention of swarming, but it would be a pity if it ever entirely succeeded, for a swarm is one of the sights of country life. It is true that there is something rather sinister about it, as always when well regulated automata get out of hand. In the ordinary way the forty or fifty thousand bees in a good stock pack themselves so tightly into their hive that one forgets what a lot of them there are. In the air they take up a great deal more room. The dark snowstorm is composed, instead of snowflakes, of thousands of tiny stinging entities on the move, nobody knows whither. Beekeepers will tell you that swarming bees never sting. Few outsiders would care to put this to the test. And just as there are people who always think that bats will get into their hair, so there are many who expect that a swarm of bees will settle on their heads.

Whatever feelings it may inspire, a swarm happening close at hand is something you cannot just ignore. Even police discipline gave way, and everybody hurried out on to the lawn.

The Hon. Secretary to the Drumclash Beekeepers' Association kept carefully in the background. Mollie Gildea, who liked her husband to show himself a man, said to him, "Ned, why don't you tell them what to do?" But he only whispered with a grin that it would be a pity to spoil it.

It was a competition between Mrs. Teely and Penrose who should be in charge. Mrs. Teely jumped on to the garden seat and clapped her hands loudly, not with the idea of imitating thunder but to get herself a hearing. In the slight lull which followed, she called out, "That's no good. You must get syringes and spray them. Then they'll think it's raining."

"That's right," said Penrose, as one who had had the words taken out of his mouth. "Mickser! Stop that row and fetch a coupla syringes and a bucket of water. Bring them here to me."

Mickser loped off down the garden. The others stopped drumming and gonging, and comparative quiet fell on the garden, but for the continuous excited humming of the bees.

Mrs. Teely addressed the group of policemen. They formed a tough-looking little group, from the Chief Superintendent down to a young car driver. "Don't be frightened," she told them. "Swarming bees won't sting you. If they do settle on any of you, don't lose your heads. Just keep quite still till we bring a skep."

At this the Chief Superintendent gave ground a little, but still the fascination of the spectacle held him, hypnotized by the bees in motion.

Mickser had brought one garden syringe, one bucket of water, and one stirrup pump. He came staggering back under the load. As Penrose clung to his tin, Mrs. Teely herself seized the syringe and went boldly to work. One of the Civic Guards, entering into the spirit of the thing, volunteered to pump for Mickser, and Mickser sent his first spray over Penrose. Mickser was so small with such large gray eyes and such a timorous appearance that it was hard to believe he had done it on purpose. Penrose, however, thought he had, and this caused a diversion, Penrose abusing Mickser, and Mrs. Teely scolding Penrose for his language, and various other people taking sides. Meanwhile the bees, either having had enough exercise for the time being or having drawn the required deduction from the shower Mrs. Teely had sent over them, gradually calmed down, and when the altercation on the lawn was over they were found to have all drawn together and hung themselves in a ball on the lowest branch of the big copper beech.

Their public followed them. Everybody walked over to have a closer look.

Alarming as a swarm may be in the air, it really looks worse after it has clustered. It then forms a tightly packed brownish or blackish mass, bigger than a football, mysteriously held together in one lump, but stirring all the time with the life of thousands of tiny lives. To those who feel a dread of creeping things, the cluster is charged with menace, and indeed it looks a great deal more dangerous than does a bomb.

"Now," said Mrs. Teely briskly," somebody must hold a skep underneath, and somebody else must knock them off the branch."

Phoebe Prendergast spoke for the first time. She had been standing well back, not offering any suggestions, ready to flee if necessary. Her well-modulated voice came clearly out of the middle distance. "Why not let them alone?"

"Then they will fly off again," cried Mrs. Teely, "and you will lose them."

"Would it matter?" said Phoebe.

Mrs. Teely looked shocked. "A swarm like this is worth money. You ought to get at least fifteen shillings for it."

Phoebe shrugged her shoulders. She refrained from pointing out that she had just come into fifty thousand pounds.

"Come now," said Mrs. Teely, "if you haven't got a skep any old box will do so long as it's big enough. And we shall want a sheet to put round it, and something to hit the branch with."

While the equipment was being assembled Mrs. Teely entertained the Chief Superintendent with reminiscences of really awkward places she had known bees to swarm in, such as up a chimney and over a church porch. Edward Gildea, feeling he could not shirk taking some hand in the business, modestly produced his veil.

It was he in the end who held the skep. Penrose undertook to hit the branch on top with a mallet. Mrs. Teely said: "One, two, three. Go!"

Penrose swung the mallet high and brought it down hard just above the cluster, and the ball of bees detached itself neatly all in one piece and fell into the skep exactly in the manner desired. All went perfectly according to the textbooks, except that the Chief Superintendent gave a sudden yelp and clapped a hand to his neck.

He looked reproachfully at Mrs. Teely. "I thought you said swarming bees didn't sting?"

"You should have kept quiet," said Mrs. Teely. "Naturally any bee will sting if you go wriggling and flapping at it. It didn't want to sting you if it could help it. Don't you realize that stinging you has cost that poor bee its life?"

The Chief Superintendent suppressed his feelings. So did the junior ranks. They felt it would be good-bye to all chance of promotion for anyone who smiled. But when Mrs. Teely seized the sufferer by the neck in order to remove the sting with a businesslike thumb nail, several of the Civic Guard became very interested in the distant view.

Edward Gildea reversed the skep and wrapped it loosely in the sheet. It felt heavy, a swarm worth having. He asked Phoebe what she would like done with it.

Phoebe looked blank. It seemed as if she had force herself to attend to what was said to her. She put a hand to her forehead in the effort to think what ought to be done with a swarm of bees on a hot day in a house that was all upset. She shook her head helplessly. It was too difficult, with Mrs. Teely's voice going on and on.

Mrs. Teely, however, had a solution to every problem. The swarm was one of the things she could take off Phoebe's hands.

"I have four stocks of my own this year," she told them. "Quite enough for one lone woman to handle, but all the same I can manage one more. I have an old box I can hive it in just for the summer, and then at the end of the season I shall probably unite two of my other stocks, and that will give me a spare hive, so they will be all right for the winter." She made it seem, not as if it would be no trouble at all, but as if what would be a lot of trouble to most people would be nothing to her. She did not grudge it, if it would be a help to Phoebe. Phoebe said she could have the swarm and welcome, and refrained from reminding her that it was worth fifteen shillings.

As they all walked back to the house Mrs. Teely remarked with meaning in her voice and a faraway look in her eyes:

"Isn't it very strange that the bees should have swarmed today?"

"It's regular swarming weather," said Edward. "I thought those bees might be on for it when I looked at them the other day. Mr. Prendergast ought to have given them more room after he took off the crate."

"It may have been that," said Mrs. Teely, "but do you know what I think?" Her voice sank to its deepest tones. "I think, nobody had told them."

"Told them what?" asked Phoebe.

"Nobody had told them about your uncle's death. Bees expect to be told things. I haven't a doubt that was why they swarmed."

The Chief District Superintendent mopped his forehead.


CHAPTER FOUR


AFTER THAT things calmed down. The interrogations seemed to be over. The Chief District Superintendent left, after swabbing his neck with ammonia. He shook hands with Phoebe and apologized for the trouble she had been caused. The Gildeas soon followed. Superintendent Menapia and Sergeant Rice carefully packed the eatables for forwarding to an analyst. A plainclothes detective from District Headquarters took Mickser's fingerprints, mainly for practice. It made Mickser feel a hero, and he went home to dinner with his cap over his eyes and his coat collar pulled up, doing his best to look like a gangster. By afternoon there was nobody left at Coppermine House but the three women, Phoebe Prendergast, Vera Byrne, and Mrs. Teely, with Sergeant Rice to protect them.

Penrose drove the Gildeas home. Mollie studied from behind his thick neck and ears close set to his head, and as he opened the car door she took one good look at his face, noting his underhung jaw. Penrose's mouth was never seen to open at all. If obliged to speak, he slid the words out sideways, just loud enough to be heard. It looked as if Vera Byrne must be attracted by the caveman type.

As she watched the big saloon roll away Mollie said, "Ned, do the police think someone poisoned Mr. Prendergast? Because I don't like the look of that man at all."

Edward, however, had rushed up to the house to get out his back numbers of *The Bee World.* If he had heard he would probably have said that people's faces were not their fault. He did not set much store by his wife's occasional flashes of feminine intuition, though he did depend on her judgment of people she had had time to know. He very much wanted to ask her, when a suitable moment arrived, what she thought of Phoebe Prendergast. Edward made no strong claim to understand women; beautiful, dark, talented, self-possessed, sophisticated ones were a bit out of his line.

Mollie Gildea got the lunch, chasing Edward and his bee journals off the dining-room table. She put out a square of honey as usual. Then Edward had to tell her about his theory.

It did not sound quite so well the second time over. The theory had not had to stand up to criticism at Coppermine House, because its exposition had been interrupted by the swarm. Mollie found plenty of holes in it, though what really turned her against it was the thought of the complications it might cause.

She thought of forty-five beautiful sections stored in her own larder, the neatest of them set aside for exhibition and sale. The Drumclash Stores took all the honey the Gildeas could spare, and it all helped to make ends meet.

"Just suppose the honey of this district got a bad name," she said. "The stores would refuse to take it, and what's more, you'd have all the Associated Beekeepers down on you. People won't give in to an idea like that without a fuss. Why, if it were true, we might as well give up keeping bees. If it could happen here, surely we'd have heard of cases before now. Why on earth should honey suddenly become poisonous this season? The bees still go to the same old flowers."

Edward had two possible answers to that. The first was that the climate of the Vale, so favorable that even tropical plants would grow there, was a perpetual temptation to gardeners to import ever more weird exotics. Somebody might be growing the so-called American yellow jasmine (not a true jasmine) *Gelsemium sempervirens*, or mountain laurel, *Kalmia latifolia*, both plants to which honey poisoning had been attributed. It might be the first year they had flowered, or they might only just have been discovered by the bees. Were this the case it would not be too difficult to trace the source of the trouble and root the plants out. But it does take a large spread of blossom to provide even a teaspoonful of honey. There would have to be *Gelsemium* or *Kalmia* by the acre. The Gildeas knew most of the great gardeners in the neighborhood, and if there were anything new on that scale they ought to have heard about it.

Edward was more inclined to blame the rhododendrons. They had been mentioned in Xenophon's account, he discovered, as well as that of Mr. Kingdon Ward. There were plenty of these about. The Gildeas had one in their own garden. The bushes were often buzzing with bumblebees, but the hive bees, according to Edward's own observation, seldom visited them.

The nectar was more troublesome for hive bees to reach; bumblebees have longer tongues. That might mean that the flowers were neglected as long as there were other sources of supply, but that for some reason this year, the bees, mysterious creatures that they are, had suddenly taken to them. Or could it be that repeated crossing with imported races, like bees of the yellow Italian strain, had evolved a longer-tongued breed, which could compete with the bumblebees, and that Mr. Prendergast's bees were derived from such a cross? Fascinated by the various possibilities, Edward was tending to lose himself in speculation, when his wife brought him down to earth.

"But if you really think something like that has happened, Ned, we ought to warn people. Somebody else might get poisoned!" Mollie was very much in earnest. This time it was not only the Cafferkeys, it was the whole population of the Vale in danger,

Edward thought this over and did not like it much. He quoted his favorite proverb: " 'Don't bid the Devil goodmorrow till he comes in at the door.' No good comes of starting a scare. The Guards will warn everybody fast enough if they think it's necessary."

"Then you don't really believe in it?" said Mollie with remorseless feminine logic.

"Well," said Edward, "if you want to know, I believe in it about as much as I do in poltergeists, and more than I believe in flying saucers. I believe poisonous honey has been known to occur, and I think there might be some here as well as anywhere else, but I'm not absolutely certain it was that that killed Mr. Prendergast."

Mollie looked satisfied. She cut herself a piece of bread and spread some honey on it and ate it. Edward never even noticed.

After a short pause Mollie said: "It's queer though, what did happen to him."

Edward did not answer directly. He had finished eating and was busy getting his pipe going. Then, as Mollie began to clear the table he took a plunge.

"How does Phoebe Prendergast strike you?" he asked. "I've never really got to know her at all."

"Neither have I," said Mollie. "She's difficult to get to know. Some people think she's conceited and standoffish, but it may be just reserve. I admire her of course. Her looks, I mean, and the way she dresses. I thought she behaved very sensibly today. She did seem sorry about her uncle, but she wasn't hypocritical. In fact I liked her better today than I did before. I shouldn't like to think she was really wicked underneath."

Edward looked up. "But you think it's possible?"

"It must have been a frightful temptation," said Mollie. "In her place, I don't know what I mightn't have done."

"Oh, most likely it was an accident," said Edward. "If it wasn't the honey it was something else that got contaminated. Extraordinary accidents do happen. You've only got to read the stuff they send you from insurance companies. One must keep an open mind."

So after lunch he went and sat open-mindedly by a rhododendron bush and spent twenty minutes beewatching, but in all that time no hive bees came near it.

## II

As soon as he had got clear of work at Coppermine House, Superintendent Menapia drove over to District Headquarters, where the Chief District Superintendent was waiting for him. Colonel Tunney pushed aside a pile of forms containing the crime reports for one day in the district, offered him a cigarette, accepted a light himself, and got to business.

"You don't like the looks of it," he said.

"I don't, sir," replied Menapia. " I don't know where I am at all. I like a murder to *be* a murder, then our work's all cut and dried. This case is all in the air. Might be murder, might be accident, or he might even have died from natural causes after all."

"Have they done the P.M. yet?"

"They're at it now. I'm to ring the hospital at half past four. They should be able to tell us something."

Colonel Tunney screwed up his eyes to look at Menapia through the cigarette smoke. He had known the Superintendent a long time and thought him a good man but if anything too easygoing. He wished he would smarten up a bit in appearance; it wasn't a good example to the men. He was hardly the overconscientious type that would make a mystery out of nothing. But he was an officer of long experience, and if he sensed concealed implications in a situation, then it had to be taken seriously.

"What's on your mind?" asked the Chief.

And as he expected, Menapia had reasons to go on, no mere mystical hunch.

"Well, sir," he said, "I don't like that business about the will, coming just beforehand."

"Mr. Gildea didn't want to say much about that."

"Just what I'm saying. It's obvious, isn't it? Either Mr. Prendergast was going to alter it, or his niece thought he was. They'd had this quarrel, and next thing the niece knew, the solicitor was sent for."

"Think Mr. Gildea's likely to give trouble?"

"Ah no, he won't. He'll do what he can for his client, but he's not out to obstruct the police. He's a very decent sort of man for a lawyer."

"This idea of his about the honey," said the Chief. "To me it has a bit of a smell of red herring about it.

"Well now, do you know, sir, there might be something in it. Bees are very mysterious creatures. Mr. Gildea does know a lot about them, he's a kind of a king bee, you might say. What I was thinking was, wouldn't it be a good thing in any case to let the idea get about? It would give people something to keep them quiet."

Colonel Tunney nodded. "We certainly don't want everyone talking about it as murder, especially if it wasn't. All the busybodies would be on to us to arrest Miss Prendergast. You think it was her, do you?"

Menapia replied, "I'm trying to keep an open mind. There's the maid who got the tea ready. Not that she'd much reason to murder him. Rice says it was the talk of the village she was setting her cap at the old man."

"Then she may have had a bit of a grudge against the niece. Wasn't it the maid brought out this story of a quarrel?"

"It was. About that, I was thinking I'd better see this Mr. and Mrs. Claremorris, the two visitors who came to the house. You know who they are? They're with that company that has the Drumclash Town Hall booked for next week. It'd be as well to get their side of the story."

"I think you're right. You may find there was nothing in the incident at all. Try and get at the subject indirectly. Make some other excuse for bringing the matter up, you know what I mean. An unofficial approach might be best. Could you get in talk with them over something else?"

"I'll make out I'm a theater fan," said Menapia, who had not even been inside a cinema for the last ten years.

"You could get yourself seats for the show. Good for you. Broaden your mind."

"The wife mightn't approve of that," said Menapia primly.

"I don't mean what you mean," said Colonel Tunney. "It's classical stuff. *She Stoops to Conquer* by Oliver Goldsmith. In spite of the title I believe it's quite clean."

Superintendent Menapia agreed. In spite of not being a theatergoer he happened to have read the play. He was fond of Goldsmith. His last remark had been intended as a little joke, but he had become resigned to having his prim little jokes misfire.

"Mind you," said Colonel Tunney, coming back to business, "if the niece did it, she must have known she'd be the first to be suspected."

"Somehow they don't think of that," said Menapia. "And a girl with her looks might have the idea she could get away with murder."

"I suppose she might. All the same, isn't there anyone else?"

"There's that Mrs. Teely," said Menapia thoughtfully. "I can't quite make *her* out. I don't like people butting in on a case from the outside. Nobody asked her up to the house this morning. Miss Prendergast never sent her word. She was very quick hearing the news, and she came round offering her condolences without waiting to be invited."

"Ah well, that's only natural in a near relation."

"Actually, she's the next of kin after the niece," said Menapia.

"What good would that do her? She wasn't in the running for the fifty thousand pounds."

"That's so," admitted Menapia. "Unless the will could be upset on some grounds or other. All the same, I don't see why she wants to hang about like that. She's now actually staying in the house."

"Ah, she's only a harmless old busybody. She's a terrible talker, isn't she? I can't stand a talker."

"She'd have you mesmerized."

"Still, that's not a criminal offense," said Colonel Tunney regretfully. He looked at his watch. "How about ringing up the hospital now?"

Menapia did so, and presently the report came through.

"The stomach was reddened and inflamed," he said. "Not much doubt about that."

The Chief Superintendent nodded. "What do they think it was?"

"Won't give an opinion. He's terribly cautious. 'An irritant poison' is as far as he'll go without getting the organs analyzed. That means waiting I don't know how long."

"The organs have to dissolve." The Chief sighed. "I've spent years out of my life waiting for analysts' reports. Still, be thankful for small mercies. At least we know he was poisoned. We've that much to go on. What did he take? Where was it obtained? What happened to the container the stuff was in? We've got to find some material evidence, and ascertain the *modus operandi.*"

"A job for the Branch, sir."

The Chief agreed. All major crime in Ireland is referred automatically to the Detective Branch in Dublin. There are detectives attached to country districts who investigate the ordinary run of petty offenses, but important investigations require trained men, searchers, photographers, fingerprint experts, with the backing of laboratories and records. Colonel Tunney said he would try to get a good man sent down in time for the inquest and would also ask the Branch to produce an expert on honey toxins.

Superintendent Menapia felt relieved, except that he now had to find accommodation for an unknown number of extras and fit them into the domestic life of the barracks.

## CHAPTER FIVE

HENRY SHEED worked nowadays for the government. He was sent traveling up and down the country to examine and report on alleged mineral deposits, there being a theory widely held among the electors that Ireland is rich in industrial resources and that only (a) British oppression and (b) native lack of enterprise have kept the Emerald Isle from turning into another Black Country. If Sheed did not go quite so far as this, he nevertheless preached the development of any resources that could be found, and was on the lookout not so much for coal and iron as for new industrial applications of minerals hitherto despised. He said to Edward Gildea, "Look what Jason and I made out of this valley during the war! Till I came along, they'd only scratched the surface."

"Are you going to start again?" asked Edward. He had handed over to Sheed the title deeds of the mine, for though the mining rights belonged to the Prendergast family the partnership agreement had provided for the lease to be continued to the surviving partner if Jason Prendergast died first.

"I might," said Sheed, "if I had the time or the financial backing, but it'd need too much of both. We'd have to sink fresh shafts. These were pretty well worked out by the end of the war. It'd really take another war to make it pay."

"Heaven forbid!" said Edward conventionally, and Sheed nodded.

"I'm not asking for that," he said, "hard case though you think me." His shrewd eyes read Edward's thoughts.

"I must confess I do look on mining here as desecration," said Edward, "war or no war."

"You're entitled to your opinion, Mr. Gildea. I'm afraid I've altered a good deal of scenery in my time. I'm not romantic about Nature, and I think we should use her gifts."

They had been to the inquest, which had been adjourned pending completion of the medical report. Edward Gildea had returned to Coppermine House with Sheed, who was anxious to get on with the business of the executorship. Sheed was staying for the funeral next day but would have to leave immediately afterwards.

Henry Sheed sat at the desk in the study in Jason Prendergast's chair. He was a younger man, a well preserved one; indeed he might have been preserved by drying in the tropics, for he was wrinkled and yellowish, like a sultana raisin, but in spite of his color he was physically fit and seemed well armored against life by experience and humor. In the few business relations Edward Gildea had had with the partners he had found Sheed much the better one to deal with.

This afternoon Sheed's sense of humor was battling with exasperation. He was annoyed to find the police taking a hand in the affairs of his late friend and partner.

"You may say good-bye to all hope of getting the estate wound up," he told Edward. "Time and money mean nothing to those fellows. Did you see the two with the Super, plainclothes men down from Dublin? Reminded me of Gussie Goose and Curly Wee. What's it all in aid of anyway? Do they really think Jason was murdered?"

"It might have been an accident," said Edward. "The honey—"

"Honey my elbow," said Sheed. "Oh, I beg your pardon, it was your idea originally, wasn't it? Have a cigar?"

They were short straight Irish-made cigars called "Whiff's," of which he always carried a few loose in his breast-pocket. He held out one to Edward, who shirked it. Sheed lit it himself and squinted down it.

"What is all this about the honey?" he said. "Do you really believe that was it?"

The coroner had tended to dwell on the honey. He had got the doctor to admit that he had heard of cases of honey poisoning, though none had ever come within his own experience. And he had extracted from Vera Byrne that her master was more than ordinarily fond of honey to eat. He did not so much spread it on his bread as balance it in chunks, and would eat as much as half a section at a sitting. Edward was hurt to find Sheed so skeptical. He said, "I don't see why not. All the same I must admit we never had any trouble from honey round here before."

"Quite," said Sheed, and that seemed to dispose of the honey. He smoked for a minute in silence, then said, "Maybe he was murdered." Edward said nothing, but by now he was getting accustomed to the idea. There was a longer pause. By this time a cloud of cigar smoke hung heavy over them both, Sheed raised a hand to fan it away.

"Who did it?" he asked.

Edward shook his head helplessly.

Sheed said, "Do they suspect Phoebe?"

"They haven't said so."

"Tcha," said Sheed. " She's the obvious person to suspect. You can't blame them. I won't say she couldn't have done it either, lovely girl though she is. Do you understand women, Gildea?"

"No," said Edward. "I always ask my wife."

"You're fortunate." Sheed was a bachelor. "And what does she think?"

"Oh, Mollie has quite an admiration for Miss Prendergast," said Edward. "And one can't but pity the poor creature as things are, without their getting any worse. If it was anything but an accident, then to my mind we ought to look into the past for an explanation. Mr. Sheed, you knew Mr.

Prendergast longer than any of us. Can you think of anyone who might be his enemy?"

"Nope," said Sheed. "Nor friend neither. Jason was a man of character, but you couldn't call him a good mixer. He may have got across quite a few people in his time. I'll think about it. You never know but something might come back to me. Jason was a good man, but he had principles, and I've known men do things on principle that I wouldn't do without any."

"Did you know anything of his brother who went to Canada?" asked Edward.

Sheed shook his head. "Never heard of him till this morning when Phoebe asked me. She found a note of his address in Jason's Bible. Somewhere in Ontario. The ink looked pretty faded, but she sent a cable on chance."

"He would be the next of kin."

"So he would. If Phoebe was convicted you'd have to look out for him." Edward shuddered.

"Not a nice idea," said Sheed, "but while we're on the subject, who's next of kin if this brother's dead? Would it be Mrs. Teely?"

"Er, yes, I believe so. That is, if he died without issue. She was the deceased's first cousin."

"I'd as soon suspect her as anybody, said Sheed. "Meddlesome old witch. Seems to me it might very well be her. Temptation enough for a hard-up woman like her, with a fortune in the family."

"But she must have known it wouldn't come to her. Prendergast's intentions abut his niece were clear, and he wasn't the sort of man to die intestate."

Sheed took his cigar out of his mouth. "What about Phoebe dying intestate? There's nobody else to inherit from *her*. Hasn't it occurred to anybody that Phoebe might have been included in the murderer's program?"

Edward started. "You mean it was only chance she didn't share his last meal?"

"No. They never had tea together. Jason's tray was a routine. According to my guess, Phoebe would have had to live to inherit. Wouldn't do at all for them to die in the wrong order." Sheed leaned over the desk and rapped on it with his fingers. "Phoebe may be in danger now."

Edward Gildea, obsessed by the thought that Phoebe herself might be guilty, had never considered the situation from this angle. It was an abyss opening under his feet. He felt quite a new kind of responsibility towards his client.

Instinct told him it was absurd to suspect Mrs. Teely. When you have laughed at somebody for years it is difficult to think them capable of murder. But reasoning from another angle he began to see her behavior as suspicious. He thought of the determined way the lady had inveigled herself into Coppermine House.

Sheed had been thinking along his own lines. "Tell me," he said, "what did the late Teely die of?"

"D.T.s," said Edward with a faint smile. There was nothing suspicious about that.

"Just what you'd expect," said Sheed.

"Is Mrs. Teely staying on at the house?" asked Edward, feeling that perhaps it ought not to be allowed.

At this a twinkle appeared in Henry Sheed's eye. It was rather like the glitter of a small piece of mica in granite.

"No, sir. She's leaving. The management requested her to vacate her room by midday." He stubbed out his cigar as if to illustrate how Mrs. Teely had been disposed of. Edward was relieved but surprised.

Sheed explained that Mrs. Teely had been turned out to make room for other visitors, and none other than the theatrical couple whose first call at the house had so much annoyed Jason Prendergast.

The Humphry Madigan Company had by now infiltrated into Drumclash. The Gildeas had had glimpses of young women in trousers, young men in coats with belts or hoods or other peculiarities, and had wondered where they could all be staying. Phoebe Prendergast, knowing from experience the horrors of theatrical lodgings in country towns, had invited her friends the Claremorrises to stay with her. They had a car and so had she, to solve the problem of getting them to and from performances. They would have comfortable beds, and Phoebe provided herself at one stroke not only with a chaperone but with an extra man for her protection. There was a great deal to be said for the arrangement, but not by Mrs. Teely.

Henry Sheed said, "It was as good as a play in itself. You should have heard Phoebe thanking Mrs. T. for the way she had put herself out, and telling her she wouldn't trespass any more on her good nature. Mrs. T. said Jason would turn in his grave—not that he's in it yet. She said no girl with decent feelings would invite people to stay whom her uncle wouldn't have in the house. Phoebe didn't need to put anything in words. She just raised her eyebrows and let Mrs. T. see her thinking that *she* came in the same category. In the end, having no choice, Mrs. Teely said she would not dream of countenancing such behavior and went off to pack. That young woman's Jason's niece all right. She'll be mistress in her own house."

They finished their business. Jason Prendergast had left his papers in good order, and such matters as drawing up a list of securities and making up the estate account would not be an onerous task. They arranged for a valuation of the house and contents to be done by a well-known firm.

"What about the mine?" asked Edward.

Sheed replied: "Enter it as derelict. Yes, I know what I said just now. I get ranting sometimes on my pet topics. I've a hunch there may be more to be got, but it's all pure guesswork. You wouldn't get anyone to put up money for it under present conditions."

"Very well, if you say so," said Edward. He stood up to go. "When shall you be down again?"

"I'll try and get down again next week," said Sheed. "Meanwhile, you keep an eye on that poor girl. I daresay it's only wishful thinking on my part about the Teely woman, but if it wasn't her, I suppose it was someone else, and whoever it was he may be dangerous."

"Unless it was the bees."

"There's that too. Anyhow, a whole lot we don't know yet is bound to come out and the only thing is to keep on the *qui vive.*"

Edward would have liked to say that it was all very well putting people on the *qui vive* when you were shaking off responsibility yourself. He envied Sheed his escape from the atmosphere of the investigation. By next week, presumably, everything would be cleared up, but what might not everyone concerned have to endure in the process?

He said to cheer himself up, "Surely no one would make an attempt on Miss Prendergast's life now that the Civic Guards are sitting up and taking notice."

" I hope you're right," said Sheed. "Personally, if it was me, I'd wait and see if the Guards mightn't save me the trouble of a second murder by convicting Phoebe of the crime."

## CHAPTER SIX

THERE WAS A LARGE attendance at Jason Prendergast's funeral, because though nobody had known him well, everybody had known who he was, and besides, his death had received publicity. The idea of a man being poisoned by natural honey from his own hive had an appeal for editors as just the sort of sinister suggestion to brighten up the news, so the report of the inquest appeared in all the national dailies and even got into some of the English papers. This was a poor advertisement for the produce of the Vale of Morna.

The Civic Guards had now begun doing a round of the local beekeepers, enquiring about cases of illness which might be attributed to honey and collecting samples of honey for analysis. They found plenty of people who had had bilious attacks; some had eaten honey and some had not. It caused plenty of talk. Beekeepers who resented interference scouted the whole idea and blamed the authorities for giving it currency. But sufferers from tummy troubles who had been despised by their families for overindulgence, and wives and mothers whose cooking had been criticized, seized on the honey as an explanation that suited everybody. The dwellers in the Vale became divided into factions, and those who said it was all nonsense about honey being harmful automatically became the party "agin the government." Old ladies invited each other to tea parties specially in order to put honey on the table and see who took it, thus testing their neighbors' political convictions.

Several beekeepers attended Jason Prendergast's funeral for the sole purpose of finding out what all the fuss was about. The Hon. Secretary of the Beekeepers' Association was buttonholed by one member after another. Edward was in a dilemma. He had to choose between encouraging the honey rumors or starting talk about Jason Prendergast having been murdered.

The Superintendent, he knew, was consulting an expert, or rather at the moment he was trying to find one, because few scientists were anxious to risk their reputations by giving an opinion on such an obscure and controversial subject. If a man could be found to give a talk, that would solve one of the recurrent problems of an Hon. Secretary. He promised everyone that he would call a meeting, and members should have a chance to sift the whole question of toxic honey and decide what, if anything, could be done about it, in the best interests of the Association.

## CHAPTER SEVEN

To SAVE Phoebe Prendergast from going into Drumclash, where she was pursued by condolences and exposed to curiosity, Edward Gildea arranged to collect her money from the bank and bring her out a sum with which to pay wages and current expenses. Phoebe invited him to come to lunch and bring Mollie with him, at which Mollie was pleased, because she had not felt sure up to then that in Phoebe's mind she might not rank with Mrs. Teely, having pushed herself in the first day, uninvited. If Phoebe specially asked for her, perhaps after all her sympathy had not been wasted.

Penrose, the grim chauffeur, was sent for them again. He called first for Mollie at the little house on the hill, then drove into Drumclash to Edward's office, and Mollie was quite relieved to have her husband's company in the car. The heat was setting her nerves on edge. In Ireland people feel uneasy when the weather stays the same more than a week on end, and everyone now was talking about the drought and the heat wave. All the inevitable drawbacks to fine weather were making themselves felt; earth cracked, gardens wilted, green vegetables were scarce, baths were impossible, and some households were in sore straits from wells drying up. The hedges were overlaid with dust instead of flowers. Even the bees were out of luck, for with so little moisture in the air the flowers held no nectar. Wise beekeepers fed syrup, and Edward Gildea came prepared to put feeders on the hives at Coppermine House.

The rocks and slag heaps of the mine looked dry as old bones and reflected back the sun with a hard yellow glare. The lawn stretched on the ledge in front of the house looked parched, and the treetops of the Vale below, shimmering in heat haze, might have been a mirage of the desert.

Entering the garden, the Gildeas saw that the trapdoor which covered an entrance to the mine was open. Its wooden shutter was turned flat back on the ground, and a man squatted by it looking into the hole. The Gildeas were irresistibly drawn to look too. They saw a ladder ten or twelve feet long with its base in a stream of turbid yellow water which rushed down a straight tunnel and lost itself again underground. At the bottom was Mickser, barefoot, paddling about with a bucket. He filled it, carried it part way up the ladder, and the man at the top hauled it up, swung it over on to the ground beside him, straightened up, and saluted. Edward recognized him as one of the two plainclothes detectives from Dublin. He was the younger one, whose engaging youthful appearance and enquiring expression had inspired Henry Sheed to christen him Curly Wee after the young hero of the *Irish Independent's* comic strip.

The house seemed to look askance at visitors under its half-closed lids. One could almost feel the heat of the sun reflected from the greenish metal of the five cockleshells over the windows.

From the kitchen came a burst of incongruous laughter. Vera Byrne, appearing from that direction, said Miss Prendergast was expecting them and she was above in her room. The Gildeas showed themselves up.

Phoebe was sitting sewing in a chic black linen frock. With her was a peach-skinned blonde, with plenty of skin in evidence, for she was dressed only in a pair of flowered cotton shorts and brassiere top to match. She was sitting on the table trimming a Victorian poke bonnet. A pair of stays, and other fragments of Victorian costume were littered about the room.

"Do come in, Mr. and Mrs. Gildea," said Phoebe, getting up to greet them and sending a slower of ribbons to the floor. "This is my friend Mrs. Claremorris, who is staying here with her husband. They're with the Humphry Madigan Company you know. I'm afraid you won't meet Lionel. He's over at the Town Hall putting up scenery. Grania, Mr. and Mrs. Gildea."

Phoebe looked a little self-conscious over the introduction. She could not help guessing what effect her flamboyant friend would produce on anyone acquainted with old Mr. Prendergast's prejudices. The actress herself, however, was prepared to put everybody at their ease.

" 'Scuse the informal beachwear," she said, extending her hand without getting up. "Stifling in here, isn't it? We're sitting indoors working our fingers to the bone because the Show must go on."

The Gildeas said politely that they were looking forward to seeing some of the plays and asked which were the best. They had thought of *She Stoops To Conquer.*

"I hope you don't object to stunts," said Phoebe.

"Experimental drama, dear," said her friend, and winked at the Gildeas. "We're doing it in modern dress. You'd be surprised how contemporary it turns out. All that about mistaking a private house for a hotel seems so much more plausible. I mean, so many houses are, nowadays. Humphry thinks an unbiased approach to the classics is educational."

Phoebe laughed. "And it's cheaper to tour than a period production."

Mrs. Claremorris looked pained. "Now, Phoebe, you know whatever Humphry is, he isn't mean. And don't you go giving the impression that we're just common barnstormers. We have a mission to bring art to the people of Ireland."

"Nonsense, you're only having fun and games. Humphry wants to keep the company together and give the younger ones experience."

Mollie Gildea liked plays in which everybody dressed up. "Aren't you doing some in period costume?" she said, indicating the poke bonnet.

"*The Wicklow Miners,*" said Phoebe. "That's the one you ought to see. The most absurd old piece they've dug up, specially intended for local consumption."

"Well, what would you give them?" said Mrs. Claremorris pouting. "*Thérèse Raquin?*"

Phoebe's expression showed she did not think this funny. "Why not?" she said carelessly. She turned to Edward. "Would you like to come down to the study now?"

Edward and Phoebe departed to talk business, leaving Mollie with the actress. Mrs. Claremorris was not difficult to talk to. She seemed a sociable soul. Her face, at a close look, appeared made up to look more fashionable and less good-natured than it naturally was, and once one had got used to the beach costume one had to admit that she had the figure for it.

"Said the wrong thing then," she remarked, making a face at the door after Phoebe had gone out. "Why did I have to pick on *Thérèse Raquin?* Except that she was marvelous in the part. One of her very best performances."

"Who was Thérèse Raquin?" asked Mollie.

"Oh, just a murderess," said Mrs. Claremorris. "Those sort of parts were always Phoebe's best. She had the intensity. I could just as well have said Salome, though, or Mrs. Tanqueray. You know, it's a crime, Phoebe wasting her talent."

"Don't you think she may return to the stage?"

"Well, she says not. Of course that may be all talk. I've been telling her she should, and that for me means putting self last, because if Phoebe rejoins the Madigan company I know who'll play most of the leads. Not all. I'm better than she is in comedy parts. But I don't know how it is, I just haven't her tragic gifts. Though I think, myself, my best part ever was Scarlett O'Hara in *Gone With The Wind*. How's that now, with the feather?"

Mrs. Claremorris put on the bonnet she had been trimming and stood up to look at herself in a wall mirror. The bonnet looked odd with the beach costume, but was becoming in itself. Mollie Gildea said so. Mrs. Claremorris said it wasn't so much that as whether the feather would catch on the branches of the old oak in the woodland scene. After a calculating scrutiny she seemed satisfied, for she doffed her headgear, found a cigarette, relaxed in an armchair, and went on talking.

"Isn't this a darling house?" she said. "Lionel, that's my husband, is crazy about it. He has such a feeling for atmosphere."

"You don't think it has a bit too much atmosphere?" said Mollie. "Some people would tell you it was haunted."

"But of course it is," said Mrs. Claremorris. "I knew that at once. I'm terribly sensitive to anything like that. Do say you're psychic! "

But Mollie, though Irish born and bred, had to apologize for her deficiency in this respect.

"Well, I can't say I've ever *seen* anything myself," said Mrs. Claremorris kindly. "I can feel a presence, though. I often do. I might even *see* something here. I hope though," she added, "it won't be old Mr. Prendergast. He was quite enough for me in the flesh. Lionel and I met him, you know, a day or two before he died."

"Oh yes?" said Mollie, hoping to be told what had really happened. She was not disappointed.

"We came to see Phoebe," said Mrs. Claremorris, "and ran into the old gentleman himself. My dear, there was quite a scene. He tried to turn us off the premises. Rogues and vagabonds, that was his attitude. Said his niece had broken off all connection with the theater. I was terrified not only of him but of Lionel, my husband, having one of his rages. Men, you know. Lionel's so temperamental, and he wouldn't stand by and see me insulted. Luckily Phoebe came out, and oh my dear, when she found out what was up she was raging. I never saw anyone so furious, and dear knows I'm used to rows in the theater. One thing, Phoebe certainly wasn't afraid to stand up to the old man. Lionel and I were terribly embarrassed. And then to hear of his dying so soon afterwards. The police actually came round asking us questions, but of course we couldn't tell them anything."

"Mr. Prendergast was very much against his niece having anything to do with the theater," said Mollie. "I'm afraid he was very old-fashioned."

"I don't know how Phoebe stood him," said Mrs. Claremorris. "I don't care how much money he had to leave, I wouldn't have stayed here if I'd been her. Though of course she had her reasons."

The last words were accompanied by an arch look, but Mollie failed to notice this, and thinking of Vera Byrne she asked, "Has Miss Prendergast decided yet to sell the house? I suppose she'll hardly wish to stay here."

"Well, I don't know," said Mrs. Claremorris. "She won't stay here forever of course, but you see, just at present, there's an Attraction."

Mollie pricked up her ears. From the way Mrs. Claremorris gave the word a capital letter there was no doubt that, of all the attractions of nature, she meant a young man. This was news. It was not much to be wondered at if Phoebe's allure had found a victim, but who could it be? Bachelors in the Vale were under close observation, and not a whisper concerning Phoebe had come over the grape vine.

"Well, maybe I'm jumping to conclusions," said Mrs. Claremorris. "I don't say it's an affair, mind you. But yesterday evening he came climbing up the footpath over there by the big rock, and Phoebe met him in the garden and they stayed out talking till nearly midnight. Doesn't that look to you like romance?"

"By the Bell Rock?" said Mollie. "Had he come up from the road then? Who is he?"

His name, Mrs. Claremorris said, was Michael Canavan. He was a lodger in a cottage on the main road, just at the foot of the rock. He was taking a Forestry course, which accounted for the Gildeas never having come across him, for foresters spend their lives not in the tangled old woods round Morna, but out on the high hills, knee high in little trees that are being planted everywhere in tidy rows. After digging holes and drains or putting up rabbit wire all day it would take some energy to climb up another hillside. It did look to Mollie like romance.

"And that's why she never walked out on the old man," asserted Mrs. Claremorris with conviction. "Though what he thought of it, or whether he even knew, is your guess as much as mine. Phoebe may have met her fate, or thinks she has, and that's why she says she won't go back to the stage. But you never can tell, my dear. Between ourselves, it's not so long since everyone was talking about her and Humphry Madigan. I don't know why nothing came of that, but they must have had some sort of row, and that was the real reason Phoebe left the company. Her uncle was just an excuse, if you ask me. Most likely this chap, Canavan, caught her on the rebound. So what I'm wondering is," she leaned forward confidentially, "what will happen when Phoebe and Humphry meet again? Won't that be a situation?"

Mollie knew what Humphry Madigan looked like, for his photographs were all over the town. He had fair wavy hair and half-closed eyes, and an excellent nose and chin. But then one can't always look at one's husband in profile. She asked for a description of Mr. Canavan. Mrs. Claremorris said that for sex appeal there was no comparison.

"Are they likely to meet?" asked Mollie.

"Well, I don't know," said Mrs. Claremorris. "Phoebe being in mourning makes a difference. She says she won't go to any of the performances, and he won't came here unless she asks him, and she hasn't yet. But there's a week to go, and who knows what that may bring forth?"

"Oh dear," said Mollie, "I do hope she'll choose the right one and be happy."

"Oh, she may marry somebody else altogether," said Mrs. Claremorris. "She's very attractive to men."

## II

Meanwhile, in the study, Edward was urging Phoebe Prendergast to make her will. He would have done so in any case on general principles, but he put it all the more strongly because Henry Sheed's remarks were preying on his mind. He could hardly bring himself to believe that Mrs. Teely harbored designs on the family inheritance and on Phoebe's life, but if the possibility existed, the obvious safeguard was for Phoebe to make a will and let it be known that she had done so. There must be somebody to whom she could safely bequeath her property; it did not much matter whom she named as legatee so long as she put her affairs in order. But he could not give Phoebe the reason why he pressed the matter now. It would be going too far to make criminal insinuations against a lady of irreproachable respectability. Phoebe did not see that there was any hurry. She said she would think it over.

" 'Do it now' is a good motto," said Edward. "It's so easy to keep putting these things off. You might fall and break your neck or be run over on the road. 'We know not the day nor the hour—' " He broke off, remembering who had last said that to him.

"One can't hope to provide for every emergency, can one?" said Phoebe. "You haven't said that I might be poisoned accidentally, which is perhaps my most likely fate, under the circumstances."

She was sitting on the windowsill again, hands in lap, ankles crossed. It was a low sill and her legs, nylon clad and extended towards him, were all Edward could see of her except a dark shape against the glare out of doors. He still did not feel at ease with her. He could not say what intimidated him, her looks, her clothes, or her self-possession. If she had been hysterical and red-eyed, at least he would have been at less of a disadvantage.

"Do the police tell you anything, Mr. Gildea?" Phoebe asked.

Edward shook his head. "Nothing they don't tell you. I don't think there's anything to tell, as yet."

She frowned. "I feel they could be more communicative. It's not comfortable, you know, wondering if anybody else is likely to collapse. Of course we all avoid honey, but then, it might not be that after all."

"Why not shut the house and go to a hotel?"

"And be stared at by all the other residents?" Phoebe's head moved impatiently. "Oh, no. I'd rather be here. Besides, I've invited the Claremorrises. They don't seem to think the dangers are any worse than those of lodgings in Drumclash."

" I'm sure the Civic Guards are doing their best. It takes some time, you know, to get reports out of analysts. I hope they'll have news for us soon," said Edward.

"That's all very well," said Phoebe, "but I should like to know what's at the back of their minds. I want to ask you something, Mr. Gildea. Why did my uncle send for you the other day?"

Edward looked at her, puckering his brows because of the light in his eyes. "He wanted to add a codicil to his will."

"A codicil? But he didn't add it."

"No. He hadn't time."

"I see. What was it?"

"Does that matter now?"

"Surely. I should like to know his last wishes." She spoke casually, but she leaned forward, waiting for an answer.

"Your uncle contemplated making one condition about your inheriting his property. You were to bind yourself not to return to the stage."

"Was that all?" Edward was surprised that she took it so calmly. "Poor Uncle," said Phoebe, "he had his *idée fixe*. I wondered what he was up to that day. He might have cut me off with a shilling. Or is it half a crown nowadays?"

"Oh no, nothing like that. He always intended you to have the money."

"Poor Uncle," she said again. "Do the police think I murdered him for it?"

"My dear Miss Prendergast—"

Phoebe raised her hand to stop Edward Gildea's protest. "Don't look so shocked. They're at least bound to take the possibility into consideration. Did you tell them about the codicil?"

Edward shook his head.

"But they asked you, didn't they? You'd better tell them, to stop them imagining something worse. If you like, you can tell them it wouldn't have made any difference. I'm not thinking of acting any more. I've had all I want of the theater. I prefer the simple life."

Edward must have looked unconvinced, for she added sadly, "Not that they'll believe you, any more than you do me."

Edward took refuge in the professional manner. "You are not legally bound by your uncle's wishes. The codicil is unsigned and therefore invalid. Had he lived he might have changed his mind. You are free to do exactly as you like."

Phoebe's mood seemed to change, as if she had got a weight off her mind. She spoke quite gaily. "At any rate I have something to look forward to, when at last we've muddled through. When you've lived from hand to mouth like I have, it's a relief to be rich. Poor uncle! I'm sorry about him. I hope he didn't suffer much at the end. But it would be hypocritical to pretend that life won't be easier for me from now on."

"That's right," said Edward. "Look forward to the future. Don't worry more than you can help. All this upset will pass."

Phoebe nodded. "One must divide one's mind into compartments and seal off the unpleasant ones."

They talked business. There was not much of it, but Edward wanted Phoebe to understand what he and Henry Sheed were doing. By now he had a rough list of Jason Prendergast's securities from which he could give her an idea of the amount of her fortune. They discussed the sale of the house, and also the arrangements for getting it and its contents valued for probate.

"Well, I think that's the lot," said Edward, putting papers together. "Er, the Civic Guards aren't being a nuisance, I hope?"

"Oh no," said Phoebe, "not at all, we're glad to have them. The sergeant's splendid company for Vera, and as for the young man from Dublin, he's invaluable. He mends everything he can find that's broken. He actually got the carpet sweeper to work again, after Penrose said it was only fit for the scrap heap."

"Did he really?" Edward was impressed. "And what did Penrose say to that?"

"Penrose," said Phoebe, "is suffering from his nose being out of joint. You see there was some kind of understanding between him and Vera— more on his side than hers, I fancy. I'm afraid our Vera's a flirt. No, I don't think either of our two protectors is very popular with Penrose."

"I wonder Vera never got married, a good cook like her," said Edward.

"Thought too much of herself, I expect," said Phoebe. It crossed Edward's mind to wonder if the same could not be said of her.

He stood up, thinking they might rejoin Mollie and Mrs. Claremorris, but Phoebe still had something on her mind. She tucked her legs under her bur did not rise. He could see her face better as she looked up at him. She had fine long eyelashes.

"Mr. Gildea," said Phoebe, "do tell me what I ought to do about Mrs. Teely. Cousin Clementina, I suppose I ought to call her. Poor old dear, I've offended her mortally. I don't want to start a lifelong feud; we've had too many in our family. I'll do anything within reason, short of having her back in the house. Don't you think that was a bit too much ·to endure? I'll apologize if she likes, though I wasn't in the wrong. I'd have done so already, only I was afraid of being snubbed, which would only make matters worse."

"I should think that would be a good move," said Edward. He had sympathized with his client over the Mrs. Teely episode, but he had not altogether approved of her behavior to an older woman. For even though one might hypothetically consider Mrs. Teely's inducement to murder, it was always possible that she had meant well and deserved more gratitude than she had got. "You could do it by letter," he suggested. "Write it now, and I'll deliver it to her and put in a word for you at the same time. Or better still, I'll get Mollie to do it. She's more of a diplomatist."

Phoebe went to the desk, and as she sat down in her uncle's place Edward was struck by a sudden fleeting resemblance to Jason Prendergast. It was one of those elusive family likenesses that are difficult to define; something in her pose, or the carriage of her head. Sheed had said she was like her uncle. He was thinking of their determination to get their own way and their self-reliance. Yet just at that moment it occurred to Edward Gildea that self-reliance in mortals has something of the pathetic.

### III

Edward remembered the feeders for the bees and went to the kitchen to ask Vera Byrne to let him dissolve some sugar in hot water to make syrup for them. The kitchen was reached by a passage at right angles to the hall, a narrow, ill-lit passage. Edward found it blocked at its darkest point by human forms.

At his footstep one obstacle divided into two. There was a slight scream and the sound of a slap. One form detached itself from the other with a push which sent the latter staggering back into Edward. It was no lightweight, either. It was Penrose.

Edward said, "What's all this?" Penrose growled, "Beg your pardon, sir," and stalked off out of the back door. Edward never saw his face but his neck was red. He found Vera Byrne in the kitchen, also with a high color. She made no reference to the incident, but seemed to be so busy getting lunch that Edward said he would come back afterwards.

IV

Mollie Gildea said she wanted to call on Mrs. Teely anyway, about gooseberries for bottling. Penrose could drive her round and she would get back to Drumclash on the evening bus. She willingly took charge of Phoebe's letter, as it always gave her satisfaction to kill two birds with one stone.

That being settled, Edward attended to the bees. He was thinking of buying the stocks off Phoebe, so he cared for them like his own, though it meant getting very hot in a bee veil while Phoebe and Mollie relaxed in the shade of the big tree and Mrs. Claremorris sunbathed scientifically on the lawn.

While they were all so engaged a telegram arrived, brought by an exhausted bicyclist who demanded a glass of water and two and six delivery fee. Phoebe opened it carelessly, thinking it was a belated condolence. Then she saw it was from Canada.

Blankly, she read aloud:

"NOTIFICATION DEATH RECEIVED STOP APPRECIATE GESTURE STOP FLYING IRELAND ATTEND FUNERAL STOP PRENDERGAST."

"It can't be my Uncle Hector," said Phoebe. "He's over seventy. He wouldn't be flying the Atlantic."

"They do, you know, dear," said Grania Claremorris. "Seventy's nothing nowadays."

"But just to attend a funeral?"

"And he's missed it too. Couldn't you hold a special memorial service?"

"And where is he to stay?" said Phoebe. "I could give him Henry Sheed's room for a night or two, but he'll want it at the weekend. Perhaps Mrs. Teely would put him up. Or wouldn't that do, without a chaperone?"

Mollie Gildea undertook to broach the matter with Mrs. Teely, thus making three birds with one stone. Failing her, the septuagenarian would have to go to a hotel, and if he could afford to travel by air, he could probably afford to put himself up in comfort.

Though the cable caused some perplexities, it set Edward Gildea's mind at rest on one point. Mrs. Teely was not, after all, Phoebe's next of kin.

## CHAPTER EIGHT

THAT SAME morning Superintendent Menapia had received a message which surprised him. Guinea pigs fed on the remains of the honeycomb that Jason Prendergast had had for tea had died.

He discussed it with Inspector Grace of the Detective Branch, who was closeted with him at the barracks, while Grace's young assistant, Detective Officer Lemon, spent a pleasant day at Coppermine House. Grace was a stern but handsome man, whose neat dark ready-made suit looked tailored to fit, so well did his proportions correspond to the tailor's ideal. He made a striking contrast to the thin, gray, shabby country Superintendent, but this did not worry Menapia.

"Well, there's for you," said Menapia, having his little joke. "A whole hive of suspects."

"The honey might all the same have been doctored," said Grace.

"What you mean is," said Menapia, "it was done by a two-legged bee."

"Well if not," said Grace, "why is this an isolated case? There's been no other death from honey poisoning, sure there hasn't?"

"Not in these parts, but you'd better see what the professor has to say." An expert had at last been found to give an opinion that honey poisoning was a possibility, if not a probability. He was coming down to talk it over both with the police and the Beekeepers' Association. Meanwhile the Guards kept enquiring after beekeepers' health and begging samples from their hives. After much patient work there was a considerable store of honey sections in the Superintendent's cupboard, waiting to be sent off to the analysts. Menapia had been showing them to the Inspector. From the open door of the cupboard there came a warm rich smell of honey, like the smell of a hive in summer. A solitary bee, passing the window, flew in and helped itself unobserved.

"It's early days yet," said Menapia, answering the Inspector's question. "People haven't begun on this year's honey. Some of them say it's too soon to take it off the hives. We should be in time to prevent another casualty."

"What system are you working on?" asked Grace. "If you take only one section from each hive, can they tell from that if the rest's poisoned?"

"No, not for certain. What they can tell is roughly whereabouts the bees have been working. Pollen analysis, they call it. They want to watch out for any out-of-the-ordinary pollen. The flight of a working bee, according to Mr. Gildea across the way," the Superintendent nodded in the direction of Edward's office, "is one and a half to two miles. To do the right thing we should get a section from every hive within a two-mile radius of the hives at Coppermine House."

"I see you believe in being thorough," said Grace. Menapia looked at him quizzically. He knew the plainclothes man was anxious to keep on the right side of him.

"We have to," he said primly, "in the interests of public safety. Two men's full time taken up and every beekeeper in the place with a grievance against us, and according to you it's all for nothing."

"I never said that," said Grace. "Even negative evidence is something. To my mind, it's detail that counts. If you don't find what you're looking for you may stumble on something else. Time and again I've known that to happen. A chemical stain on a piece of cloth, or a piece of dust from a trouser turn-up—things like that can hang a man." The marvels of scientific detection were a pet subject of Grace's.

"Pardon," said Menapia yawning. To show he had been attending he said, "As you say, the means is a better indication than the motive."

"That's right. You can't argue much from a motive. A person may have the best motive in the world for murder and yet not commit it. There's at least three people in this case with some reason to wish the old man dead, and yet perhaps none of them did it."

"Three?"

"Yeah. There's the obvious one, the niece. A bit too obvious in my opinion, though you never know. Then there's the chauffeur." Menapia looked up. "The reason I suspect him is," Grace continued, "he's engaged to the cook, more or less, and the cook, they say, was after the old man herself. She wouldn't be the first who married her employer. So there you have sexual jealousy, the commonest motive for murder next to money, and Penrose looks the type."

"The man's not Irish, of course," said Menapia, refusing to allow for four generations of the family having lived in the Vale. "Who's your third? Mrs. Teely? "

"No, I don't see that she had much to gain. My third's his partner, Mr. Sheed, the owner of the mining rights. Maybe they're worth more than he says."

"You'd have to prove that."

"I don't know that we need pay much attention to it. As Sheed wasn't on the spot there's nothing to connect him with the death." Grace sat back in his chair and put his fingertips together to recapitulate. "Here's how it was," he said. "The old man took the honey off the hive himself about the middle of the morning. He brought it in himself to the larder and packed most of it away in tins, leaving one section out on a plate for his own tea. The only other person to have handled that section was the maid, Vera Byrne, when she laid the tea tray. She admits to having touched it to take the bits of wood off that were round it. The niece says she never even saw it. She went over to Cranbay in the morning to get her hair washed. In the afternoon she went for a walk. She was in the house from about ten minutes before lunch to about half an hour after and during that time she never went near the larder, so she says, and nobody saw her near it either. She might have been, all the same."

"Ay," said Menapia.

"One other person did go into the larder," said Grace, "the garden boy, Mickser. Just a kid up to mischief. I rule out him and the maid, for lack of motive. No, apart from the niece my most likely suspect is the chauffeur. He drove Miss Prendergast to Cranbay in the morning and brought her back. In the afternoon he took down the engine of the car, a job to last him all afternoon. A dirty job too. If he was at that, he'd have to stop and clean up if he was to go in and out of the house and leave no trace. But he could have done it all the same, with a bit of management."

"Like the niece," said Menapia.

"As you say."

"What you want," said Menapia, echoing Colonel Tunney, "is the *modus operandi.*"

"How about this?" Grace reached over and took a section of honey out of the cupboard. Honey dripped out of it on to the table. Most of the samples were only part sealed, this early in the season. Many of them had been put away the wrong way up, for the Superintendent was not familiar with the niceties of honeycomb architecture. As a section is built in the hive, the cells have a slight upward tilt, perceptible only to a close observer. Turn them the other way up and the honey runs out, which was why the cupboard shelves were a sticky mess. Now honey was spreading itself on the table too. The wandering bee who had been in the cupboard came back with a pair of friends. Menapia flapped at them aimlessly, but it was too hot to get up and chase them out.

"See what I mean?" said Grace, looking at the section. "It's got holes in it, empty cells here and there. What's to prevent anyone dropping in poison? A few grains of arsenic would do the trick."

"Wouldn't it have been noticed?"

"His sight can't have been so good at seventy."

"It was, though. He could still read without glasses."

"Is that so?" Menapia had the pleasure of seeing the Dublin detective look baffled. Grace tried again. "Could it have been something injected through the wax?"

"No room for it," said Menapia. "A cell wouldn't be waxed over until it was full to the top."

"Wait now!" This time Grace really thought he had got it. " I have a better idea altogether. Say your man didn't wait till the honey was in the house. Say he tampered with it while it was still in the hive. Drop the stuff in an empty cell and leave the bees to seal it over. Wouldn't that do the business? Know what I mean, the honeycomb would be completed by the bees and there'd be nothing for anyone to notice. And do you know what?" The Inspector sat up with excitement. "Do you see the implications, man? It alters the time factor. If the honey was poisoned before it left the hive,

anyone could have done it any time since the beginning of the season. We'll
have to look beyond the last few days."

Menapia's unresponsive expression damped his enthusiasm. "What's
wrong with it? "'he asked.

"Oh, nothing at all," said Menapia politely. "You might be right, I don't
say you aren't, but if I were you I'd check that with Mr. Gildea. I have heard
tell that if bees find any dirt of any kind in a cell they clean it right out before
they put any honey there. They wouldn't just put the honey in on top."

They sat in silence for a minute or two, the country Superintendent re-
flecting on the wonderful ways of bees, and the town Detective on the devi-
ous ways of human beings.

There was a knock on the door and in came the Sergeant and Guard who
were on the job of collecting honey samples. They had been trailing round
in uniform all that hot morning, tracking down beekeepers who one and all
pretended to be out and persuading them against their wills to open their
hives on a day when it looked as if thunder might be coming. The Sergeant
had a swelling on his neck, and the Guard's cheek bulged as if he had tooth-
ache. They asked if they might buy themselves bee veils and charge them to
expenses. The Superintendent looked dubious. Headquarters might not sanc-
tion it. Bee veils would hardly look right in uniform. The dignity of the
Force has to be maintained.

"You have no need to get stung," he told them. "You shouldn't approach too close to the hive." They went out, looking gloomy, and Menapia
remarked to Grace that things weren't like they used to be in the Force. The
men were getting soft.

But Grace was still intent on his honey section. He felt he was getting an
idea if he could only nail it down.

He looked at Menapia with a challenging eye. "Lookah here! He wouldn't
need wait for the bees to seal the poisoned sections, would he? The man
could do it himself. Anyone a bit neat with his hands could melt a bit of wax
and drop it in on top of the poison and smooth it over, know-what-I-mean?
Who's to know the difference? Then he could put the honey in the larder, *or*
in the hive."

Menapia could find nothing wrong with that.

"The hive might tell us something," said Grace. "A grain of powder on
the floor, fallen hair, or a thread of a coat caught on a nail. There might even
be a fingerprint. I'd like to get that hive up to the Technical Bureau."

"You'd have to get Miss Prendergast's permission, of course." The Superintendent meditated. "How would you set about moving it? Mr. Gildea'd
do the job for us, I'm sure, but maybe he's too closely connected with the
case."

"Haven't you anyone in the Guards?" asked Grace, not favoring the introduction of outsiders. "Some of these country chaps must know about bees."

"I never knew such an ignorant lot as we have at present," said Menapia. "Don't know what the Force is coming to. Some of them wouldn't know a chiffchaff from a willow wren. Wait though, we had a sergeant here once who kept bees. Had a hive in the back of the barracks. I wonder is he still in the land of the living?"

A telephone call to headquarters eventually located the beekeeping sergeant. He was now in charge of a small remote Guard station in the hills. If things were quiet there he might be borrowed. To drive out and consult him would be a pleasanter occupation than sitting in the office waiting for news.

Menapia replaced the honey section in the cupboard, locked the door and put the key in his pocket. He had already invited the Inspector to his own house for dinner. He left word that they would not be back for an hour or two, and ignoring the sticky mess on the table, the two senior officers tramped out.


II


Inspector Grace's assistant, Detective Officer Lemon, was acting as liaison between Coppermine House and the headquarters of the investigation at Drumclash. Since there was no telephone at Coppermine House—the only telephones in those parts being at Civic Guard stations and post offices—he had to carry messages between the two points. He covered the distance on a push bicycle, his application to hire a motor bicycle having been turned down as putting too much of a burden on the taxpayer.

Tired of inactivity, D/O Lemon had sprung to the saddle to bear the news of the cable from Canada which had arrived for Phoebe Prendergast. Up till then the police had not taken much interest in Jason Prendergast's long-lost brother. A next of kin last heard of fifty years ago in a distant country is one thing, but a next of kin flying home the moment he knew his brother was dead is another. D/O Lemon had found out all there was to find out about him, namely his home address. The Inspector might want to consult the Canadian police about him. After all, he seemed to be the family black sheep. D/O Lemon hoped he had earned a pat on the back.

D/O Lemon had worked with Inspector Grace on one other case. When Grace asked for him again, he took it as a compliment, but the Inspector spoiled it by telling him he looked on him chiefly as a mascot, and that it was better to be lucky than clever. He also kindly said that Mick Lemon's innocent appearance might prove an asset if he stopped being as innocent as he looked.

Pink with exertion, D/O Lemon pedaled through the beautiful scenery of the Vale of Morna, and wished he was back in Dublin trailing a shoplifter round Woolworth's, or doing anything with a definite object in view and some hope of arresting somebody for something. Cycle rides in the country were not what he had in mind when he joined the Force. It wasn't like going out with the Flying Squad.

But there was action in store for him. A police officer never knows when he may be confronted with a situation demanding courage, ingenuity and resource. Such a situation confronted D/O Lemon when he reached Drumclash Civic Guard barracks.

The Superintendent and the Inspector were still out. The Sergeant in charge said Mr. Lemon could go into the Superintendent's office if he wanted a place to write out his report. D/O Lemon opened the door and shut it again quickly. He turned to find the Sergeant and the rest of the barracks staff watching him with interested anticipation.

The Superintendent's room was alive with bees.

## III

Penrose drove Edward Gildea back to his office. When Edward got out of the car Penrose said unexpectedly

"Could I speak to you a minute, sir?"

Edward was intrigued at the prospect of a glimpse of the human being behind the chauffeur's grim correctitude. He brought him up to his room, put him in the client's chair, and waited to be told what the trouble was.

Penrose, that silent man, had a struggle to find words. His face worked, and Edward noted that his fists were actually clenched. Was he bringing evidence concerning the death of his master? For a wild moment Edward thought he was going to confess to a crime. At last he muttered, "It's about a woman."

"Explain yourself, man," said Edward. "What woman? What's the matter with you?"

"The cook above at the house, sir. Vera Byrne. I want to have her in Court." He was red with fury. " I want to sue her for breach of promise."

Edward felt let down. He had long ceased to be interested in other people's matrimonial muddles. When Mollie, his wife, wondered what attraction Vera could possibly find in Penrose, Edward had reminded her that rural romance rests as much on savings as sex appeal. All the same, he was not altogether surprised that she had gone back on her choice.

"Have you anything in writing?" he asked.

"I have not," said Penrose, "but I have witnesses."

Edward looked dubious. "Well, go on, tell me all about it. When did she promise to marry you?"

"She promised to marry me whenever the master died."

Edward's question had been ambiguously worded. He had meant to ask when Vera had made her promise. However, he gradually extracted the whole story.

Vera Byrne had been the reason why Penrose became Mr. Prendergast's chauffeur. He had formerly worked in the mine, in the days of Prendergast & Sheed, and when the works closed down he had remained in Mr. Prendergast's service. His idea had been to marry Vera Byrne at once. She could keep on as cook, and he would get his meals in the kitchen, while she shared his rooms over the garage. But Vera did not fall in with this plan. She said she wanted a house of her own.

Houses were scarce round Morna and Drumclash. The kind of home they wanted was what the County Council struggled to provide for agricultural laborers, but it was no use applying for one unless you had seven children already, and as Vera refused to cooperate in this respect the position was a deadlock. Then Penrose heard of a cottage he could rent near Dublin. He proposed that they should both give notice and find themselves work in the city. Vera had replied that she did not like to leave old Mr. Prendergast stranded.

It was difficult to make out how much Penrose had to go on in the way of encouragement from Vera. He seemed inclined to take a good deal for granted. The nearest she seemed to have got to a promise of marriage was to declare, "before witnesses" as Penrose insisted, that she would marry Penrose if it was not for old Mr. Prendergast. Penrose repeated this several times word for word.

" 'I'd marry you if it wasn't for the Master.' These were her words. Mickser's mother and father were there listening to her. 'I'd marry you if it wasn't for the Master,' she says. And now she says she never thought of the Master dying so soon."

"Of course she didn't," said Edward. "It's been a shock to her. You must give her time."

"Amn't I after giving her three years' time, the strap! It's not time she wants. I would give her time only for the way she's carrying on with the Civic Guards. It's a disgrace to the world."

Edward recollected that Phoebe had said Vera was a flirt.

"Why don't you look elsewhere yourself, Penrose?" he said.

Penrose struck an attitude. He said he wasn't going to stand for being made a fool of.

"Oh come," said Edward, "a woman has a right to change her mind. Besides, you haven't suffered any financial loss."

"I have so. I could have got a better job, many's the time. I could have gone to England and got a job at ten pounds a week. And haven't I a right to get damages for my broken heart?"

"I'm afraid you haven't a case," said Edward Gildea in his most downright way. "You'd be making a fool of yourself to bring an action on no more grounds than you've got. Think what it would sound like, read out in Court. You'd have the whole town laughing at you. Have sense, man! You're not the first to be crossed in love."

Penrose was hard to convince. He went on muttering about his rights in a threatening tone, till Edward lost all patience with him. Having tried all civil means of getting rid of him, he was beginning to think he would have to turn him out, which would make their relations more awkward than ever afterwards, when his clerk came running upstairs to say that he was wanted at the barracks.

## IV

The bee that had visited the Superintendent's office that morning came from a hive in the backyard of a shop farther down the street. It was a mismanaged hive that had reared a large number of young bees on the honey flow, and now that these were of age to go out to forage, the honey flow had temporarily ceased and they were short of supplies. Hedges that a little earlier had offered a variety of small flowers close together to choose from, like the counters of a multiple stores, now had shed their blossom. The chestnut candles had wasted in the heat. The young bees toiled round ragweed and charlock, bringing home a poor harvest of bitter honey. Then came a sudden revelation of plenty at their door.

The first scout that had been at the honey cupboard came home and danced a dance. It was not just dancing for joy. The bees have their code of communication, expressed in movements. It has even been interpreted by human observers, notably Dr. Otto Frisch. Had Dr. Frisch been there to see this bee go up and down, to and fro, waggling its tail in a particular direction, he might have known that it had discovered ample supplies nearby on a line southwest. But no human eye witnessed the performance in the darkness of the brood chamber, on the empty combs.

Another bee returned with the scout to investigate. Then it too danced the dance, and the news spread through the hive. Bees returning from toilsome flights farther afield sped off to the new source. Soon there were hundreds of them cleaning up the honey on the Superintendent's desk.

But the first scout knew there was more. The cupboard door was shut, but the bee had been in once, and it was baffled only for a moment. The keyhole (from which the Superintendent had thoughtfully removed the key) made a perfect beeway. Bees love to crawl through little dark tunnels. They queued up for it, buzzing to and fro. Once inside they wasted no time. They lingered not to sip for themselves but loaded up, buzzed off to the parent hive and returned for more, bringing still more bees with them. They worked with the determined concentration on business that has made bees an example with moralists and a byword with ordinary human beings.

"No, they aren't swarming," said Edward Gildea. "I only wish they were, they'd be easier to deal with. These bees are robbing. If you leave quantities of honey about where they can get at it, only a few hundred yards from a hive at this stage in the season, what else do you expect?"

"Robbing?" said the Sergeant, and his hand reached automatically for a crime sheet.

"That's right," said Edward, "and I should leave them to it, if I were you. They'll quiet down when they've cleaned the place out. The Superintendent can't have honey for his tea, but that can't be helped."

It is one thing to take a peaceful contented swarm when everything is going well, and quite another to interfere with a bad-tempered band of robbers out of a strange hive. Swarming bees may or may not sting, but with robbers there is no doubt. The Hon. Secretary of the Drumclash and District Beekeepers' Association felt there were jobs at which one had to draw the line.

But the full impact of the situation at last struck the Sergeant. "Holy Saints!" he exclaimed. "The samples! That honey wasn't for eating, it was for sending up to Dublin this evening. They're destroying evidence!"

Something had to be done, and by Edward Gildea. The owner of the bees, a garage man, had gone out testing a car, and his assistant disclaimed responsibility. The County Horticultural instructor was far away instructing backward farmers in filling up forms. There was an extraordinary absence from Drumclash that afternoon of other members of the Beekeepers' Association. In fact Edward did not know where to turn for an assistant, unless he enlisted one of the barracks staff, and there was no rush to volunteer.

Then forth stepped bold Mick Lemon, ambitious for promotion and ready to try anything once. "Mind you," he said, "I don't know one end of a bee from the other."

"You will," said Edward Gildea.

The garage owner's wife lent equipment: a smoker and a goose's wing, a veil, and a pair of old gloves with the fingertips cut out. A syringe was commandeered from the General Stores. Edward warned his assistant to put on his bicycle clips; nothing impairs a beekeeper's efficiency so much as the suspicion that a bee may be crawling up his leg. Another thing calculated to sap his morale is a hole in his bee veil. The borrowed veil was pinned together in one place with a twisted hairpin; the pin held the pieces together, but every time it bobbed against Mick Lemon's face he thought a bee had got through.

With all their armor on, such as it was, Edward and Mick went into action. The rest of the barracks staff left them the field to themselves. They showered water from the syringe over the room in general. They puffed smoke through the keyhole of the cupboard. They opened the window wide and swept out bees with the goose wing. The bees buzzed vigorously round their heads and against their veils, forming themselves into suicide squads and leaving stings on the hats and collars of the attackers if they failed to get on the target. Edward and Mick were soon panting with exhaustion. It is surprising how hot one can get in a bee veil, even out of doors, let alone in a room not much bigger than a meat safe.

Meanwhile those in the neighboring houses saw puffs of smoke issuing from the barracks windows. Word went round that the house was on fire. A crowd collected in the street. Business in the shops was at a standstill and through traffic was held up. Cars, buses and lorries, hooting their indignation at being delayed in their nationally important business, added to the turmoil. While the fire rumor was being contradicted several others started. Some said a bomb had been thrown in at the window of the barracks, others that it was a time bomb and had been smuggled in along with the Sergeant's washing. Most people believed it was some kind of political demonstration, and almost turned it into one by arguing about the various topical grievances that might have provoked it. Only the truth was too improbable a story to be accepted.

This was the position when Superintendent Menapia and Inspector Grace returned from their country drive. They left their car at the end of a long queue and pushed their way through the crowd. They were just in time to see D/O Lemon stagger to the front door, his veil wreathed round his hat, his face dripping, and a goose wing in his hand. He had come out for a breath of air, not knowing what to expect and when he saw the crowd his mouth dropped open and stayed open, as he stood transfixed on the threshold. A camera clicked. It belonged to a member of the Humphry Madigan company who dabbled in free-lance journalism. "Just a minute," he called, "could I have your name please?" D/O Lemon pulled himself together and saluted gallantly. Just as the camera clicked again, he caught the eye of Inspector Grace and ducked for safety.

Superintendent Menapia reached the barracks and made some terse remarks to the sergeant in charge. The Superintendent's arrival had a moral effect on the Guards who were trying to disperse the crowd, and at last they managed to clear a lane for traffic. Reluctantly the citizens of Drumclash concluded that whatever had or had not happened it was all over now.

Edging his way cautiously into his own office, Menapia found Edward Gildea trying to pick the lock of his cupboard, which still sheltered an unknown quantity of bees. Menapia gave him the key, and took cover. There was a further engagement with the bees, lasting about twenty minutes. Then at last Edward Gildea ventured to pronounce the situation under control, and even as he pronounced it, one last bee that had been in ambush stung him on the ear.

The Superintendent found his office one damp sticky mess of water and honey with a sprinkling of dead bees. Inspector Grace found his assistant exhausted. Detective Officer Lemon was afflicted for some time after with a kind of St. Vitus' dance—a tendency to start suddenly and brush off imaginary bees, and he complained of a humming in his ears.

But the samples were saved, and Menapia lost no time in getting them packed and despatched to the analysts.

The Superintendent further sanctioned the purchase of one bee veil, to be put in charge of the Station Sergeant and issued for use in emergencies.

Detective Officer Lemon's photograph subsequently appeared in a weekly paper, with a brief account of the incident. He cut it out and sent it to his mother. Later on a more colorful account appeared in *The Garda Review,* which likes comic relief.

It may as well be added in conclusion, though slightly in anticipation of events, that when the report came from the analysts all the samples of honey were guaranteed pure and fit for human consumption.

## CHAPTER NINE

FROM BEES at the barracks to bees at the bungalow: while Edward Gildea was battling with the robber horde, his wife Mollie was scientifically observing bee behavior in company with Mrs. Teely.

The bungalow, called for some reason "El Jireh," was on the main road, where the road and river emerged from the mine into green fields. It had battlements round the roof and pointed windows like a church, a blend of defensiveness and piety which somehow suited the owner. It stood on about half an acre of ground. The small piece in front was almost filled by two large old rhododendron bushes, while the back garden was intensively cultivated with fruit, vegetables and the saleable kinds of flowers. The beehives were on a flat part of the roof. Whatever the time of year there would be a notice on the gate offering something for sale. These notices changed like the leaves of a calendar: "Daffodils" and "Cabbage plants" were taken down when "Lettuce" and "Gooseberries" went up, while "Tomatoes" and "Windfall apples" waited their turn.

As Mollie Gildea walked up the path between the rhododendrons she noticed a good many bees on them and made a note to tell her husband. She went closer to look, and brushing a leaf with her hand she found it sticky. It seemed odd, but she did not think much of it at the time.

The door was on the latch and she walked in. The house smelled of paraffin lamps and furniture polish. It was crammed with furniture and bric-a-brac. Mrs. Teely among other things dealt in antiques. Most people pitied her for having from time to time to sell her family heirlooms, but Mollie knew she was a regular attender at auctions, and most of her goods and chattels were things she had picked up herself with an eye to profit. Squeezing past a linen chest and a Welsh dresser, the visitor made her way through the back door into the garden, where the mistress of "El Jireh" was generally to be found.

Mrs. Teely was sitting on a camp stool stooping intently over something she had in front of her on the top of a chicken coop. She wore a dun-colored overall and round her head a colored cotton head-square, and looked very much like a gypsy crystal gazer. She jumped at Mollie's voice, but recovered herself at once and assured her that she did not mind being interrupted.

"I am busy," she said, "but then I always am, and that's no reason why you should have your journey for nothing. Do find yourself something to sit on—there's a butter box over there—and excuse my not getting up, because I have to concentrate. I shall not let it distract my attention."

It did not seem a good opportunity to broach a delicate subject, but Mollie hoped to propitiate Mrs. Teely by a sympathetic interest in whatever she might be doing and so pave the way for the peacemaking mission she had undertaken for Phoebe Prendergast.

The objects on the chicken coop were mysterious: a stop watch, a notepad and pencil, a saucer containing something sticky, and two bottles of nail varnish, which last Mrs. Teely never used on her nails and always professed to scorn.

Mrs. Teely's attitude grew tense, and the visitor saw that her eyes were fixed on a bee which had buzzed down over their heads, no doubt from one of the hives on the roof. It circled round the saucer and presently alighted and began to suck. Mrs. Teely reached for the nearest bottle of nail varnish—a bright red shade—and unscrewed the top which had the usual small brush attached. She held the brush poised, and deftly dropped a spot of varnish on the bee's tail. The bee did not seem to mind; having finished its drink it flew straight off towards the hives. Mrs. Teely quickly set the stop watch going, glanced at her own wrist and made a note. She said, "Now we must watch for it to came back. It will most likely take between three and four minutes. Ah, here comes another!"

She reached for the other bottle of varnish, which was a pale pink, and decorated the second bee in the same manner as the first.

"A contrasting shade," she said, "for purposes of comparison. One has to be careful not to touch their wings or heads. I find this little brush so handy. The girl at the Medical Hall thought I was completely mad when I told her why I wanted nail varnish. I was afraid she might imagine it was intended for my hands."

The stop watch was still timing the first bee, which now appeared again. Mrs. Teely, busy making a note on Bee Number Two, became very agitated, scribbling with one hand and stopping the watch with the other. Keeping her eyes fixed on the bees she said to Mollie, "I'll tell you how you could help, dear. Write down the times for me. Number One Bee, three and a half minutes exactly, and forty seconds to drink."

Mollie reached meekly for the pad, and asked what exactly Mrs. Teely was trying to do. She had by now a glimmering of an idea, for Mollie had the advantage over the girl at the Medical Hall of having lived with a beekeeper and witnessed various forms of beekeeping eccentricity. She even knew that the sticky saucer was called an artificial flower, though it was hardly the kind one would pin on an evening dress. Mrs. Teely looked important. She replied, "It's a mass experiment by readers of *The Apiarist*. We have to fill up a form. Results will be sent in from all over Europe. The object is to ascertain how long bees take coming and going and taking up nectar, and also how quickly the news of a source of supply becomes communicated to others. See, here is a third bee already. Soon there will be many more, and every ten minutes I shall count how many there are on the saucer."

It was a pity Mrs. Teely was not in Drumclash to observe the bees at the barracks.

Mollie Gildea thought this looked like taking all afternoon. At first there was a certain sporting fascination in watching for Bee One and Bee Two to arrive, as they did alternately every two or three minutes. Mollie dutifully clocked them in, while Mrs. Teely chatted about ways in which one could test the bees' sense of direction, color preferences and quickness in the uptake, and generally assess their intelligence quota. The garden baked in the sun. All life but the insects' succumbed to the heat and drowsed. Sweet scents pervaded the air. No sound came from all the valley but the hum of the toiling bees and Mrs. Teely's voice chatting on. At last a train whistle sounding at the tunnel between Drumclash and Morna warned Mollie that the afternoon was getting on, and she sought in her mind for a way to introduce more personal topics.

She remarked casually that she had been lunching at Coppermine House. Mrs. Teely stiffened.

"I'm not sure that I want to hear anything about that house," she said.

"Oh, I know how you feel," said Mollie warmly, "and I can quite understand it. But dear Mrs. Teely, are you being quite fair?"

"It is not my feelings that matter," replied Mrs. Teely. "There are some kinds of behavior that leave a bad taste in the mouth."

"Phoebe Prendergast is very sorry she has offended you," said Mollie. "She has written to apologize."

"My dear, please leave me out of it. I make no complaint for myself. What does hurt is to see poor Jason's memory so little respected, and by one who owes him so much. His home thrown open to riffraff, yes, riffraff. People who would never have crossed the threshold in Jason's lifetime. And a member of the family shown the door."

"But Mrs. Teely, Phoebe never saw it in that light. Her friends, I believe, are a perfectly respectable couple, and she only thought what it would be like for them in Drumclash lodgings: damp beds, fleas or worse, the windows never opened—"

"I daresay," said Mrs. Teely, "and no keys to the bedroom doors."

"That's just what I mean," said Mollie, though this last disadvantage had not occurred to her.

"But stage people are used to all that."

"Well, it's not what one would like for one's friends," said Mollie firmly. "But apart from that, I know Phoebe was thinking of you as well as them. She was worried at the thought of you putting yourself out for her, leaving your own house empty at night, with your bees and all your lovely old things."

"That was nothing to me compared with the duty of standing by a younger relation and protecting her reputation."

"But if Mrs. Claremorris was there to act as chaperone—" After all, Mrs. Teely had not seen Mrs. Claremorris in her sunbathing costume.

Mrs. Teely's reply took Mollie aback.

"Oh my dear Mrs. Gildea," she said, "as if a chaperone was all she needed! Surely you guessed that was the merest pretext. I don't mean that she ought not to have one, indeed she ought. But matters may be far more serious than that. I could not very well say it in so many words to the girl herself, but surely the same thought is in all our minds." She dropped her voice. "Phoebe may have to face a murder charge."

"Mrs. Teely!"

"Yes dear, facts must be faced. What are all these detectives doing, hanging about the house? You and I may think the idea is preposterous, but what can we prove? All we can do, especially myself, is to lend her all the moral support of respectable connections. That is precisely what I hoped to achieve by staying in the house. I cannot think the presence of casual theatrical acquaintances is of equal value."

Mollie gaped at Mrs. Teely, wondering if she had misjudged her. Then she felt angry with her. Need she be so quick to assume that people would think of Phoebe as a murderess? The idea might cross one's mind, but that was another thing from believing in it. And what Mollie could not believe was that all this had been in Mrs. Teely's mind so early as the first morning, when she had rushed round to Coppermine House immediately on hearing the news of Jason Prendergast's death. No, her original reason for staying had been something more selfish; economy, perhaps, or sheer curiosity, or designs on Vera Byrne. She had never thought of labeling Phoebe a suspect until she had a grievance against her.

"I thought you thought it was the honey," said Mollie.

"Certainly," said Mrs. Teely. "But it is what the police think that counts, as Phoebe will find out for herself."

She looked so forbidding and so like her deceased Cousin Jason that if Edward Gildea had been in charge of the peace parley he would have given up.

Bees Numbers One and Two had by now spread the news of the artificial flower to a number of their friends and relations, or these had discovered it for themselves. The saucer was thickly clustered with bees, and Mrs. Teely became very busy counting and ostentatiously determined to concentrate. Mollie counted too; it was as good as going through the alphabet to prevent oneself losing one's temper. But after making an entry on the notepad, she took advantage of an off moment to reintroduce the subject of Phoebe's affairs. She still had a card to play.

She said, "I was going to tell you the news. Who do you think may arrive any minute? He meant to be here for the funeral and will be sorry he's missed it." Mollie looked expectantly at Mrs. Teely as she spoke, and saw that she had made her sit up.

Mrs. Teely said, staring: "You can't mean—"

Mollie nodded. "I do. Hector Prendergast. Phoebe had a cable, I saw it myself. It arrived while we were there to lunch. He's flying the Atlantic."

"Flying the Atlantic at his age!"

"But he didn't say when he would arrive. And now the question is, where is *he* to stay, as Phoebe has no room for him?"

The news had thrown Mrs. Teely into a trance. She sat staring at the saucer of bees, but Numbers One and Two got by unobserved, and their friends and relations proceeded to mop up the remains of the syrup without either lady taking any more notice of them. Mollie ventured a question.

"How old is he? Can you remember him at all, Mrs. Teely, or were you only a child when he went away?"

Mrs. Teely collected her thoughts with a start. "I was a child of seventeen and my cousins, Hector, Horace and Jason, were all young men in their twenties. I remember them all perfectly well, especially Hector, because he had a motor car, the first that was ever seen in the Vale, and he used to give me rides in it. He was a general favorite, I think. I for one was very sorry he had to go, but of course there was nothing else for it."

"Did he do anything very dreadful, Mrs. Teely? If it isn't being too inquisitive."

"He meant no harm," said Mrs. Teely, "but he was always inclined to be too optimistic. When he took an interest in mining (as was natural for anyone in our family) he made sure there must be gold in the hills here, as we know there was at one time. He formed a company to look for it and sold a whole lot of shares to people we knew, and then it all came to nothing. I don't think Hector really understood business. Some of the shareholders wanted to be paid back, but I don't think he was legally responsible; what made it awkward was knowing the people, for of course shareholders are generally just names on paper. Some of Hector's turned quite nasty, and he had to go away, if only for the sake of the family. He hated leaving Ireland. He told me so the night before he went." At the memory of that parting Mrs. Teely breathed a sentimental sigh.

"How sad," said Mollie, but she was thinking of Mrs. Teely rather than of the defaulting Hector. Had there been a broken romance? There did not seem much hope of mending it after fifty years. But Mrs. Teely had been the one to make Phoebe send word to Canada, and now here was Hector flying home.

"He must have done well for himself out there," she said, "if he can afford to fly."

"Oh, he may have borrowed the fare," said Mrs. Teely. "That would be quite like Hector. But it seems as if home still means something to him after all these years. He must have been lonely out there. He was such a dear, affectionate, thoughtful boy."

"How strange it will be for you to meet again!"

"Strange, my dear, and sad," replied Mrs. Teely. "Neither of us will have changed for the better. I'm not sure it isn't a meeting I shall try to avoid. After all, it is not me he is coming to see. I daresay he will have forgotten my existence."

Mollie Gildea saw through this. Mrs. Teely was all agog to meet Hector Prendergast and was only afraid she would not be asked. This, therefore, was the moment to produce Phoebe's letter. She produced it out of her bag, pretending to have forgotten it till searching for her bus guide.

Mrs. Teely graciously consented to open the letter, and as she read it her attitude softened.

"Well, well," she said, "one must make allowances. Phoebe has not had our advantages. Her education, poor child, must have been very irregular, but she has some nice feelings after all, for she invites me to choose a memento of poor Jason from among his personal things. I am really touched that she should think of it. I wonder what sort of thing she had in mind?"

Mollie, who had not known what was in the letter, could not tell her, but she was amused to think that Phoebe had summed Mrs. Teely up pretty well.

"Just some small personal trifle, I suppose," said Mrs. Teely. "Hardly anything so considerable as a piece of furniture. I should not have room for anything like that. I always admired the potato ring on the dining room sideboard that was presented to Jason by his Masonic Lodge, but it's not old silver, only a reproduction. There's a nice cream jug that really is old. I think one ought to choose something that will be often in use, if one wants to keep a person's memory green. A thing I do need is a letter scales, for weighing out the tea in ounces for my daily. There was a brass one on Jason's desk, but I daresay I might pick up one like it anywhere fairly cheap. I think on the whole the cream jug—" She folded up the letter and put it in her handbag. "I'll just pop round there some time and consult Phoebe herself."

Mollie saw that her mission was a success, but she thought it might help to preserve friendly relations between the cousins if she warned Phoebe of the direction of Mrs. Teely's ideas on mementoes, in case Phoebe's were different.

Her bus was due, so she took her leave. As they passed through the small front garden she noticed that there were still plenty of bees on the rhododendrons, which showed that Edward's observation did not cover everything. She was about to ask Mrs. Teely what made the leaves sticky, but the bus came and she had to run for it.


## CHAPTER 10


FINDING the police so much interested in honey, Edward Gildea began to have hopes of his theory. At least he was hopeful on his client's account, and he was also mildly excited at the thought of the case figuring in bee journals and proud of having a small piece of bee history made in the Vale. But there was another side to the picture, and he had to recognize that, from the point of view of local beekeeping, it might spell disaster.

Edward, in fact, had a good deal to answer for when the Drumclash and District Beekeepers' Association finally met to discuss the matter. For years the members had been congratulating themselves on having such a loyal, zealous, efficient, knowledgeable secretary, and now they felt they had been cherishing a snake in their bosoms. For they all knew now who had been putting ideas into the Superintendent's head, or in other words, how he had got bees in his bonnet.

For once the Hon. Secretary could not complain of the attendance. The Association turned out in full strength, but instead of the usual friendly atmosphere there were groups muttering together in corners, and dark looks and worried expressions. To add to Edward's troubles, the speaker was late. The Superintendent had promised to meet his train and drive him down, but time went by and there was no sign of either of them. Then Inspector Grace, slipping in unobtrusively at the back, told Edward the Superintendent had been delayed by a call from headquarters, and the Professor with him, but they would both be along soon. As this sounded vague and people were looking impatient, Edward suggested to the President of the Association that they might open the meeting with a general discussion, while waiting for higher guidance.

Beekeepers make almost as interesting a study as bees. It would be difficult to find any other bond that would collect such a varied lot of individuals together in one room. On the whole they were backyard beekeepers in the Drumclash Association, though there was Brother Aidan from the monastery, who had charge of five hundred hives and ran out-apiaries, hiring hives to farmers to pollinate orchards and pastures. The President, Lord Cranbay, had been elected more as a distinguished resident than a bee-man; he had one hive, which he placed on the portico of his Georgian mansion to keep out visitors. Miss Bryony, the librarian, had bought a hive after reading Maeterlinck's *Life of the Bee,* and cherished her bees like a mother, nursing sickly ones in tins, and filling hot-water bottles to put in with them on winter nights. Mrs. Grant-Kimberley, the richest member, just hated to think of all the honey that must be going to waste in her large garden, so bought half a dozen new hives and all the latest kinds of equipment and re-queened her stocks every year with American queens at a guinea each. Father Banim, the parish priest, kept bees for the odd reason that he was fond of carpentry. Mr. Emoe, the schoolmaster, thought them educational. Young Peter Smythe, who was at a public school, kept them because pets were allowed and he wanted to be original. Old John Hargreaves of the General Stores found it paid to know something about bees if you stocked beekeeping appliances. There were also farmers, farm laborers, retired colonels, maiden ladies, and other such natives of the countryside, who kept bees because it seemed the natural thing to do if you were fond of honey.

Lord Cranbay was on Edward Gildea's side about the poisonous honey, but then he had nothing to lose. He never opened his own hive nowadays, he just let the bees consume their own stores. He was intrigued by the idea as something new and also had a fellow feeling for the Prendergasts as landowners, and hoped there would be no scandal. He began by asking members to stand and pass a vote of condolence with the relations of the late Mr. Prendergast, for he thought this might bring home to everybody that it was a serious matter. It caused him some embarrassment, though adding to the effect, when Mrs. Teely took it on herself to make a speech of acknowledgment, more or less in tears, and promised to convey the sympathy of the meeting to Miss Prendergast. When this was got over, the President called on the Hon. Secretary to speak for himself.

Edward had brushed his hair and straightened his tie before he left home. He now took a firm hold on both lapels of his tweed coat and launched out. He was not going to waste time apologizing, whatever members might expect of him. He wanted a full discussion, he said.

"While we're waiting for Professor O'Moore (who should be along any minute now), perhaps we might pool our own knowledge. What we want to do today is to get at the facts. We don't want a whispering campaign. If there is poisonous honey in the district we want to trace it to its source, so that it can be got rid of. If it's all a false alarm, we want the rumor officially contradicted. And whatever we may feel about the idea as beekeepers, I hope we're all out to do our duty as citizens." Sad to say this exhortation met with no applause.

Edward had come furnished with extracts from articles in *The Bee World*, which he now asked permission to read aloud. The principal authority was a Russian writer who said that cases of honey poisoning were common in the Caucasus. People were often taken ill and fell down in paroxysms ending in a long swoon or death. It was sealed honey in the comb which seemed to be to blame for the symptoms, and, moreover, the poison might be confined to a few cells, since more than one person could eat from the same comb and not all be affected. Cases were more frequent in dry seasons; popular opinion attributed the poison to rhododendrons, but many bee-men said that it was not honey at all, but a honeydew deposited by insects on the leaves.

By the time Edward sat down the meeting had plenty to chew on. Before the President could call on anybody else, up rose Mr. Hargreaves of the General Stores. He was anxious to remove any misunderstanding about his own position as representing the trade. The Stores would not be in the market for honey until all allegations, as he put it, were withdrawn. "There's a glut this year anyhow," he said. "The price won't be economic, it's only taking it off people's hands to oblige. If the honey's poisonous into the bargain, I can't be running the risk. It isn't as if I could send it to England." Mr. Hargreaves was a believer in letting the world know where he stood. His declared intention not to handle any more honey for market without a certificate did nothing to lighten the atmosphere.

His voice, gruff with a slight northern accent, had hardly ceased when the theme was taken up by the shrill voice of Mrs. Grant-Kimberley, like an imperfectly tuned violin giving the reply to a somewhat heavy-handed cello. Mrs. Kimberley demanded what right the Guards had to interfere with things they knew nothing about. The idea of wanting honey at this stage in the season! Hers was not capped nor even ripe, yet they seemed to imagine one had only to lift the roof off a hive and take out a perfect section. The men who called at her house had never even heard of a super-clearer. Such ignorance! She had said, "If you want honey, go and take it. Help yourselves!" and she was glad to think they had got stung for their pains.

This speech was regrettably popular, and punctuated by laughter. It gave the cue to an elderly farmer with a lifelong habit of demanding his rights to ask what was being done in the way of fixing compensation. Obviously the government ought to pay for the honey beekeepers would be unable to sell. It was the Hon. Secretary's job to point this out to the authorities. The Hon. Secretary cursed inwardly, but the President came to his aid. He soothed the speaker by saying that this very important question must be put on the agenda for the next committee meeting, but that what they had to do that afternoon was to collect evidence for or against the occurrence of poisonous honey.

Two people stood up together, Mr. Emoe the schoolmaster and Father Banim. Mr. Emoe politely deferred to the Church, and the reverend Father proceeded gravely to warn everyone against paying too much attention to any scientific pronouncements that came from Russia, a country where not only had they abandoned all religion, but even truth on the materialistic plane had to be distorted in obedience to the dictates of a ruling clique. After this Mr. Emoe looked sorry he had caught the President's eye, but on being pressed to say his piece he diffidently explained that he too had read the article in *The Bee World* and it had interested him because of what Xenophon said on the same subject. He was also interested in the reference to rhododendrons, of which there had been such magnificent displays in the Vale this year. It might just be worth drawing attention to the coincidence, because in spite of the Iron Curtain, it was all one world.

"But do bees work rhododendrons?" asked Lord Cranbay. "There are banks of rhododendrons ail round my house, and I don't know that I ever saw a bee on them."

The question started a series of arguments all over the room. Apart from certainties like hawthorn and fruit blossom and clover, everybody had their own ideas as to which plants bees prefer. Honeysuckle, for instance, in spite of the song, is of no more use to bees than a tin to a man without a tin opener. Some held that rhododendrons presented the same difficulty of construction, having long tubes that bees cannot get their tongues down. Others asserted that Italian bees have longer tongues than the commoner strains and can collect nectar from a wider range of flowers. This led to the old controversy about the merits of Italian versus native bees. Arguments went briskly round in circles and there was a danger of national prejudices being aroused, when fortunately the Superintendent arrived, and with him a spruce old gentleman in black, who looked, and was, the Professor.

The Professor beamed at the class, apologized offhandedly for being late, and came straight to business. He launched into an account of an outbreak of honey poisoning which had occurred in New Zealand and which had been investigated by the New Zealand Department of Agriculture. In April 1945 some of the honey of the Pongakawa Valley was found to be poisonous, though some was harmless, and though all of it alike appeared to be derived from the tutu tree. Pollen of this tree *(Coriaria arborea)* was found in both toxic and nontoxic honey. It was noticed, however, that the trees were covered with honeydew and that the bees were collecting this as well as nectar from the flowers. Experiment proved that the nectar from the flowers was safe to eat, but the honeydew, excreted by insects which had sucked the leaf juices, contained a hitherto unknown poison, which was isolated and called by the chemists "mellitoxin."

"And it is, I think, worth noting," said the Professor, in a high, precise voice, his eyes fixed on the ceiling, "that the prevalence of honeydew is linked with particular climatic conditions. In dry years there is more of it, whether it is that heat causes the insects to multiply, or induces them to suck the leaf juices, or that shortage of water induces the bees to take to the honeydew, the point is that the trouble seems unlikely to arise except in time of drought."

He brought his gaze back to his audience. It was now looking more cheerful. There was a buzz of talk when the speaker paused. Most people welcomed this new explanation. The drought had certainly been phenomenal. Anything might happen if you had fine weather in Ireland for six weeks on end. At least there was no need to root up rhododendrons or destroy stocks of Italian bees. Only the President, while thanking the Professor, said dubiously that he had never noticed honeydew on anything in his garden, any more than he had seen any bees on his rhododendrons.

Mollie Gildea then made her contribution. She did not often speak at meetings, for fear of disgracing Edward, but this time she felt really justified. She told how she had noticed stickiness on some rhododendron bushes at Mrs. Teely's, not more than half a mile from Coppermine House and within easy reach of Mr. Prendergast's hives. All eyes turned to Mrs. Teely, who looked put out and turned rather red. She said, "You all know what it's like; the house to run and the busiest time of year in the garden, and the parish fête on top of it all, one job after another from morning to night. I don't have time to notice things." So the hypothesis rested on Mollie's assertion, but that was good enough for most people.

The President asked if the Superintendent or the Detective Inspector would care to say anything before he closed the proceedings. Superintendent Menapia, who seemed to have been wrapped in meditation, woke up with a start, thanked everybody for their kind assistance, and apologized for the trouble they had been caused. He reminded them that a theory is only a theory until it is supported by facts, and that this one had yet to be tested by analyzing samples of honey for mellitoxin.

The President then dismissed the meeting, saying, "I won't keep you any longer because I'm sure you're all as anxious as I am to take a look at your trees and shrubs and see if you can find traces of honeydew on them."

He spoke too late. As the meeting was on the point of breaking up a startling change came over the day. It was heralded by a tremendous thunderclap. The oppressiveness of the weather had reached its culmination. Clouds had been piling up slowly all afternoon; now they burst under their own weight, and rain sluiced through the streets of Drumclash and pelted the country for miles around.

Everyone was delighted to see it. The whole atmosphere of the meeting changed with the freshening of the air. Members who had been glaring at each other a few minutes earlier sat back and relaxed, thought how they could have baths again, and how with a day or two of rain like this they would be saved carrying water long journeys to thirsty cattle and gardens. The pastures would revive, the crops come on, the clover flowers would again secrete nectar and the bees have wholesome occupation. The schoolroom hummed like a hive during a honey flow.

"Well, Superintendent," said the President, waving his hand towards the streaming windows, "if the Professor's right you won't have any more trouble. This will wash all the honeydew away."

"And we shall never know for certain that there was any," said the Superintendent. He did not seem to care.

He collected Inspector Grace and the Professor and bundled them out to his car, without giving members a chance to buttonhole them.

Mrs. Teely also left at once, safe and dry in her little Austin. She slammed the door and started the engine with an angry buzz.

"Oh dear! Now I've offended her," said Mollie Gildea to her husband. "Perhaps I shouldn't have said anything about her rhododendrons, but I did think it might be important." Edward assured her that it was. The Hon. Secretary had been restored to members' esteem, which was just as well, since the Gildeas were on bicycles and had to wait for the thunder shower to be over and talk to everybody who wanted to talk to them.

Edward received congratulations from all sides. Most people seemed to think that he deserved the credit of solving the whole mystery of Jason Prendergast's death.

## CHAPTER ELEVEN

THE GILDEAS were going to the play that evening, and after the success of the meeting they felt in the mood for celebrations. They cycled home with just comfortable time for supper, but their schedule was upset by an unexpected visitor.

They were surprised to see a jaunting-car standing at their gate. A few such old-fashioned vehicles appear regularly in the Vale every tourist season, but this one had got off the beaten track. It had been in the rain; the driver had disappeared, perhaps to shelter, but the horse was philosophically munching the sopping grass of the road bank while steam rose from its flanks. The Gildeas maneuvered their bicycles round the obstacle and in at their own gate, and found a stranger looking out of their dining-room window.

He was a large young man, dressed in a loose, light-colored flannel suit weighted down at the pockets. He had sandy hair thinning over a high bony forehead, and large blue eyes. Leaning out of the window he remarked

"Guess you must be Mr. and Mrs. Gildea. I hope you'll overlook my breaking into your house, but I had no protection from your climate, and when it came on to rain, I found where you kept your key. Allow me ,to introduce myself. My name is Prendergast."

They saw that he wore a black tie.

"Not Hector Prendergast, surely?" said Edward.

"Correct, but not the one you mean. Hector Prendergast Junior. My father passed away five years ago, in Cobalt, Ontario."

They joined him indoors. Mollie gave a hasty glance round to make sure the room looked presentable for visitors, and swept some dead flowers out of a vase. Edward ascertained that Hector junior was staying in a hotel. He had landed at Shannon the previous day and come on by air to Dublin, but had to spend a night in the city before completing his journey on the leisurely train.

He had seen the report of the inquest in a newspaper. He had asked the manageress of his hotel about it and found her inclined to be mysterious. It was she who had given him Mr. Gildea's name.

"I took the liberty of calling here as your office was closed," he said. "I felt I needed somebody to put me wise. I'm going up to call on my cousin at Coppermine House, and I don't want to drop any bricks. The police seem to be kind of interested in my late cousin's death. Maybe, as his solicitor, you can tell me what's in the air!"

Mollie, thinking of the theater, said she would get supper, and perhaps Mr. Prendergast would have it with them. He and Ned could have a quarter of an hour to themselves in the garden first.

The two men obeyed orders and went out. They sat on a low wall which divided the garden from a tangled bramble patch on the downslope of the hill and looked out across the little stream at the bottom to the rising ground beyond and the distant mountains, a clear view after the rain. A cuckoo kept on calling all the time they were talking, rather an irritating accompaniment to conversation.

Edward told Hector Prendergast about the upshot of the Beekeepers' deliberations. He gave the impression that, even if the facts were not yet fully established, there was nothing to worry about. Earlier in the day he might not have been so reassuring. He was glad the Canadian had not called till after the meeting.

"You relieve my mind, Mr. Gildea," said Hector Prendergast. "Not to beat about the bush, I was afraid there might be some suspicion of foul play."

"Not that I know of," said Edward. "Of course you understand that any case of sudden death has to be investigated."

"Oh, sure. Only the police seemed to be putting in some overtime on this one. I thought you wouldn't mind my coming to you."

"Not at all. You're welcome."

"As a matter of fact that wasn't the only thing." The young man hesitated and Edward looked encouraging. "Guess it seems crazy to you, Mr. Gildea, flying a thousand miles to attend the funeral of a relation you've never seen."

"You get about the world so much more than we do," said Edward. "It's more than I'd do myself."

"Maybe so. But if you'll pardon my saying so, Mr. Gildea, you don't look to me like the hard-boiled, stuffed shirt sort of professional man. You won't think the worse of a man for telling you right out how he feels. After waiting there in your parlor, looking at the photographs on the mantelpiece, and all the odds and ends lying around, I can see you're a man with a real family life. You won't contradict me when I say that family life is about the most sacred tie a man can have." He gazed earnestly at Edward, who felt embarrassed. "That was the way my father felt, and I guess I learned it at his knee. I was a witness to the sorrow he felt at having cut loose from home ties. We even talked of it together. He said there was no going back for him, but it was the wish of his life that his son should visit Ireland and get together with any folks we had left. I'd had it in mind for years to go back sometime. I kind of built a dream castle in the air. Well now, with this dream of mine, you, can guess how I reacted when I got the cable inviting me to participate in the family grief over the death of Mr. Jason Prendergast. It seemed like the call I'd been waiting for. I just fixed to take a fortnight's vacation and lit out for the airport."

"Lucky you were able to get away," said Edward.

"Well, it was strange how things turned out just right. In all reverence, Mr. Gildea, it looked like Providence. Seemed like I was meant to go. The reason I'm telling you all this is to make you understand it means a whole lot to me. I feel I was sent for a purpose. And now I have to touch on a painful subject. I don't know how much you know about my father?"

Edward only knew what Mollie had told him of her conversation with Mrs. Teely, from which he had gathered that Hector Prendergast Senior had cleared out in a hurry after defrauding his friends and relations right and left. His son proceeded to show him in a more favorable light.

"He had that money on his conscience, Mr. Gildea. I guess a good moral upbringing stands to a man throughout life. He always intended to make restitution but"—Hector junior smiled indulgently—"somehow he never got around to doing anything about it. It was a lot to fork out at a time. It wasn't till he was dying that he told me all the story. 'Son,' he said, 'you're independent of what I leave. You're earning your own paycheck. I lay it on you to put aside twenty thousand dollars out of my estate to clear me with the folks at home in Ireland.' Well, sir," concluded Hector Junior, looking Mr. Gildea in the eye. "I regard that as a sacred trust."

Edward had an uneasy feeling that this story was following lines identical with stories he had heard before. He thought he knew what was coming. But as he was expected to say something and Hector's blue eyes, so different from the rest of the Prendergasts', were fixed on him, he said it was all very creditable to both of them, and he wished Jason Prendergast could have known about it.

"I guess that was just the irony of life," said Hector Junior. "But as I hold that money on trust, Mr. Gildea, I'd appreciate your advice on how to pay it back, and who to."

"You haven't a list of the shareholders?"

"It isn't necessary. The family got together and paid them off. The real sufferers in the end were Jason and the other brother, Horace—father of Miss Phoebe. Instead of inheriting anything, Jason made his own pile, but Horace died in debt."

Hector Junior certainly seemed to be fully informed about the family.

"Miss Phoebe Prendergast is her uncle's heiress."

"Yeah, I know. She's got plenty. She doesn't need another twenty thousand dollars. But there's another member of the family, a widow lady, and by what I hear she's having a real hard financial struggle. She might have expected to find her name in the will but didn't. To make ends meet, she sells stuff out of her garden and even sometimes has to part with her household treasures." These simple facts, familiar to all who knew Mrs. Teely, took on added pathos on an alien tongue. "How would it be," said Hector, "to look on that twenty thousand dollars as more of an obligation to the family than to my Uncle Jason as an individual, and pay it out where it would do most good? Isn't it a case where strict legality might be disregarded in favor of human considerations?"

"If your father's wishes were merely expressed verbally, you aren't legally tied down," said Edward. "You can interpret his instructions according to the spirit rather than the letter."

"My father often spoke of his little Cousin Clementina," said Hector Junior. "I guess he'd have liked her to have it."

"Well, I don't see why she shouldn't."

Edward saw Mollie looking out of the window and glanced at his watch, but his visitor had not finished yet. He wanted to know whether the debt ought to be reckoned in American or English money. His father had spoken of twenty thousand dollars, but the original capital had been five thousand pounds, and nowadays they were not the same thing. It would be cheaper for Hector Junior to translate twenty thousand dollars back into pounds at present rates. Edward said he was not legally bound to pay in dollars, since he was not legally bound to pay at all, but suggested that if he could afford it he might as well do the thing handsomely. Oddly enough Hector Junior did not seem to see this point of view. The way in which he argued the matter out so as to save both his money and his conscience reminded Edward Gildea for the first time of his Uncle Jason.

But he had still not quite finished. There was another trifling difficulty in the way of his paying anything to anybody—at present he had no money. Not wishing to carry too much on him, he had arranged for a letter of credit to enable him to draw on a Dublin bank, but it had not yet come through. Moreover, the journey had cost more than he expected because of having to break it in Dublin, and he was down to his last couple of pounds. The joke, he admitted smiling widely, was on him. Unused to foreign travel, he had not given sufficient attention to preliminary organization.

"Anywhere in Canada or the States," he said, "there'd be some guy would know who I was, and after that I'd have no trouble."

Edward looked quite openly at his watch and said that after all there was no hurry about paying over the money; it could wait till the letter of credit came through.

Hector Junior said it wasn't so much that. What riled him was to be here in Ireland at last, and the Garden of Ireland at that, with no way of getting round to see places, because he just didn't have the money for car hire. The crowning absurdity was that in order to get to Dublin to enquire about his credit he would have to lay out his last pound on the train fare. Then if the letter still hadn't come, it would be just too bad. He added that he didn't want to have to apply to his cousin Phoebe. He didn't care to borrow from a woman.

It was all too plain where this was leading. The story had gone according to formula. Edward was prepared, however. He was able to say with his most pleasant smile that he never kept any money in the house over the weekend, and regretted he could do nothing to help. Hector Prendergast, to do him justice, took this well. He said he guessed he could get by for a few days; he was only temporarily in a fix; he had not intended to touch Mr. Gildea, merely invited him to share the humor of the situation.

Mollie then called them in to supper. Over the meal the stranger chatted so agreeably that his hostess at least was sorry to have to cut the evening short. He took leave with a firm frank handshake, thanking the Gildeas for what he called "a real Irish welcome."

"What are you looking like that for?" asked Mollie, watching Edward watch the guest off the premises.

"Just my nasty suspicious mind," said Edward. "I can't help wondering if he really comes from Canada at all. You'd expect somebody from the New World to produce something more original and up-to-date in the way of a lead up to a confidence trick."


## II


Mollie had a cocktail frock; Edward, not to be outdone, pinned a rose to his buttonhole. They found the old Town Hall had also undergone a transformation. It was Georgian, and dignified though dingy; it repaid a little trouble. One or two large flower arrangements in conspicuous positions and a scattering of playbills and photographs on the walls distracted the eye from peeling paint and stained distemper. Humphry Madigan's own curtain, green with gold tassels, made a satisfying patch of color and gave the impression of things being done regardless. This impression was helped on by an evident man of the world in a sleekly tailored suit who hovered about the aisles, unobtrusively superintending the filling up of the seats with mere ordinary humdrum specimens of humanity. He came up to the Gildeas, having identified them by some supernatural means, and introduced himself as Mrs. Claremorris's husband. They were ushered into places of honor and presented with programs free. Mr. Claremorris also had an invitation for them from Phoebe Prendergast.

She wanted them to come back to supper after the play. They could drive out with the Claremorrises, and later on Penrose would take them home.

It sounded gay, and Mollie's cocktail frock too seldom had an opportunity to live up to its name. Yet the Gildeas looked at each other, thinking in their provincial, old-fashioned way, that it was rather soon for Phoebe to be giving a party.

"It isn't a party," said Mr. Claremorris. "There's a chap she wants you to meet, and he can't get off earlier in the day. A fellow called Canavan."

Mollie Gildea promptly accepted for both of them. Edward still looked bewildered, and murmured as Claremorris departed, "Who is this Canavan?"

"Why, the man I told you about," said Mollie. "You can't have forgotten. The one Mrs. Claremorris was talking about the other day. Phoebe's young man. I'm sure she's going to announce the engagement." And Mollie felt her best frock fully justified.

Edward was glad of the invitation for a different reason. It would give him a chance to drop Phoebe a gentle hint about her Canadian cousin, without making a special errand of it or putting anything on paper. He did not think she ought to lend that young man anything more than a sympathetic ear.

The play exceeded expectations. The Gildeas, out to enjoy themselves, were prepared to make allowances, but no condescension was called for. The Humphry Madigan Company, which had had the courage to break new ground by coming to Drumclash, was young, keen and out for experience and a lark. It deserved applause and got it.

The recipe for success in 1798, the date of *The Wicklow Miners,* was fairly simple, but still seemed to work. It all centered round a Good Young Man, wrongfully suspected but finally exonerated, with a heroine who believes in him because she loves him (Mrs. Claremorris in the poke bonnet). The hero, having discovered gold in the Wicklow hills, uses it to do good, but other characters with evil minds accuse him of highway robbery; he is thrown into prison, escapes into the mine by a secret passage, and returns to enrich all the kind neighbors who have turned out to rescue him. Everybody bursts into song at intervals, and the hero and heroine in particular have several most affecting duets. It was a lively piece of nonsense put over with a swing, and had a special appeal, as Phoebe had said, to the Drumclash audience, on account of a perennial hope in the district that gold might be found there again. Had not these hills been the source of the gold collars and ornaments in the National Museum, the castoffs of kings and priests long ago? O'Keefe, the forgotten constructor of *The Wicklow Miners,* had been working on a theme that was topical in his day, though the only person ever to do anything practical about it in recent years was Hector Prendergast Senior, and that had proved a disappointment.

It was the male star who ran away with the show. Never before had such an exquisite young man as Humphry Madigan been seen in Drumclash. His fair wavy hair, chiseled features, swift smile, expressive hands, shapely legs (displayed to perfection in riding breeches), and his melting tenor would have set a new standard for masculine charm, if they had not seemed rather to belong to another world. His photograph, postcard size, was on sale in the interval, and unresentful Drumclash husbands bought copies for their wives.

Edward bought one for Mollie, and one of Grania Claremorris for himself; just to keep even, though he did not want it in the least.

"To think of Phoebe having a past like that," whispered Mollie, more curious than ever to see the young Mr. Canavan who had replaced this Adonis in that young woman's experienced heart.

The show ended in the right way, with several curtains, a huge bouquet for Grama Claremorris, and a graceful speech from Humphry Madigan, in which he thanked everybody and took no credit to himself. He said the splendid reception they had had in Drumclash proved what he had always maintained, that there was a large potential audience for drama in rural Ireland, and that it paid to bring them the best.

It was the last performance. Next week the company moved on to Seaport, a town where there would be summer visitors eager for entertainment. It was a mere fifteen miles away at the other end of the Vale. The Gildeas found themselves considering possibilities of getting there by bus.

After the last applause had died away and the audience had dispersed, the Gildeas waited for the Claremorrises, and were introduced to Humphry Madigan. He came out from behind the green curtain, wrapped mysteriously in a hooded duffle coat, and still with his makeup on, so that they hardly felt even then that they were meeting the real Humphry. Nevertheless they enjoyed their brief conversation with him, for he greeted everything they said as if he found it extremely intelligent and interesting, and left them feeling as if they had been as much an event in his life as he had in theirs. It was an illusion that wore off in the light of common sense, but it was agreeable while it lasted.

Then when Grania Claremorris floated out, in a red corduroy coat, with a scarf over her hair, Humphry Madigan carried her bouquet to the car, and kissed her hand and thanked her for a marvellous performance. It hardly seemed as if this could still be Drumclash.

They drove off, smothered under all the flowers. Mr. Claremorris seemed quite philosophical about his wife's glamorous leading man. He was not an unattractive man himself, but much solider and more silent, and altogether more like a husband.

"It's all very fine kissing my hand, Mr. Humphry Madigan," said Grania Claremorris as the car moved out of earshot, "but I haven't forgiven you for taking the only decent digs left in Seaport. The town's packed out, Mrs. Gildea, which is all to the good from the box office point of view, but there's simply no accommodation left. A flock mattress, my dear, in the dampest room of the dirtiest boarding house in Ireland. That's what Humphry

Madigan's leading lady has to put up with. While he has a double bed with spiral springing all to himself in a decent pub."

"Why not go on strike?" said her husband.

"I'm too good a trouper," said Grania. "The show must go on. But don't you imagine I'm taking it lying down. Not on a flock mattress. I'll find some comeback, so Humphry can look out."

This was disillusioning, but glamor clung to the evening all the same. It was a perfect summer night. Daylight lingered, for it was not far from the longest day. There was still light over the open country which the main road traversed before it plunged into the darkness of the Vale, and windows of scattered houses twinkled like the first evening stars. The faraway mountains still kept their shapes and made shadowy masses in the west. A new moon was rising. Mollie Gildea turned her money for it. Grania Claremorris began to sing:

> "The young May moon is beaming, Love,
> The goldworm's lamp is gleaming, Love,
> How sweet to rove through Morna's grove
> While the drowsy world lies dreaming, Love!"

## CHAPTER TWELVE

THE GAIETY of the party subsided as they approached Coppermine House, where a Civic Guard saluted them and watched them up the path. The hall, with one small oil lamp burning, was darker than the moonlit dusk, and the heavy mahogany furniture and dark moralistic engravings on the walls suddenly conjured up the personality of the deceased owner. Even the lighted drawing room, whither Grania Claremorris led the way, reflected Jason Prendergast's personality, though it could never have seen much of him. The Gildeas had never been in that room. It had a heavy gilt overmantel mirror and a grand piano, draped, with a lamp on it.

Five people sat there, looking as if they had been a long time making conversation. It was now obvious that Phoebe meant this to be a family reunion. Her guests were Mrs. Teely, Henry Sheed, who had come back for the weekend, and Hector Prendergast. The fifth, besides herself, was a stocky, brown-faced young man with chunky features and thick black hair, and she lost no time in presenting him as Michael Canavan.

Phoebe tonight looked serenely content, too happy to imagine that anything could be wrong anywhere in the scheme of things. Yet Mrs. Teely sat shrunk into a sofa corner as if she felt ill, and Henry Sheed looked sour. His eye caught Edward Gildea's and then traveled towards Hector Prendergast with a bleak absence of expression. Evidently he did not feel that the overseas visitor improved the party.

The first thing Phoebe said, welcoming the Gildeas with both hands, was, "We've heard all about the Beekeepers' meeting. What a relief! Everything seems clear now, and Uncle Jason's affairs can all be settled."

"A good afternoon's work, Gildea," said Henry Sheed. "Have a cigar."

Edward was a little taken aback. Though he had little doubt that honeydew collected by the bees would turn out to be what had poisoned Jason Prendergast, he knew it was not yet proved. Superstitious instinct suggested it might not be lucky to jump to conclusions. Word had gone round very quickly. The fact was, the meeting had been held over again afterwards in various Drumclash bars. Lionel Claremorris had got an account of it from two farmers over their pints and had came home with the good news to Phoebe. And Phoebe had seized the opportunity to give this party. She was longing to announce her engagement, and nothing hindered her but the atmosphere of uncertainty she lived in since her uncle's death. Now the sky was clear to her, and the moment specially appropriate. All the people she wanted were at hand. Henry Sheed would be off again on Monday, and the Claremorrises were moving on next day. Hector Prendergast's arrival also seemed like a good omen, since he made the family circle complete.

Phoebe and the Claremorrises poured drinks for everybody; sherry for the conservative, a cocktail of the Claremorrises' concoction for those who would risk it, whiskey for Henry Sheed. Then Phoebe put her arm through her brown-faced young man's and said very simply, "I expect you've guessed that I had a reason for bringing you all together. I want you to meet Michael, because he and I are going to get married."

Congratulations followed, and the drinking of healths. The Claremorrises were in their element, and it was they and Hector Prendergast who between them carried off the great moment in the appropriate way.

Out of the tail of his eye, Edward saw his wife kiss Phoebe and turn away to the window, and knew she was surreptitiously wiping her eyes. Mollie always cried at weddings and on similar occasions.

Phoebe told him and Henry Sheed that she and Michael Canavan had been unofficially engaged for about six weeks, unknown to her uncle. She said, "It wasn't that Uncle Jason would have had any reason to object, but you know what he was like. We did feel it was important to choose the right moment, and somehow it never came."

When she turned away to fill someone's glass, Henry Sheed faced Edward with skepticism written plain on his face. He said, "Jason damn well would have objected, and she knows it."

"Oh, I don't know," said Edward. "Might he not have been glad to see her marrying someone unconnected with the theater?"

"Not him. Jason was a business man. He'd bargained for feminine company in his old age."

"But he couldn't have expected her to stay single forever."

"Maybe not, but he'd have had his money back. He mightn't have refused his consent to the match, but he wouldn't have subsidized it. Phoebe'd have been cut off with a shilling."

Edward Gildea did not think so badly of the old man, though it was hard to argue with one who had known him so much longer. Somehow he did not think Jason Prendergast would have shown his softer side to Henry Sheed, even if it existed. Sheed's view of the whole world was cynical in the extreme. He obviously regarded Michael Canavan as a fortune hunter.

"Jason passed on just at the most convenient moment," he said. "It'd make anybody think. I hope there are no holes in that solution of yours."

Phoebe's two men of business were hardly entering into the spirit of the celebrations. They kept their own counsel, however. It would have been better if Grania Claremorris had observed the same rule of discretion. Whether tactlessness or mischief inspired her, or drinking the health of the engaged couple several times running, she brought up a subject that would have been better left alone.

"Darling," she said, "may I break it gently to Humphry Madigan?"

"Who?" said Michael Canavan.

"An old flame," said Grania, teasing.

"All over long ago," said Lionel Claremorris. "Quite a thing of the past."

"You mean that actor chap?" said Canavan.

"Who else?" said Grania. "There's only one Humphry Madigan. Phoebe's onetime leading man."

"Was he? I didn't know."

Michael Canavan was no actor. He failed to disguise the fact that he was surprised, puzzled, and hurt.

"Darling, you are deep," said Grania to Phoebe. She turned back to Canavan. "Don't mind my chatter. I must have had too much already."

"You can tell Humphry if you like," said Phoebe. "He'll see it in the paper, I suppose."

The brown-faced young man was looking sulky. Lionel Claremorris took his wife by the elbows and shook her. Mollie Gildea, standing at the window, caused a diversion.

"Do look, somebody," she said. "What can that be? Something white, moving in the garden."

Mollie was not merely being tactful. There was something in her voice which caught everybody's attention. Grania Claremorris glided across the room to join her at the window and peered out through the glass, making blinkers with her hands to shut out the light from the room. Then she called her husband to open the window for her. It was a heavy sash. Lionel Claremorris and Hector Prendergast between them freed the wood where it had swelled with damp, and flung up the bottom half. They leaned out, Mollie and Grania hovering behind them. Phoebe called, "What is it, Lionel, for goodness sake?"

Lionel Claremorris, coming back into the lamplight, announced with relish, "A shapeless Thing in human form."

"What do you mean, shapeless and in human form?" asked Sheed, but nobody else minded about verbal precision.

"A ghost?" said Phoebe. "What nonsense!"

"Well, Cousin Phoebe, you just come and take a look," said Hector Prendergast.

He and Lionel were half joking, but Grania when she turned round was intensely serious. "I knew it could happen here," she said in a voice of awe. "I felt I was entering a psychic field. This is a clear case of extrasensory perception."

The rest of the party joined them at the window. Some of them stepped out over the low sill into the garden. The dark had descended now. They breathed the perfection of a summer night and sensed the suggestion night in the country always holds of wild creatures astir and a different order of existence coming into play. And there was something strange down by the beehives. It was what Lionel had described: something shapeless but with a human look about it. It stood upright and had legs and arms. They could not actually see through it, but there was an impression of transparency; it was certainly less substantial at the edges. It stood still, and seemed to have its back to them.

Mollie Gildea took her husband's arm, and he could feel that she had not much psychic curiosity. Henry Sheed said in his ear, "If ever a man had reason to walk it would be poor Jason."

It flashed across Edward's mind that if anybody there present had anything to conceal in connection with Jason Prendergast's death, and if they really imagined they saw his ghost walking, their reactions might be interesting.

Grania Claremorris was straining her eyes into the gloom, but made no move to go any nearer, partly because her husband had his arm round her. Lionel Claremorris looked as if he was enjoying the situation. Hector Prendergast shut his eyes and opened them again. Henry Sheed lounged against the side of the window with his hands in his pockets. Michael Canavan crossed himself, and Edward registered the fact that he must be a Catholic. As for Phoebe, she was fully occupied with Mrs. Teely, who seemed to feel faint.

The Thing, whatever it was, turned round. From the back it had seemed to be headless, or rather neckless, for above the arms it grew into a vague mass. But now the group by the window received an impression of peculiar horror, for, though the apparition seemed to be looking towards them, it had no face. There was darkness where a face should have been.

"Doesn't look like Jason," said Henry Sheed.

If he meant to break the tension he only succeeded in doing the opposite. Mrs. Teely's nerves, at least, were strung up to breaking point, and at Sheed's remark she shrieked aloud.

"It was my fault," cried Mrs. Teely. "All my doing. Oh, Jason, Jason! I never meant to kill you."

This was enough to cause everyone to forget even the apparition.

As they crowded round the weeping lady, Phoebe said sharply, " It's pure hysteria. Don't believe her. Better get her indoors."

"And what's the trouble here?" broke in another voice, reassuringly steady, official, and matter-of-fact. It was Sergeant Rice. He came looming out of the dusk and stood shoulder to shoulder with the apparition, while behind him hovered Detective Officer Lemon.

The apparition could now be plainly seen in the light from the drawing-room windows. It wore blue serge trousers. Its upper half was solid, but achieved a ghostly effect through being covered in a one-piece garment of white muslin, draped over the top of the head, including a brimmed hat, and gathered in with elastic at the waist and wrists. A square of black net was let in over the face, to enable the wearer to see out. Edward Gildea recognized it as the Beekeepers' Blouse of which a full description with directions for making had appeared in *An Beachaire, The Irish Beekeeper,* for July, 1950.

A little later he identified the wearer as one Sergeant Sylvester, who used to come to the meetings of the Beekeepers' Association when he was stationed in Drumclash.

At a less anxious moment everybody would have laughed. As it was, only Grania Claremorris let a sudden giggle escape her. Sheed swore under his breath, and Mollie Gildea gave a gasp of relief. Phoebe Prendergast said, as if she knew all about it, "Oh, you're the man who's come for the hive."

"That's right, Miss," said a gruff voice from behind the veil. "I have it all fixed now, if you wouldn't mind signing the form." From somewhere inside his blouse he produced a duplicate form of receipt.

"Hold on, Mr. Sylvester," Sergeant Rice intervened, "there's something the matter here." He was looking at Mrs. Teely, who crouched on the windowsill, a handkerchief to her eyes. She did not offer to repeat her wild confession, but obviously they had to have the matter out. Edward Gildea took it on himself to say to the Sergeant, "This lady thinks she knows something about Mr. Prendergast's death. I think you'd better hear what she has to say."

## II

Back in the drawing room, Mrs. Teely calmed down, dried her tears, and became more her usual self. There is always some relief in matters being brought to a head, or even to a point where the abscess can be lanced. She said she wished to speak before the whole party and would sign a statement afterwards in whatever form the Sergeant wished. Her guilt had been preying on her mind ever since the realization of it had first come to her, which was that afternoon when Mollie Gildea gave her evidence at the meeting of the Beekeepers' Association.

There was nothing criminal about it. The harm she accused herself of having done could hardly have been foreseen by the most prudent person in the world.

What was in Mrs. Teely's mind was the stickiness of the rhododendron bushes. It was not honeydew, as Mollie Gildea had supposed. It was sugar syrup, the remains of another experiment.

"I was trying to see if my bees could be conditioned to visit certain flowers, flowers that in the ordinary way they seemed to neglect. It's been done. Mr. Gildea will bear me out."

"The Moscow experiments?" said Edward.

Mrs. Teely nodded tearfully.

"Interesting," said Edward. "They claim to have increased the pollination of red clover thirty per cent. Or was it thirty-fold?"

"Makes a difference," muttered Sheed.

"Anyhow, they increased it," said Edward. "The point was, it worked. But I thought that was done by feeding bees on an infusion prepared from the flowers."

Mrs. Teely shook her head. "I tried that, but it didn't work for me. Oh, if only it had! Then my own bees would have been the only ones to get the taste and gather the poison, and I should have been the one to die." She broke down again.

"Take it easy now, ma'am," said Sergeant Rice in his, most fatherly manner. "Sure, what's done is done, and it'll be all the same in a hundred years. Take your time now, and tell us what exactly you did do."

"I sp-sprayed the bushes with sugar syrup," sobbed Mrs. Teely. "They did that in Germany. It brought ever so many bees there within the hour. There must have been some of poor Jason's among them. I chose the rhododendrons because honey bees didn't seem to go near them, though bumblers love them. I never dreamed they were p-poisonous."

"Sure how could you?" said D/O Lemon, but he was a townsman. Sergeant Sylvester knew more about such things. He was sitting in on the interview clad informally in shirt and trousers, having removed his protections. Clearing his throat he remarked:

"When I was a boy I used to be always looking for the bumblebees' nests and robbing honey out of them. I mind the time it made me as sick as a dog."

Edward Gildea said that the idea of any danger from the rhododendrons would never have occurred to him until recently when he had begun to look up information about honey toxins. Henry Sheed declared, "If I'd nothing more on my conscience than you have, Mrs. Teely, I'd be a happy man this day."

But people with confessions to make are inclined, once the worst is out, to let go and enjoy themselves. Mrs. Teely showed a disposition to dwell on her iniquities and keep on talking. She said, "I can't undo what I've done, but when I came home from the meeting this afternoon, tired as I was, I couldn't sit down until I'd removed the cause of danger. I went to work on those bushes and pulled off every flower. I picked and picked until I'd stripped the branches." She showed her hands, which were stained brown and green, like many a gardener's in summer. "But that's not enough. Other hives may have been contaminated. I saw I must confess, not only for poor Jason's sake, but so that others might be warned. Don't think I meant to evade the consequences of my folly. I came here on purpose to tell. All this evening, in the midst of the gaiety of you all, I've sat here, loath to dampen your spirits but waiting for the moment to speak. Arrest me, Sergeant. Take me where you like. I'll pay any penalty the law demands, but I beg you to lose no time in making the facts known to all."

The kindly policemen assured her that there was no need for her to worry. Henry Sheed said, "My dear madam, we all ought to be most grateful to you, especially Miss Phoebe."

It was a double-edged remark, though made in the most innocent tone of voice. Only Edward Gildea frowned, but then he was getting to know Sheed's peculiar sense of humor.

Detective Officer Lemon felt no time should be lost in letting Inspector Grace know of the latest development, and he asked for a lift back to Drumclash with Sergeant Sylvester and the beehive. Sergeant Sylvester had charge of a station wagon. A seat had been taken out and the beehive stood on the floor at the back. The front seat next the driver looked better to D/O Lemon than his bicycle.

Sergeant Sylvester flashed his torch on the hive to see that all was safe. Edward Gildea, glancing in with the natural interest of a fellow beekeeper, casually observed, "I see you believe in ventilation."

"It's better moving them late and open in this weather," said Sergeant Sylvester. "They might be suffocated if you shut them up."

"Holy Mother!" said a stifled voice out of the dark. It had just dawned on D/O Lemon that he was expected to ride with a beehive of which the doors were wide open.

"Sure we'll have no trouble," said Sergeant Sylvester. "They've all settled down for the night."

"Don't bees ever walk in their sleep?" asked D/O Lemon faintly.

"Why, Lemon," said Edward, "this is not the form you showed the other day at the barracks."

"But I had a veil on then."

"Wear mine if you like," said Sergeant Sylvester.

D/O Lemon looked at the Beekeeper's Blouse and pride visibly struggled with cowardice. In the end pride got the upper hand.

"Keep it for yourself, thanks," he said. "I'll take a chance. For the love of God will you drive carefully?"

Not for the first time he wondered why he ever joined the Force.

## CHAPTER THIRTEEN

INSPECTOR GRACE was not pleased to be waked up in the middle of the night to be told the solution of the mystery, especially as it was not the right solution.

"Rhododendrons, how are ye?" he said with Dublin disdain. "Listen, how could it be the rhododendrons? Did you not read the analysts' reports on the samples?"

D/O Lemon, crestfallen, remembered that there had been rhododendron pollen and sugar syrup among other things in honey that was guaranteed harmless. Rats and guinea-pigs throve on it.

"Never mind that now," said Grace. "There's more news you didn't hear. The report on the P.M. came in this afternoon. It changes the look of things. What that man died of was arsenic."

This was what had delayed the Superintendent on his way to the meeting of the Beekeepers' Association. When the news came, he had rung up the Chief Superintendent to ask if he should allay the Beekeepers' anxieties, but the Chief thought there would be time enough for that later and asked for the expert to address the meeting as arranged. Least said, soonest mended.

"Arsenic?" said Mick Lemon. "Why wasn't he sick?"

"There's a cerebral form. Sudden and deep insensibility. He was lucky, but it put the doctor off the track. They found powder in the cells of the honeycomb too, but that's another funny thing. Arsenic ought to be colored blue. This was white."

"Purchased abroad?" suggested Mick.

"Not necessarily. But it might be a pointer."

"So it's murder, all right," said Mick.

"Yeah," yawned the Inspector, and went to sleep again.

## II

Edward Gildea, as yet uninformed of the latest development, woke up next morning with the matter of rhododendron honey very much on his mind. He had his duty to the Beekeepers' Association; he ought to warn them where the danger lay. Sunday though it was, he thought he had better get hold of the Superintendent and find out what the Civic Guards were going to do about it.

He was just pumping the tires of his bicycle when Henry Sheed turned up. He came sauntering up from the gate with his usual short cigar in his mouth Edward stopped pumping and they sat on the low garden wall.

"Nice little place you have," said Sheed, looking round him at the small house tucked into a fold of the hill, the garden sloping behind, the view in front over the valley, the wooden beehives in a weedy corner away from the house, and the inevitable rhododendrons. "Well," said: Sheed, his eye resting on the rhododendrons, "was I right about you know who?"

"Poor Mrs. Teely," said Edward. "At least she's ready to take the blame."

"Sure, after she's been found out by your observant little wife."

"She didn't know what had happened herself till then."

"Apparently not." Sheed puffed cigar smoke over a rose that grew near the wall, to fumigate some greenfly. "In the interests of logic," he said, "I can't resist pointing out that she might have done it accidentally on purpose. Who could prove anything? But I don't want to bring on an action for slander. And there wouldn't be much point, if she isn't the next of kin."

Edward smiled. "What do you think of our overseas visitor?"

"You didn't seem much smitten with him," said Sheed. "What was that you were telling Phoebe last night?"

"Not to lend him money. I shouldn't be surprised if a touch was contemplated." Edward told Sheed about Hector Prendergast's benevolent intentions and his temporary lack of money to carry them out. Sheed was much amused.

"That one has whiskers on it," he said. "But you look out, or next thing he'll be selling somebody a gold brick. He was at Phoebe for permission to go down the mine, but she referred him to me and I turned a deaf ear. He seems a chip off the old block."

"You don't think he could be an impostor?"

"Maybe he's a detective in disguise," said Sheed. "There's so many new faces around. What do you think of Phoebe's intended?"

"I didn't see much of him, what with everything," said Edward. "He seemed all right. She's free to marry whom she likes."

"And has the looks to pick and choose too. And picks on him. Ah well, women are a mystery. By the way, I've a letter for you from Phoebe. Instructions about her will. She meant to give them to you last night."

"Oh yes. I was urging her to make one, on general principles."

"And for particular reasons?"

"Those don't seem operative now."

"Phoebe'll be alone again after tonight," said Sheed. "The theater crowd has moved on."

"Well, I don't see there's much to worry about. I hope everything's on the brink of being cleared up. Matter of fact I was just going down to have a word with the Superintendent."

"I thought you might be. That's really what brought me over. Mind if I come with you?"

"By all means," said Edward politely.

They went in Sheed's car, not the Coppermine House saloon, but his own car, a muddy, dinted, much-enduring Ford.

The Superintendent and Inspector Grace were both at the barracks. Menapia was in uniform, about to go to Mass. At the sight of their visitors they exchanged glances.

"Sit down, Mr. Sheed. Sit down, Mr. Gildea," said the Superintendent, but remained standing himself. "I have some news for you. But your own business first. What happened last night, I suppose?"

Edward asked if the Civic Guards would give him early notice of any steps they proposed to take to get rid of the contaminated honey in the district, and whether the Association could help.

The Superintendent cut him short.

"Make your mind easy, Mr. Gildea. There isn't going to be any need for restrictions or regulations."

Edward asked, surprised, "But are you satisfied there's no risk?"

The Superintendent tapped the report on the post mortem, which lay on his desk. He told them what was in it.

"Jason Prendergast was poisoned by arsenic."

Sheed drew in his breath and coughed on his own cigar smoke for quite a while. They left him to recover himself, while the two policemen went on explaining to Edward Gildea about the cerebral symptoms and also about the quantity of arsenic taken. There had been a microscopic amount of it left in the bottom of two honey cells. Suddenly Edward interrupted, thumping the table.

"I knew it," he said. "I ought to have thought of it. Spraying crops with insecticides made of arsenic. I knew it was dangerous. The Association protested against it. I went on a delegation myself. The department wouldn't listen. Now there's been a death, perhaps they'll make up their minds to do something about it."

The Superintendent shook his gray head.

"No, Mr. Gildea. This isn't the fault of any farmer spraying his crops. We've two reasons to know that. First of all, the bees themselves weren't affected."

"How can you tell? The sick bees would crawl outside the hive. Many may have died on the wing."

"Granted, but there was no sign of anything at all the matter, according to Sylvester. That particular stock was at full strength. You know that, Mr. Gildea. Didn't it throw a swarm?"

Edward's lead sank forward.

"Secondly," continued the Superintendent, "these arsenical sprays aren't as deadly as all that. They only contain a percentage of arsenic, and they're further diluted in use. But the organs of the deceased contained two grains of pure arsenic—arsenious oxide—in powder form. That's enough for a fatal dose."

Inspector Grace, who till then had been a looker-on, took up the tale. "It was packed in a few of the cells," he said. "Then the tops were sealed over—you could melt the wax with a taper—and the combs were put back in the hive for the bees to fill the rest. They wouldn't break the sealed cells, would they?"

"Not when honey was coming in freely," said Edward. "What a diabolical—"

"First time it's ever been done, to my knowledge," interrupted the Inspector. "The case ought to make history." He spoke with professional enthusiasm.

Henry Sheed looked at the Inspector with dislike. He had recovered from his fit of coughing, and now, putting away a clean handkerchief, he asked, with a complete departure from his usual hard-boiled manner, "How are we to break the news to Phoebe?"

There was a pause.

The church bell was ringing. The Superintendent reached for his hat. He said, looking at Inspector Grace, not the others, "Were you thinking of going out there this afternoon?"

Grace nodded. "I'll be having a talk with Miss Prendergast. We'll have to search the whole place. Perhaps Mr. Gildea would like to come too?"

Edward had intended to spend the afternoon preparing nucleus boxes for queen rearing, but he sighed and said of course he would come. The Inspector promised to call for him.

Henry Sheed drove Edward home, and went back alone himself to Coppermine House, not looking as if he liked being the bearer of the bad news.

Edward told Mollie. She was deeply shocked, but she said, "Well, at least we can have honey for lunch."

Edward took out the envelope Sheed had given him. Before seeing Phoebe Prendergast he thought he had better glance through her instructions. They were not complicated; a single sheet of notepaper contained them. She wished to leave everything of which she died possessed to her fiancé, Michael Canavan.

### III

"Before we get there, Mr. Gildea," said Inspector Grace, as they wound their way down to the Vale in the Superintendent's car, "I wonder would you mind telling me a little more about that last interview you had with the deceased? Things look serious now, you know. The Superintendent didn't want at the time to press you to disclose your client's affairs, but I'd be interested to know now, what was in that codicil?"

Edward did not mind this question.

"I don't think it matters," he said. "You know what the old man was like. He wanted to make a condition about his niece's inheritance. She was to promise never to return to the stage."

"Did Miss Prendergast herself know of this?"

"I don't know. I think not."

"And where was the harm in telling us about it to begin with?"

Edward looked apologetic. "I admit I was afraid at first the information might be rather to Miss Prendergast's prejudice. You see, I believed her one desire was to act. As it turns out, I was quite wrong. She means to marry and settle down."

"So I hear. Mr. Canavan, isn't it?"

"I see you're up to date, Inspector."

"We have to be, in the Force." The Inspector smiled.

"I hope the police have nothing against him?"

"Not so for," said the Inspector. "Not so far." He spoke heavily and looked serious, but Irishmen often do when they are joking.

Edward also had a question he wanted to ask. It related to Hector Prendergast. He wondered if the Civic Guards would be checking his *bona fides*.

"Just a matter of routine," murmured the Inspector who had cabled to Canada the day before. "Any reason to think there's anything wrong?"

Edward repeated Hector Prendergast's own story. The Inspector did not need the point underlined.

"I'll be looking forward to meeting the gentleman," he said. "I hear he's putting up at Mrs. Teely's."

Edward had not gathered this fact, but it had been arranged the night before that the Canadian cousin should transfer himself from his hotel to "El Jireh." Mrs. Teely had invited him the moment they met, in spite of the mental anguish which she afterwards turned out to have been suffering at the time on account of the rhododendrons. Probably she wanted someone to cling to, and Hector Prendergast seemed the natural person, even though he was not the one she had expected and was not, she said, very like his father.


## IV


Henry Sheed was walking about the garden, laying a trail of cigar butts. When the police car drove into the yard he came to meet Edward Gildea and the Inspector.

"I've told her," he said, holding the garden gate open. "She didn't say much. She's expecting you."

Detective Officer Lemon came up and saluted. All four men walked in silence up to the house.

Phoebe met them in the hall. She said quietly to the Inspector, "This doesn't make things easier for you."

"It's all in the day's work," he answered. "We have our routine you know. I'm afraid I'll have to ask you all some more questions."

"Mr. Sheed says you want to search the house."

"House and premises, please. We'll have trained men on the job who won't cause you too much inconvenience."

"Oh yes. I don't mind about inconvenience. You must do everything you think necessary. When do you want to start?"

"There'll be a search party down some time in the afternoon. I'd like to have a look round myself, too." The Inspector reflected. "I expect you'd like a word with Mr. Gildea," he said considerately. "Suppose you take him into the study while I'm talking to Mick here, and we'll join you later."

Phoebe brought Edward into the study and Henry Sheed followed, carrying in an extra chair. It was lighter there than in the hall, and Edward saw Phoebe wore more makeup than usual. She had been trying to hide the traces of tears. She looked from one man to the other, hands clasped in her lap, the fingers nervously clenched.

"I can't believe this horrible news," she said. "Who could have done such a thing? There's only one person I can think of, and that's Penrose, and yet I've no right to say that, it's just his manner. He's been worse lately, but that's because of this trouble between him and Vera. I was really sorry for him over that. Do you think he could have done such a thing?"

She was chattering nervously, repeating herself. Edward had never seen her like this before. He felt horribly inadequate, and was grateful for the support of Henry Sheed's presence.

"Why him rather than Vera?" said Sheed.

"Oh no, not Vera!" cried Phoebe. "She's a most respectable woman, and she was genuinely attached to my uncle."

"That's just it," said Sheed. "This is no time to beat about the bush. 'Attached' is right. Before you came I made no doubt she was setting her cap at Jason. I told him so. One reason he sent for you."

Phoebe was completely taken aback. She was shocked and angry and could not find the right words to express her disgust.

"Sorry if I'm upsetting your ideas about things," said Sheed. "It's no disrespect to Jason. It wasn't his fault. I don't mean, either, that he didn't welcome you for your own sweet sake. Damn it, he could have had Clementina Teely, couldn't he? You don't need to look so old-fashioned about it." He grimaced at Edward. "I've put my big foot in it."

"No, no you haven't," said Phoebe. "I'm glad you told me. I suppose I ought to have guessed, though marriage is the last thing one would think of for Uncle Jason. Surely you don't think she murdered him out of disappointment?"

"Or Penrose did, out of jealousy."

"I can't believe it," said Phoebe with a sudden revulsion. " Vera never cared in any real sense for Uncle Jason. She flirts with everyone. It would only be his money, and killing him wouldn't help. As for Penrose, he'd have to murder half the men in Morna to make sure of Vera."

"Have it your own way," said Sheed, sitting back with his arms folded. For once he had let his cigar go out.

Edward glanced out of the window. The two detectives were still prowling about the garden. He supposed he ought to give Phoebe some professional advice on what to say to them, but it was difficult to begin. She must know what she was up against. Once before, she had said to him, half joking, that she knew they suspected her.

She read his thoughts and said it again. "Of course they, the police, think I did it."

Sheed rounded on her before Edward could speak. "Don't you go dramatizing yourself, my dear. They're not such fools as that. They're bound to be judges of human nature, it's their job. Nobody who knows you would ever imagine anything of the sort. You haven't the guts. You, the tender-heartedest girl on earth! Why, you wouldn't kill a—a bee if it stung you."

His logic might be weak but his partisanship was comforting, and his look and tone of voice said more than his actual words. Edward was grateful to him again, because he himself felt unable to rise to the same heights. He stuck to his role of sober professional adviser, and told Phoebe she could not do better than go on as she had been doing, giving the police every assistance and not looking as if she expected to be accused. "Remember, it's up to them to prove somebody guilty. Nobody has to prove themselves innocent."

"So don't go sticking out your pretty neck," said Henry Sheed.

Phoebe thanked them both so much they both felt embarrassed, and Edward looked out of the window again. The two detectives had lifted up the trapdoor in the garden and were peering into the mineshaft.

A map of the mine hung on the wall behind Sheed. It was a cross section, a complicated system of vertical and horizontal lines with curious names marked here and there. "Doghole," "Madam's shaft," "O'Brien's shaft," "North, South and Middle Whim." These had no connection with any place that Edward knew on the hill, but he did know there were any number of old openings among the rocks and slag heaps where a small object might be thrown down. A tin or a bottle would drop deep, deep down, perhaps into water. The police would have their work cut out if they meant to search the mine.

"Before the Inspector comes," said Phoebe suddenly, "there's something else I want to talk about. My—my engagement to Michael. I'm afraid I was too impulsive last night."

Sheed looked at her and said, doubling his fists, "If that young man shows signs of letting you down, you just send for me."

"Nothing of the kind," said Phoebe. "Michael would marry me tomorrow if I gave in to him. I only meant that I was in too much of a hurry to announce the engagement to all and sundry. You know how one longs to tell the world. I might have known it was unlucky." She sighed. "I promised Michael I'd send the notice to the papers today, but now I think it had better wait a little. I don't want to entangle him in my troubles."

"I mentioned it to the Inspector," said Edward diffidently. "I thought he was bound to know."

"Almost one of the family, isn't he?" said Phoebe. "But I'd rather the news didn't spread round the valley just yet. It's perhaps all to the good that the Claremorrises have left."

"Tell us a bit more about your fiasco," said Henry Sheed. "Sorry, the word slipped out. Spill us the inside story of your romance. Where did you fish him up?"

He winked at Edward. His idea was to get Phoebe talking and make her forget her troubles, and he was a good judge; Phoebe was as ready as any girl to talk of her lover. Her drifting days were over; she clung to the certainty of her feelings about Michael; she knew he loved her because she loved him. She did not put all this in so many words for such a cynical listener as Henry Sheed, but she left no doubt of it, as she described how she had met Canavan six months before on one of her long solitary walks, how they talked, how they met again, first by chance, then by arrangement, then regularly. No wonder she had been independent of the mild social life of the Vale. She said she had known from her first conversation with Michael Canavan that here was someone with whom she could share every thought.

"Well, it's your own business," said Sheed. "I suppose he has no private means."

"No more than I had at the time when he proposed."

"You had expectations, my dear."

"Michael didn't mean us to depend on Uncle Jason. He wanted to elope. It might have come to that if Uncle Jason had disapproved, but I thought we owed it to Uncle at least to give him the chance."

"But you hadn't much hope."

"Oh, you never could tell with Uncle Jason," said Phoebe.

"Well, you're on the pig's back now, anyhow," said Sheed cheerfully. "But you still haven't  told us who the fellow is and his people, if he has any."

"If you want to know," said Phoebe, "his father keeps a shop. They're Canavans the chemists, in Cranbay."

"The what?" cried Sheed. "Oh, all right, I heard you the first time. Well, well. Let's look on the bright side. You'll be able to get your cosmetics at a reduction."


V


The Chief Superintendent arrived, and later the search party. The interviews dragged on. Phoebe was self-controlled, Vera Byrne was sensible and calm, Penrose was truculent. The Inspector knew how to handle them all. Nothing new emerged. At long last Edward Gildea found there was nothing more for him to do and he might as well go home.

He said good-bye to Henry Sheed.

"I'm on my way tomorrow," said Sheed. "Got to be. I'm sorry to leave with things in this mess. Phoebe'll have police protection at the house, that's one thing." He looked meaningly at Edward. "For protection, read surveillance, but what's the odds so long as somebody keeps a lookout. You can phone my home, Gildea, if you want to get in touch with me. I shan't be there but the landlady'll know where I am. I'll do my best to get down again during the week."

He held out his hand, meeting Edward's eyes with a look full of foreboding. Edward had no reason to doubt his sincerity, but he could not help envying him his escape. The fog of mistrust and suspicion was thickening. Sheed would breathe better in a different atmosphere than that of Coppermine House.

Penrose was to drive Edward home. As he moved towards the car, Phoebe stopped him.

"Do something for me," she said. "Go round by Mrs. Teely's. Poor Cousin Clementina; she still thinks she was the death of Uncle Jason with her experiments. It would only be kind to give her the good news about the arsenic."

She pressed his hand with a bitter smile, and turned back to her gloomy house.

## CHAPTER FOURTEEN

ON THE DRIVE from Coppermine House to "El Jireh," not a word was exchanged between passenger and chauffeur. Penrose's silence was far more impenetrable than the mere not speaking till spoken to of the well-trained servant, and Edward did not attempt to break it. It oppressed him, however, and that with the stuffiness of the saloon car combined to give him an idea of what it might be like to suffer from claustrophobia. He was glad to get out at Mrs. Teely's garden gate. Penrose opened the door for him, then climbed back into the driving seat and sat staring unseeingly ahead.

The lean-to shed at the side of the bungalow which served as a garage had its door wide open, and the baby Austin had gone. This seemed to mean that Mrs. Teely was out, but Edward, in no hurry to reenter the car, stood a while in the garden looking round him, taking in the sorry sight of the rhododendron bushes stripped of their flowers, and all for nothing. Mrs. Teely's onslaught on them must have been fierce, for they were not merely bare of blossom, but torn and broken; flowers, leaves and twigs strewed the ground. Edward brushed his hand over the nearest branch, but of course there was no trace left by now of either syrup or honeydew; he merely got a shower of raindrops up his sleeve. The weather was still broken, and there had been another shower during the afternoon. It was a consolation to think that it would not, after all, have been a good day for opening hives.

The look of the countryside had changed since the rain. Nothing made much alteration in the strange region of the mine, but down here in the valley it was now high summer, the trees in full leaf displaying variations on grayer, bluer greens than those of spring. The broom along the river had shed its gold on the water. Elder trees drooped out of the hedges under their panicles of swelling buds. Fields of poor land near the water were full of buttercups. There must be clover somewhere. Edward glanced up at the hives on Mrs. Teely's roof and followed the flights of one or two bees that were now emerging after the shower.

"Why, Mr. Gildea!" said Mrs. Teely's voice behind him, and he jumped. She came out of the house door in her garden overall. "I couldn't think whose the car was," she said. "I was afraid it might be the police."

Mrs. Teely looked more her usual self, but her manner was still nervous. "What a fright you gave me," she said. "Why didn't you come in?"

"I thought you must be out when I saw the car was gone," Edward explained, feeling rather as if he had been caught spying, for no reason at all except that Mrs. Teely looked so much on the defensive.

"On the contrary, I'm immobilized for the day. I've lent my little car to Hector. I am sure he's a careful driver, though I thought he started off rather fast. He's gone up to Dublin for the night."

"For the night, has he?" said Edward, wondering what Prendergast was up to. "It was decent of you to let him have the car for so long."

"Oh, I don't need it much on Sunday," said Mrs. Teely, "not once I've been to church, and he'll be back by tomorrow afternoon. As a matter of fact he's doing a little errand for me, something I should have found it rather painful to do myself. Some old silver, Gildea, not the kind of things I should ever have any use for, and you know I always say, what is the sense in keeping things put away in boxes? But all the same, it hurts a little to part with family treasures. Old silver fetches good prices now, if one knows the ropes. One must know what to ask for and hold out for one's rights. Hector will be able to hold his own with the dealers better than I should. Not that I am a bad hand at a bargain, Mr. Gildea, but you know," Mrs. Teely looked archly at him, " there is an advantage in being a man."

Edward frowned. "Prendergast's taken up some silver to sell for you, has he? May I ask if it's of much value?"

"I never count my chickens," said Mrs. Teely, "but the salver is worth thirty pounds at least, and the candlesticks ought not to go for less than twenty-five for the pair. There's some table silver too, and that fetches a very good price nowadays. I really don't think it could be less than a hundred pounds in all."

"Silver to the value of a hundred pounds!" said Edward. "Excuse me,

Mrs. Teely, but haven't you been rather trusting? He's almost a total stranger."

"By no means a stranger," said Mrs. Teely haughtily. "Whom should one trust, if not one's own flesh and blood?"

"His father—"

" There were extenuating circumstances," said Mrs. Teely.

"But are you sure he is his father's son?" said Edward. "We've only his word for it. And there isn't much resemblance between him and anyone else in your family."

"Oh, don't you think he has Phoebe's forehead? And I see a look of Jason in him too, though of course it makes a difference being fair instead of dark and tall instead of short. Why, who else could he be, Mr. Gildea? You can't really imagine he's an impostor! Oh, no! You must give me credit for some knowledge of human nature. Hector has wide and cultured interests; he's an educated man. Forgive me for saying your profession makes you suspicious, you lawyers. But I am not a babe in arms, and I ought to know by this time whom I can and cannot trust."

Edward saw he had upset the unfortunate lady. "Well, well," he said, "there's no reason to think the worst. When do you say he'll be back?"

"Tomorrow afternoon. Was it Hector you came to see?"

"Good Lord, no!" said Edward. "No, I came to give you the latest news. I'm afraid it may come as rather a shock, though it'll relieve your mind in one respect. It's the medical report on the post mortem. They say now it wasn't the honey, it was arsenic."

Mrs. Teely blinked at him. "I don't understand."

"There was arsenic mixed with the honey Mr. Prendergast had for tea. There doesn't seem any doubt it was done deliberately. In plain words, it's murder."

"Murder!" repeated Mrs. Teely. She turned so pale Edward was afraid she felt faint and took her arm to steady her. "Hadn't you better sit down?" he said awkwardly. "Can I get you a glass of water?" He wished Mollie was with him.

"No, no thanks, nothing," said Mrs. Teely. "Have they said who?"

"At present I don't believe they've the slightest idea."

"Has Phoebe been told?"

"I've just come from there." Edward indicated the Coppermine House car outside the gate. He wondered if Penrose was listening, or if he was too full of his own troubles. "Miss Prendergast's keeping calm. She's wonderful, really. Oh, one thing I was forgetting to mention: she doesn't want her engagement talked of till she's clear of this mess."

"Ah, poor girl! What a surprise that was to us all! Such a romance, an idyll of the mountains! Can it go on, Mr. Gildea? Will the young man's loyalty be proof against this test? Can Phoebe's love stand the strain?"

Edward did not feel equal to discussing all these psychological reactions. Seeing that Mrs. Teely looked a better color, he declared he must go. "By the way," he said, "what's the number of your car?"

"NI 3412," said Mrs. Teely. "Why?"

"Might be useful to have a note of it," said Edward evasively. "Goodbye, now, Mrs. Teely. Take care of yourself. You can set your mind at rest about the honey anyway." He wrung her hand and retreated towards the car.

"My poor rhododendron bushes," said Mrs. Teely, and tears came to her eyes. Edward made a cowardly escape, and left her mourning among the fallen flowers.

## II

Edward told Penrose to drive him into Drumclash. He went to the barracks and found Superintendent Menapia there, though normally on a Sunday evening he would have been walking the mountains, or sitting under a hedge watching birds, or taking a supper of small trout out of the upper reaches of the streams beyond the polluting influence of the mine.

Edward told him of Hector Prendergast's departure and gave him the number of the car.

"It may be quite all right," he said. "I just thought it looked a bit queer."

"What time did he leave?" asked the Superintendent. Edward had forgotten to ask. Menapia sighed patiently and proceeded to put a telephone call through to Dublin. When he had given his instructions he turned back to Edward. "I suppose you thought we hadn't enough work to do for a Sunday, Mr. Gildea."

"I thought I might be giving you a push along," said Edward.

"That's very decent of you," said Menapia, not sounding grateful. "And what do you expect us to do about it? We can't charge the man with anything. He took the car with the lady's leave."

"He obtained valuables on false pretenses."

"What evidence have you of that?"

"None," said Edward cheerfully. "Do you always insist on evidence before you do anything? Isn't prevention better than cure?"

"Now, you know as well as I do, Mr. Gildea, that we can't go locking people up on suspicion. The police would have an easier job if we could."

Menapia needed an excuse to let off steam. The latest development in the Prendergast case had let loose on him several extra helpers from the Detective Branch who had to be fed and accommodated and who raised all sorts of domestic problems. The murder of Jason Prendergast was being given first priority in his concerns, and he wrote off Hector Prendergast as having an alibi for that.

"For all we know," said Menapia, "the man's on the level. He did come off the plane from Canada, we checked that. If he can afford air travel, why should he take the risk of stealing a few candlesticks from an old lady?"

"Might be a habit," said Edward, "or just a hobby. But if you don't think that story sounds phony, Superintendent, doesn't it strike you as odd that he should clear out in a hurry just when things begin to happen?"

"I've seen a lot of coincidences in our work," said Menapia.

"If he is up to anything," said Edward, "this would be the day to choose, when you have your hands full already."

"And if anybody else is up to anything," said Menapia, "wouldn't it be a good time to send us off on a wild goose chase? Just what did the lady say about it, Mr. Gildea? I suppose there's no fear she invented it all, just to throw a spanner in the works."

They went over it all again, with a Guard to take notes. Before they had finished the telephone rang. Menapia listened, and looked pleased.

"They've picked him up," he said, still holding the receiver. "Radio patrol car reported him entering Dublin by the Bray road. Doesn't look like trying to dodge." He listened again, and spoke into the mouthpiece. He said, "Suspected of making away with goods and also of driving without an Irish license." This happy thought had just occurred to him and he winked at Edward. "He may be implicated in a murder down here. No, we've no proof. Just keep under observation. Don't let him get away with the goods. If you want to pull him up you can have him over the license."

Edward went home feeling that he had earned some time off. After tea he instinctively made for his beehives, not to work at them—it was too late in the day, or he told himself it was because he was tired—but to watch the bees working, which he always found a rest.

From the time when men first kept bees in straw skeps, beekeepers with problems to solve will have been found in the neighborhood of their hives, staring at the bees going in and out. From this no doubt arose the superstition of "telling the bees." The modern mass-production apiarist with a thousand hives may scorn the idea that they can ever be a spiritual resource, but then he does not keep bees, they keep him. It is the backyard beekeeper who enjoys the privilege of communing with life in another realm.

If the world grows stale, imagine for a change how it must appear to beings with three simple and two compound eyes. The compound eyes of worker bees are made up of about twelve thousand hexagonal lenses, pointing in every direction. They must see a great deal that we miss.

Edward's bees were hard at it, enjoying the flowers freshened up by rain and making up for lost time. The outgoing ones circled high and vanished, but his eye could trace in the air the lines of returning foragers flying straight to each hive. There were still as many going out as coming in; the entrances were wide open, but there were more bees than could get in and out all at once, and a buzz went on round each alighting board like Edward's thoughts buzzing in his head.

Who had poisoned Jason Prendergast? Penrose? The man looked hangdog enough. Why had Vera Byrne thrown him over? Did she know or suspect anything? With a man of that type one would expect a blunt instrument murder, rather than the subtlety of a doctored honeycomb, but a mechanic is neat with his hands, and Penrose had some knowledge of the ways of bees. He had known what to do on the day of the swarm.

Vera Byrne? Had she gone out of her way to invent a way of poisoning her employer which would not point to the cook? But Edward could not see that Vera had any reason to kill the old man. Besides, she knew nothing about bees.

Phoebe Prendergast was nervous of bees; she would not have gone near the hive. But she had helped her uncle prepare crates of sections. She could have put poisoned comb in place beforehand, if she knew enough for the idea to have occurred to her.

Michael Canavan's father was a chemist. Could he have obtained arsenic for Phoebe? Could he have done it himself?

Mrs. Teely knew more about bees than all the rest of them put together. The method of the crime seemed very much in line with her famous experiments, and had not her whole behavior since Jason Prendergast's death been strange? She had clung to Phoebe like a limpet till Phoebe dislodged her, and then, after being out of things for a time, had made the most of that silly business about the rhododendrons to draw attention to herself. When the police took no notice she seemed disappointed. Was it a form of neurosis, similar to the urge which makes innocent lunatics confess to crimes they never committed, or was it a shrewd maneuver to keep herself near the center of events, drawing red herrings across the track? If Mrs. Teely had had a motive, Edward would have certainly suspected her among the first, but he could not see how she had anything to gain.

In spite of everything, he could not help feeling glad the bees were exonerated. He watched them jostle at the entrances; it looked as if they had found a good source of honey somewhere, probably the clover, and it was pleasant to be able to look forward without misgivings to a bumper harvest.

## CHAPTER FIFTEEN

HECTOR PRENDERGAST drove to Dublin's four best advertised hotels and found a room in the fourth. He entrusted the box of silver to the manager, left his suitcase in his bedroom, and went to Evensong at St. Ann's Church, Dawson Street. Then he went back to his hotel and had a cold supper. Afterwards he looked out of the front door, saw that it was raining again, and retired to the Residents' Lounge, where he got into conversation with five American maiden ladies on their first trip to Europe. They all talked hard till eleven o'clock, then the ladies went to bed, and so did he.

Next morning he reclaimed his box of silver and set out in his car about half past nine. This being Dublin, he had about an hour before the streets became too busy for car shopping. He did a brisk round of antique shops and jewelers. In each shop he displayed the silver and asked for a valuation. The lowest he got was forty-five pounds, the highest, fifty guineas. Each time he put all the silver back in his case and walked out again.

After the fifth shop he looked at his watch and drove to the Bank of Ireland. There he presented a letter of credit, which did not produce the right reaction. After being kept waiting while a good deal of whispering and popping in and out of gilded cages went on, he was informed by a civil and apologetic official that no confirmation had come through, and was politely requested to call back.

The official, when approached by a detective a few minutes later, was guarded in his comments. He said there was not necessarily anything wrong. The gentleman had been in twice to present a letter of credit, but no advice concerning it had yet come through. Delays sometimes did occur. If the instructions had been mailed instead of cabled that might account for it. Naturally the Bank could not pay out money on demand to every traveler who found a hitch in his arrangements, but it would most likely all be explained in a day or two.

Hector Prendergast meanwhile was threading his way through increasing traffic to the Quays. Detectives followed him when he took the silver to a pawnshop and pawned the lot for twenty pounds. One detective then telephoned for instructions, the others kept following.

Prendergast's next step mystified them. He went to a tool shop and bought a small hand pick, a miniature weapon about ten inches long. Next, he visited a shop that supplied laboratory requisites, and bought a blowpipe—a small brass tube about a quarter-inch in diameter, fitted with a pinholed nozzle at one end. Also a carbon block, a two and a half inch cube. Also a packet of borax.

Then he went to a café and had a large ice cream.

When he came out of the café he got into trouble with the police. The detectives following him watched with interest while he was reprimanded for parking where parking was not allowed. But they did not want competition, so one of them caught the eye of the uniformed Civic Guard, and he accepted Prendergast's excuse of not knowing the Irish language and let him off without asking to see his license.

The incident, however, had put ideas into Prendergast's head, for he drove back to his hotel and had a consultation with the hall porter. Then he walked to the Motor Registration Office in Kildare Street, filled in a Form of Application for a Driving License, handed over ten shillings, and came out in a stronger legal position.

It was now about one o'clock. Prendergast went back to his hotel for lunch. The two detectives also had a good lunch and entered it to expenses. Prendergast then settled his bill, entered his car and drove off.

A patrol car followed him. It followed him all the way back to Drumclash and then on to Mrs. Teely's. Then, leaving one man behind on watch, it drove back to Drumclash to report to Superintendent Menapia.

The Superintendent called on Mrs. Teely at teatime. He asked to speak to her privately. Hector Prendergast was having tea in the front parlor, which left them only the kitchen. There Mrs. Teely and the Superintendent had a heart to heart.

He found her all of a twitter. Her guest had told her a tale which she might have accepted unsuspectingly, but for Edward Gildea's intervention. Edward Gildea had poisoned her mind against the stranger, even though he was a relation. When Hector Prendergast said that he had left the silver with an expert who wanted time to consider his valuation, Mrs. Teely did not know whether to believe him or not.

"I'm so glad you're here to advise me, Superintendent," she said. "I didn't like to say I didn't believe him for fear of hurting his feelings. It would have sounded like accusing him of theft, and then supposing it had been true after all—! But, oh dear, I suppose it does amount to stealing after all."

"I'll have a word with him," said the Superintendent. Mrs. Teely took him into the parlor where Hector Prendergast was sitting on a low cane-seated nurse chair at a table made of a brass tray on legs. He could not easily get up without sending the tray flying. The room was crammed with Mrs. Teely's "nice old things," and three people filled it to capacity.

Mrs. Teely sank on to a wool-worked footstool that ran across the front of the fireplace. The Superintendent towered over both of them. He took a high-backed rush-bottomed chair, but only to lean on the back of it.

Hector Prendergast was very much surprised to find that the Superintendent knew all about his transaction with the pawnshop.

"My, that's smart work," he said admiringly, "but it's just too bad of you to expose my little subterfuge. You might have asked me privately first."

"Well, Mr. Prendergast," said Menapia, "perhaps you wouldn't mind telling us just what was your idea."

" Sure." Hector took a sip of tea and set down his cup. He smiled up at the Superintendent with his wide friendly smile. It included Mrs. Teely too. "My idea, Cousin Clementina, was to buy that silver myself. I kind of took a fancy to it, and besides, I felt I'd like to keep it in the family. The trouble was, I'd gotten into difficulties through the inefficient functioning of the machinery of international credit. I expected to be able to get cash from the Bank of Ireland in College Green, Dublin, but so far they have no knowledge of me, and I shall have some questions to ask back home till I find the individual responsible for landing me in this position. A stranger in a strange land, like myself, does not find it the easiest thing in the world to raise a loan. I've been operating on a shoestring basis, and the shoestring looks like snapping. So to bridge the gap in my financial resources I pawned the silver. I reckoned it would be safe till I was ready to offer cash for it."

"But, Hector, dear, why didn't you tell me?" Mrs. Teely wailed.

"Well, Cousin Clementina, it appeared to me as if a lady might have a prejudice against the sordid associations of pawnshops."

The childlike innocence of Hector Prendergast's large blue eyes made a strong appeal for belief in his story, but Mrs. Teely looked at the Superintendent and hardened her heart.

"I don't think much of that for a reason," she said, "and I'd like to have my silver back."

"As soon as my credit comes through—"

"What have you done with the money they gave you at the pawnshop?"

Hector Prendergast spread out his hands. He said in a patient voice: "Why, I just explained. I needed some cash for current expenses. A driving license and one or two little things I had to get, and the hotel bill, of course. Oh, and I filled the car with gas for you."

"I wish you hadn't," said Mrs. Teely. "I'm sure petrol's safer."

The Superintendent looked from one to the other of them. Mrs. Teely's face was red and she was on the verge of crying from sheer temper. Hector Prendergast, sitting on his low seat with his long legs half across the room, looked mild, long-suffering, but deeply injured. It was going to be embarrassing for them to spend the evening in each other's company.

"Do you wish to lay a charge against this person, Madam?" asked the Superintendent.

"No, no," said Mrs. Teely hastily. Then she changed her mind. "Yes, I do. I charge him with stealing my silver, Superintendent, if he doesn't give it back."

So Hector Prendergast accompanied the Superintendent back to Drumclash.

## CHAPTER SIXTEEN

COPPERMINE HOUSE was swarming with detectives. Six men in pairs searched room by room for traces of arsenic. A photographer took pictures of the study and the larder, interiors and exteriors, and of the situation of the beehives. Inspector Grace went through papers already gone through without result by Henry Sheed.

A fingerprint expert took the prints of the whole household for comparison with some found on the hive and some on the broken slips of wood which had enclosed the fatal honeycomb. Some of those on the wooden section belonged to the deceased and some to Vera Byrne. There were others, underneath, so fragmentary that they were impossible to identify with certainty, though it could be said whose they were not. They were not Mr. Prendergast's or Vera's; they might belong to Phoebe. But if they did there was an explanation, for Phoebe had helped her uncle prepare the crate of sections before it was placed on the hive, folding the wooden slips into squares and fitting them with a wax foundation.

It was on the 10th of May, according to a record card, that the crate had been placed on the hive. At first it had been thought that this was the earliest date when the poisoner's trap could have been laid. But Phoebe remembered that the crate had contained, besides new sections with flat pieces of wax foundation, some old part-finished sections with cells drawn out and empty and a few already filled and sealed. These were leftovers from last year, such as a thrifty beekeeper puts aside and uses to encourage the bees to start work again. In one of them the arsenic might have been concealed. They had been kept through the winter in a box in Jason Prendergast's workshop.

This room was in the servants' quarters, and in the passage outside the detectives made another discovery. They lifted a piece of linoleum in the passage and found a trapdoor in the floor, similar to the trapdoor in the garden, and also covering an entrance to the mine. There was really no secret about it; it was marked on the map, but few ever bothered to trace details in that complicated crisscross of lines. By way of two twelve-rung ladders it gave access from the house to a tunnel below the level of the one opening from the garden, and running in a different direction. The upper tunnel was bored into the hillside northwest of the house, the lower one ran north and south and came out at a small wooden door concealed by bushes about two hundred yards down the lane.

"That would be the way Hector Prendergast Senior got out when his creditors were after him," remarked the Chief Superintendent, who had been digging up the past history of the family.

Phoebe Prendergast had not known of this passage. She was interested but rather alarmed, and asked, "Could people get in by it from outside?"

"Not unless somebody left the door unfastened," said the detective who had been along. "The door at the far end is bolted on the inside and this one here has a bolt on top."

"Vera Byrne knew all about it," remarked Sergeant Rice after Phoebe had gone. "It was no surprise to that one. I'd go bail she's used it herself in the past."

"It's handy-looking, all right," said Inspector Grace, "so near the place where the sections were stored. But it wouldn't have been any use to anyone in the house already, and it wouldn't have been any use to anyone outside unless somebody in the house let him in."

He was thinking of Mrs. Teely, who was on such good terms with Vera Byrne.

Vera when questioned was as straightforward as ever. Her manner with the Inspector and the Chief Superintendent was always respectful, sensible, and without a sign of the flirtatiousness with which she alleviated the hard lot of Sergeant Rice.

"I been down there half a dozen times since I came," she admitted. "I'd slip out that way and in again to get to a dance. The Master didn't give permission for late dances, and sure, you're only young once. I never told anyone how I got in and out, but some of the miners know all about it. They say there's other passages too."

The Chief peered down the ladder into the darkness. "You'd have your work cut out to search the mine," he said.

"It may come to that," said the Inspector.

II

Phoebe sat in her bedroom trying to read while the police searched her sitting room. She looked out at the sound of yet another car in the lane. Then her face brightened. This time it was the Claremorrises. They parked in the yard, next to the Chief Superintendent. Grania and Lionel got out, Lionel in snow-white shirt and gray flannels, Grania in the bolero-dress that topped her sunbathing suit. She gave a dazzling smile to the plainclothes man who intercepted them.

"I left something behind," she said. "If you must know, officer, a pair of nylon step-ins. They should be hanging over a rail in the bathroom."

"They are, miss, I noticed them," he told her, and let them pass.

"What an observant man you are, officer," said Grania over her shoulder. "Thank you so much." Then "Hello, darling," to Phoebe, as she came to meet them, "what a lot of people! Are you having a Police Annual Outing or something?"

"I must talk to you," said Phoebe. "Don't rush off at once. Stay to tea."

But the Claremorrises shook their heads and both explained at once that they had to get back to a special rehearsal. Word had reached the Humphry Madigan Company that a talent spotter from Hollywood was coming down incognito to watch a performance.

"His name's Marcus Bowman, but he calls himself Johnson," said Grania. "Fancy his coming all the way down here!"

"Wants to take a trip in the country and put it on his expense sheet," said Lionel. "Ever hear of him, dear? "

Phoebe had never heard of him.

"Legs are what he'll be looking for," said Grania with a sigh. "Mine are as good as Kathleen Ryan's any day, but they don't get a chance playing period stuff: Humphry wants to do *She Stoops To Conquer* in costume, so he can wear a powdered wig."

"Never mind," said her husband, "if I get a chance I'll show him that snap of you playing Hamlet with the Holy Faith Past Pupils Dramatic Society."

"Humphry's gone right off the deep end," said Grania, "calling afternoon rehearsals in this heat. It's slavery. I've a good mind to ignore it."

But Phoebe understood that not for worlds would Mrs. Claremorris impair her own chances of making an impression on the film executive.

"I must talk to you before you go," she insisted. "Sit down for a minute. Something terrible has happened."

"I haven't told Humphry about your engagement yet," said Grania. "To tell you the truth Humphry and I aren't on speaking terms, except on business. But I've thought of a way to come back at him for the dirty trick he played us over the bedrooms."

Phoebe had maneuvered them over to the garden seat, and as they all sat down she managed to get a word in.

"You needn't go spreading the news about me and Michael," she began. "That's partly what—"

"Darling, you're not all washed up already?"

"No, of course not. Something's happened, I tell you." Both Claremorrises were now gazing at Phoebe in eager anticipation of disaster. She said, "Uncle Jason's death wasn't an accident. It turns out now he was poisoned, deliberately poisoned, with arsenic."

She looked hard at them and let it penetrate.

Grania's jaw dropped. Lionel gave a very long whistle like a tire going flat. For once neither of them found anything to say.

"So there's going to be talk," said Phoebe. "There'll be those who think I did it. I may be arrested. I don't want our engagement to add to the story. I don't want Michael to be involved in any of this. Time enough for us to put the banns up when it's all over and I'm a free woman."

"But why do they think you did it?" asked Grania.

"Shut up, you fool," said Lionel.

"How can they help it?" said Phoebe. "It doesn't matter. They're all very kind about it. But they're all over the place now, and I don't suppose there'll be much peace till they've found out all there is to find out."

"I thought there seemed to be a few more than usual," said the observant Lionel.

"They're searching the house for clues," said Phoebe with a little laugh. "They took all our fingerprints."

"How too terribly authentic!"

Grania had got her second wind. "Can we do anything to help?" she said earnestly. "Shall I talk to the inspector for you? Could we give you an alibi or anything? What are friends for, if not to stand by at a crisis? And I must say, I do think your fiancé's place now is at your side. What's love worth if it can't face the first trial?"

"Let's hope it won't come to a trial," said Phoebe dryly.

"Darling, of course I didn't mean—but if it should," said Grania, struck by a thought, "you can depend on us to give evidence for the defense. So don't hesitate to call on us."

She saw herself in the box, in a chic black frock and a little hat with violets and a veil.

"I know a terribly good lawyer," said Lionel. "He's expensive, but he'd get anyone off."

Phoebe pressed both their hands and thanked them with tears in her eyes, and reminded them they must not be late for their rehearsal.

"I just wanted you to know," she said. "Try and believe the best of me, whatever you may hear. It's good to know one has friends."

"Count on us," said the Claremorrises. What exactly they meant by that and why Phoebe found it comforting might be hard for anyone outside the theater to understand.

As they walked back to the gate, watched by two plainclothes men on duty there and by the Chief Superintendent and the Inspector from the study window, Phoebe held her head high before the world. She enquired after her friends' comfort in their Seaport lodgings.

This revived Grania's grievance. She said, "There aren't actually bugs, as far as we've noticed. There's pretty well everything else. But never mind. I'll have my revenge. Humphry shall have his share of insect life."

"Whatever are you going to do?" asked Phoebe.

"Fill his room with bees," said Grania. "Remember what happened at the barracks here? I thought of it the moment I saw there were two hives in the garden not twenty yards from the window. All I need do is slip in and leave a section of honey there and the window open. I'll do it this afternoon, while he's at the rehearsal. Mr. Humphry blooming Madigan can look out."

"I can't stop her," said Lionel. "I've no control over her. I'm only her husband."

Phoebe laughed heartlessly. "Poor Humphry, he deserves it. A case of 'revenge is sweet.' "

"Women!" said Lionel.

Phoebe's parting words were: "Do let me know how it works."

### III

The detectives were all still there when Michael Canavan climbed up the hillside to the garden that evening. He too had to be interviewed by the Inspector. They took his fingerprints. It was all routine.

Afterwards he and Phoebe escaped from the house and climbed to the top of the Bell Rock, where fir trees grew raggedly in a little wood. They sat on dry pine needles and had the choice of two contrasted views, one of the valley, the other of the mine. Michael's eyes rested on green treetops and hedgerows, the road and river with a field's width in between, leading the eye on to the woods into which both road and river disappeared. Tiny vehicles passed along the road, smoke spired up from cottage chimneys; these signs of human beings, safely occupied at a safe distance, increased the attraction of the scene.

Phoebe stared the other way, into a chasm where, some time in the last century, part of the mine had fallen in. Precipices of sheer slate towered above a heap of tumbled rocks half buried in slag, and in the face of the rock were two black orifices, the openings of tunnels which had been sheared across by the landslide. These tunnel mouths, opening on the scene of desolation, added to it the horror of deeper darkness in lost regions underground, the suggestion of endless grim possibilities open to human experience, beyond the bleak world view seen by the light of reason and day.

"Have you sent the notice to the papers?" asked Michael.

"Not yet," said Phoebe. "I think it had better wait for a day or two, Michael. Just till I get out of this mess."

"What do you mean? There's all the more reason to put it in at once. You ought not to be alone. Let everybody know I'm with you."

"You'd only make matters worse. Think what a headline our engagement would be if I was arrested."

"They daren't do that," said Michael fiercely.

"They might. Then how should I feel? I don't want you dragged into this, Michael. Things are bad enough without. I wish I hadn't got engaged to you."

"You couldn't help yourself."

Michael spoke with calm assurance. Phoebe's dark eyes flashed.

"I could if I'd wanted to. I temporarily lost my head. I felt myself sinking and clung. But I'm not a clinger, Michael. I prefer to fight my own battles."

"See here," said Michael, "we're as good as man and wife—"

"We are not," said Phoebe.

"What's the matter with you this evening?" said Michael. "Anyone would think you were trying to break it off."

"No, Michael, don't be stupid. It's only that our engagement belongs to a different order of events. It has nothing to do with all this. Forget about it. It's in abeyance. It must wait till—"

"Till when? Tibb's Eve? I don't see anything to wait for."

"Till we know what happened to Uncle Jason. Till everybody knows I had nothing to do with it."

"Oh shut up!" said Michael. "You're only frightening yourself with talk."

He put his arms round her, but Phoebe twisted herself out of them.

"Don't!" she said. "That only makes things worse. How can I think?"

"What do you want to think for? We had it all settled. We've told the family. You can't back out of a thing like that. The situation hasn't changed since yesterday. We didn't know then either what happened. You don't imagine the police were taken in by all that about the bees? Nothing's changed, unless you've changed your mind. Tell me this!" Michael's voice sharpened with suspicion. "Has it anything to do with this fellow Madigan?"

"With Humphry? Don't be absurd!"

"Just what was all that about you and him?"

"All what? Nothing that matters. I may have once thought I was in love with him. I know better now."

"Was he in love with you?"

"Humphry?" said Phoebe with a scornful laugh. "He's never been in love with anybody but himself."

"How long ago was all this?"

"Oh, two years at least."

"Only two years? And you never said a word about him to me."

"Why should I? It's all dead and done with. I was a different person in those days. People change. I've never asked you if you were in love with anybody before me.

"I'd have told you if I had been."

"I wonder."

"Oh well," said Michael after a pause, "don't let's quarrel about it."

"I'm sorry, Michael," said Phoebe. "It was my fault. I'm all on edge. I just can't stand being argued with or cross-questioned. I'm not fit for human company just now."

"Of course," said Michael gently. "I understand."

"Then don't touch me!" said Phoebe. "Please, my dear."

Michael stayed put. Phoebe stood up and walked slowly away from him towards the edge of the cliff. She stood with her back turned staring out over the rocks.

There was a crash of footsteps behind her. She felt herself seized by the arm and hauled backwards.

"Michael!" she cried, indignant. Her free arm whirled round with momentum behind it. The slap landed on a face, but it was not her fiancé's; it was Detective Officer Lemon's.

Detective Officer Lemon also found himself gripped from behind by Michael Canavan. After a confused moment, they all three disengaged.

The plainclothes man apologized. He explained that he thought Phoebe was about to throw herself over.

"Have you been spying on us all the time?" said Phoebe.

"I was only keeping an eye on you from a distance," said the miserable youth. "I didn't listen in."

"You can take yourself off now," growled Canavan.

Phoebe promptly changed her tone.

"It's not his fault, Michael," she said. "I suppose he had orders. It only proves what I was saying just now. What's the use of pretending we can be engaged or do anything in a normal way?"

Since Saturday she had been wearing a ring, a modest affair for an heiress, just one small diamond. She took it off and held it out.

"Take it back, Michael," she said. "Keep it for me till I ask you for it."

Michael began to protest. He glared at D/O Lemon who tactfully faded out. But Phoebe kissed the ring and held it out.

Soon after, the disengaged couple came down from the rock, walking side by side with plenty of room for a third person between them.

## CHAPTER SEVENTEEN

ON TUESDAY MORNING Edward Gildea went early into Drumclash in order to tackle arrears of work that had piled up while he was busy with Phoebe Prendergast's affairs. As his foot was on the step of his office he was hailed from the Civic Guard barracks and told that the Superintendent would like a word with him.

He knew the moment he entered the inner room that the Superintendent, who was looking particularly prim, had some joke up his sleeve.

"Morning, Mr. Gildea," he said. "I believe you were anxious to see a certain gentleman arrested."

"I never said that," said Edward. " I only suggested you should keep an eye on him."

"And a nice runaround he gave us," said Menapia. "Mind you, we don't complain. We're devils for work. If a fellow goes off with an old lady's valuables and pawns them we like to be told. It's good for the young ones to have someone to follow around for practice, and of course we're always glad of the chance to make a pop."

"So I did you a good turn," said Edward. "What's the matter?"

"Well the matter is, Mr. Gildea, that as you should know, there's one law for the rich and another for the poor."

Edward wiggled his eyebrows.

Menapia said casually, "We just heard from Canada that Hector Prendergast, senior, died a millionaire."

Edward blinked. "How on earth did he manage that?"

"He was in the right place at the right time. They had a mining boom out there in the twenties and thirties, maybe you've heard. He did a bit of prospecting and struck lucky. He left his pile to his only son. Hector Prendergast, Junior, has no need to steal old ladies' teaspoons."

"Do you mean to say he's been telling the truth all along? How do you know it is his son?"

"His papers are all in order and they've cabled us a full description. His signature's O.K. Everything tallies."

Edward Gildea buried his face in his hands.

"I'll never get over this," he said in a muffled voice. "From now on, God help me, I'm a mark for the most obvious touch. Say it's not too late for me to rush round and offer to lend him a few quid."

Menapia laughed unkindly. "You've missed the boat. His letter of credit's come through. The wires have been humming. They're all falling over themselves at the bank. The advice still hasn't arrived because it was mailed in the ordinary post. They found out the mistake at the other end and cabled."

"You're not making all this up?"

The Superintendent handed him a sheaf of papers: two cables and three telegrams from Dublin, also two ten-pound notes and a pawn ticket.

"We're sending a man to get the silver out for him. He's bought it off Mrs. Teely. He gave her a hundred pounds for the lot. That's her own valuation and about double anyone else's."

"Well, it's a lesson to me," said Edward. "From now on I believe the best of everyone. I'll do anything anyone asks me to—pay their fares, bury their relations, hold their babies. I won't go by their faces; appearances may be against them. I'll just let them spin me their tales and reach for my wallet."

"You'll be ruined before the year's out," said the Superintendent.

"I expect so," said Edward, "but I couldn't survive another bloomer like this. One thing I am looking forward to," he said, cheering up, "and that's telling Mr. Sheed."

The Superintendent, having had his fun, started looking busy, and Edward, being busy himself, went back to his office. Halfway through the morning he had a visit from Hector Prendergast.

Edward had no time to hide under the table. He shamefacedly took the hand the visitor held out to him. Prendergast beamed at him.

"I guess you've heard from the Superintendent," he said. "You've given over thinking I'm a con man." He raised his free hand to stop Edward protesting. "Sure, you did, and I don't blame you. I can see now how cockeyed the situation must have looked to you. Maybe the way I acted was crazy, but what would you do? My credit's good all over the States; I'd never figured out how to get cash in a place where I wasn't known. Guess I'll be all the more ready to part with a few dollars next time I fall in with someone who says he's in need."

"Then I hope you won't be imposed on," said Edward.

"I hope not, Mr. Gildea. I have faith in human nature. Rich or poor, we're all folks. 'There's so much good in the best of us, and so much bad in the worst of us—' "

"Er, yes," said Edward.

"Well, you lawyers can't help having suspicious minds. But I didn't just come in to shake hands and pass the time of day. There's something you could do for me, Mr. Gildea, if you would be so kind."

"Certainly, Mr. Prendergast," said Edward, all zeal.

"I want to go down the mine," said Prendergast. "That mine has points of interest for me. I heard a lot about it from my father that I'd like to check up on, and apart from sentiment, as a mining engineer myself, I'd be interested to have a look see. My cousin Phoebe had no objection, but the police were a mite obstructive. I thought maybe if I could get hold of Mr. Sheed—"

Edward frowned. "There wouldn't be much difficulty in the ordinary way. We could get someone to take you down. Mr. Sheed would, I'm sure, have no objection. But you see, the place is in the hands of the Guards just now. Er, I suppose you've heard the news."

Prendergast nodded gravely. "I sure have. A shocking thing about Uncle Jason. You had no idea the other day?"

Edward shook his head. "I hope you don't think I deliberately misled you. I've enough to answer for, haven't I?"

"Forget it, brother," said Prendergast magnanimously. "Cousin Clementina's mind is relieved, that's one good thing. I sure don't want to interfere with the investigation, but my going down the mine won't hinder anything the police are doing above ground. I know my way about. You can tell the Superintendent I won't go falling down shafts, making more work for him."

"It's not that. You see, they're searching high and low for clues. They want to find the container the arsenic came out of. The obvious place to chuck a thing like that would be down one of the old mine openings. It may not sound very hopeful trying to find it, but those fellows have wonderful patience. Only of course they want the whole field to themselves."

"Maybe I could help."

"They wouldn't let you. I honestly don't think it's any use asking them. If you wait a day or two—"

"I'm only staying on another week," said Prendergast. "I don't want to lose my reservation. Say, this might be important, Mr. Gildea. You don't think maybe a little palm oil would have a softening effect on the Superintendent?"

Edward visualized Menapia's insulted expression. "For goodness' sake, don't try that on. You might get into serious trouble."

"You think I might be arrested again?" Prendergast grinned.

"Yes, and lose your reservation," said Edward, who realized that this was the one threat which had an effect on the Canadian. " If they arrested you properly it might take days to get you out."

Prendergast looked like a sulky child. Edward was truly sorry he could not do more to oblige him. To cheer him up, he promised to see the Superintendent and also to wire to Henry Sheed and secure his permission, which would be necessary in any case. He said the police might not be very long about their present task, or if they were, perhaps they might allow the Canadian to go down with them, and follow on over the ground they had covered. Prendergast agreed that this would be better than nothing, though he would have liked to have a free hand.

"What's your idea about the mine?" Edward asked, but Prendergast chose to be mysterious.

"It's not an idea, just a hunch. Only when I get a hunch seems like I can't get any rest till I've worked it out."

He shook hands again and lounged moodily out. Edward took time off from his letters and deeds to entertain himself with composing a telegram to Sheed.

## II

Two hours later, Hector Prendergast was back again. Edward heard his transatlantic voice in the room below, assuring the clerk that he knew his own way up. A minute later he breezed in, came right round the desk to where Edward was sitting, laid a hand on his shoulder, leaned over, and dumped a stone on top of the pile of letters Edward was trying to sign.

"Know what that is?" he said.

Edward was no geologist. He sometimes picked up the pretty fragments of quartz, streaked pink or yellow, that he found on the hill roads, but he would not have bothered with this whitish-gray stone, which looked quite ordinary.

"Arsenical pyrites," said Prendergast.

He took from his pocket (he was always weighted down at the pockets) the small hand pick he had bought in Dublin, chipped off a corner, and held the broken piece to Edward's nose. Edward's nostrils wrinkled at a smell he could not quite place.

"Garlic, isn't it?" said Prendergast. "See those crystals: wedge-shaped. That's how you know. Easy to recognize, once you've learned the signs."

"Arsenic?" said Edward. He traced a line through the little heap of dust on his blotter where the stone was chipped. "You don't mean, this is?"

"Not exactly. What you want is the oxide, but there's no difficulty in precipitating it from this. All you want is a carbon block and a blowpipe, and something to heat it with."

Prendergast felt in his pockets again and produced a brass tube and a black cube, also a teaspoon, a candle end and his lighter. He softened the candle end and stuck it on to an ashtray. He scooped up the dust on Edward's blotter and shook it on to the black cube, which was slightly hollowed on the top. He lit the candle and put the brass tube to his mouth, and blew through the flame.

Vague recollections stirred in Edward's mind of having seen the same thing done in science classes at school. He felt the faint surprise he always did feel when any part of his education turned out to have a bearing on real life.

The air forced through the thin nozzle of the brass tube shaped a small bright cone in the candle flame. Prendergast directed the point of it to the center of the heap of dust. He held the teaspoon behind. Edward watched, fascinated, while the heap disappeared leaving only a ring of dust with a hole in the middle. And round this at a little distance another circle formed that was not grey but yellowish white.

Prendergast stopped blowing. He looked pleased.

"There you are," he said. "Arsenic settles at a little distance. If it's nearer, it's antimony. The yellow in it's iron." He opened a penknife and scraped together the powdery deposit of the outer circle. "There's enough there on the point of my knife to kill a bigger man than Jason. No Poisons Register to sign, and less than five minutes' work."

"But you have to find your stone," said Edward.

"I just walked along the lane by the house and picked one up," said Prendergast. "There's plenty lying about."

Edward wanted to laugh. There were the detectives combing through Coppermine House for tins and bottles or screws of paper, or flypapers, sheep dip, fireworks, paint or other commercial commodities containing arsenic. There were the Civic Guards through half the country patiently studying Poisons Registers backwards for twelve months past. And all the time here was what they sought, ready to the hand of the first knowledgeable passerby.

"And I learned that at school," he said. "It would never have occurred to me to make use of it. It's all very well for you, you're a mineralogist. I can hardly believe that anyone round here, any of the people in the case, would think of it."

Prendergast cocked an eye at him. "Doesn't it appear to you that this murderer has some brains? His interests may be wide. His experience probably covers technicalities of subjects other than bees. The murderer must have a good deal of perverted ingenuity."

"Penrose used to work in the mines," said Edward thoughtfully.

"Is that so?" Prendergast appeared to brood on this information. "Well," he said, "if that man isn't the killer type, his face sure is his misfortune. And it's not gang warfare. One will be enough."

"We'd better talk to the Superintendent," said Edward. "Shall we go across there now?"

Prendergast shook his head. "He's out. Conference at headquarters. I tried him first. I guess I'll go along to the house and see if I can get the Inspector interested. If I give him a hand out, maybe he'll let me go down the mine. You could put the proposition up to the Superintendent when he gets back."

He cleaned his penknife on a piece of paper, shedding the lethal dose of arsenic on the carpet. Edward looked at it with misgiving, but could not think of any way of disposing of it.

The Superintendent had not said how long he would be. It was an important conference. Edward made up his mind to wait for him, however late. He was excited by the thought that here perhaps was the key to the puzzle, and that by the time night came Penrose might be in prison and everyone else's mind at rest.

## CHAPTER EIGHTEEN

INSPECTOR GRACE had also gone to the conference, accompanied by Mahon, the head of the search party, and Sergeant Rice, the local authority. Detective Officer Lemon was left in sole charge at Coppermine House. The search in the house and garden had been abandoned; the search in the mine had not yet begun. It was an off day, the calm in the middle of a cyclone.

It was pleasant out of doors. Round in the yard by the kitchen door Mickser was holding skeins of knitting wool for Vera Byrne. Penrose's eye was off him; it was Penrose's half day off. Phoebe Prendergast took some sewing out to the seat under the big tree while D/O Lemon, ignored by everyone, paced idly back and forth along the garden path, contemplating the beauties of nature and longing to exchange them for the dusty streets of Dublin.

Then visitors arrived to break the monotony. First, Hector Prendergast in Mrs. Teely's baby Austin. He asked for the Inspector and looked thoughtful when he heard he was out. He asked where Penrose was. Detective Officer Lemon had seen him setting off on foot for Morna.

Prendergast drove off and had to back in the lane to let another car get up. This was the Claremorrises again. Detective Officer Lemon knew the rattle of their engine by now. They were welcome as far as he was concerned. Mrs. Claremorris was more worth looking at than rocks and trees. Miss Prendergast was all right, but Mrs. Claremorris came nearer to D/O Lemon's feminine ideal.

But he hardly recognized his feminine ideal when she got out of the car. She had a scarf over her head, but it fell open as she was ducking out of the door, and revealed her usually attractive features all slewed sideways, a cheek twice the normal size, and one eye almost buried. This hideous disfigurement would have shocked D/O Lemon more if he had not seen the Guard who had had the job of collecting samples of honey from beehives. In his case it had been just as bad, but only temporary. What on earth had Mrs. Claremorris been up to to get herself so badly stung?

Her husband had preserved his usual appearance, and so had a third party who had come with them, who was easily recognized from his photographs as Humphry Madigan. If confirmation had been required, Phoebe Prendergast greeted this third party as "Humphry, my dear!"

"Phoebe, my angel!" he replied and kissed her. Detective Officer Lemon thought, "Well, after all, she did break off her engagement to the other man."

Phoebe turned to Grania. "Darling! What have you done to yourself?"

"Hoist with her own petard," said Mr. Madigan. "Wash no pity on her. She wears the marks of her own infamous spite. This"—a sweeping gesture rounded out the swelling on Grania's face—"this is what she meant to happen to me."

"It just shows what one little bee can do," said Lionel Claremorris. "Not a whole swarm, just one. The silly girl caught it in the garden and carried it up to Humphry's room to give it a taste of the honey and start the rush. It didn't appreciate her kind intentions."

"Kind intentions, how are ye? " said Humphry Madigan.

"Oh, don't go on and on about it," said Grania. "I'm punished, aren't I? And it isn't fair to say I meant it to happen to Humphry. There was no need at all for him to get stung. I only meant to keep him out of his room for a bit and teach him to grab the best accommodation for himself. Yes, you did, Humphry, and if anyone's to blame it's you. As if I hadn't got enough to bear!"

"You egocentric little cat!" said Humphry Madigan. "What do you care if the Show can't go on? If you had to play your cruel tricks, couldn't you at least have waited till Bowman had been and gone?"

"Bowman?" said Phoebe, puzzled.

"Of MGM," said Lionel, reminding her.

"Oh!" said Phoebe, in a voice that registered the full extent of the disaster.

"Oh dear," said Phoebe again, after a pause. "But what brings you here? Is there anything I can do?"

"Can you give Grania anything for her face?"

"Sal volatile might help. I'm afraid it won't take the swelling down by tonight."

"Go and wash your face in sal volatile, Grania," said Humphry Madigan. "Lionel can help you, and mean while Phoebe will solace me with her sympathy. Phoebe, you look beautiful as ever, a refreshing change for my eyes. Why haven't I seen you for so long? Where can we talk?"

The Claremorrises went indoors, Phoebe calling after them to try the bathroom cupboard. Humphry Madigan led Phoebe to the seat under the tree. He began talking hard.

They were in full view of D/O Lemon, patrolling between house and gate. He did not listen, but he got an impression that Madigan was pleading for something. Phoebe seemed to argue with him. Madigan at one point went on his knees, but she laughed at him and made him get up. Madigan was nearly as good as the films. He talked and talked. He waved his arms round in circles. He clutched his hair. Then he stopped acting and sobered down, but went on talking and persuading, hardly giving Phoebe time to answer him. Everything she said he seemed to cut off short. They had it all to themselves for twenty minutes. The Claremorrises stayed indoors, and as it could not have taken all that time to bathe anybody's face, it looked as if it might be a put-up job on their part, leaving Phoebe and Madigan together. At last it began to seem as if Madigan was wearing Phoebe down. She stopped arguing and shrugged her shoulders. They talked a bit more, Phoebe saying more and Madigan less. Then he suddenly seized one of her hands and kissed it. A minute later out came the Claremorrises, just as if they had been watching. They all four talked together. Each of the Claremorrises in turn shook Phoebe's hand. Then Madigan seemed to get impatient and started hustling the others towards the car. They all said good-bye, and last thing of all, Madigan took Phoebe in his arms and kissed her.

The car bumped off down the lane, leaving the garden quieter than ever. Phoebe walked slowly back to the seat and remained there very still for about ten minutes, staring at the view. Then she sprang to her feet and hurried into the house.

When Vera Byrne called him in for a cup of tea, D/O Lemon offered her six to four against Phoebe marrying Michael Canavan.


## CHAPTER NINETEEN


CHIEF SUPERINTENDENT Tunney had called the conference, tearing himself with regret, for an afternoon, from his financial estimates for the upkeep and improvement of barracks and a new scheme for simplifying recruitment for the Force. In his heart of hearts he could not feel that the death of one old gentleman was more important than the welfare of hundreds of young, active, loyal, underpaid and overworked Civic Guards. But he saw that the case would bring publicity. From the moment when the medical report mentioned arsenic, proving the death to have been a murder, it took rank as one of the biggest ever handled in a district where major crime was rare. If they could show speedy results, it might even have a softening effect on the Department of Finance.

Nevertheless Colonel Tunney was too old a hand to be impatient. He knew that, apart from those simple crimes in which the identity of the murderer is obvious from the first, the best chance of bringing anyone to book lay in thorough enquiries over a wide field, that brilliance was useless without good staff work, and that luck rewarded those who earned it by perseverance.

Inspector Grace struck the Chief as a man who earned his luck. He was neglecting no detail, interviewing witnesses, comparing statements, going over the ground. The object of the conference was not to hustle an experienced investigator, but to stimulate morale by official interest and approval.

Five men sat that summer afternoon in the Chief's cramped, book-lined office, which had through its one large window a distant tantalizing view, over roofs and between chimneys, of the sea. Colonel Tunney, chairman and host; Superintendent Menapia, patient but worried; Inspector Grace, on the defensive; Mahon of the search party, a one job man unconcerned with other people's troubles; Sergeant Rice, to whom this was all adventure, and who sat quietly making the most of permission to smoke in uniform.

The Chief Superintendent had before him a fragment of stone, similar to the one Hector Prendergast showed Edward Gildea that same afternoon. This one had been found in a box of geological specimens at Coppermine House. It had a label pasted on it, "Arsenical pyrites." Inspector Grace had rung up the Technical Bureau about it and had been told how you could make your own arsenic at home without expense.

"So that's where it came from, you think?" said the Chief.

Grace said, "It accounts for one thing that puzzled me. The arsenic in the honeycomb was white, not blue. That looked as if it hadn't been obtained commercially in this country."

"Smart of you to catch on to it," said the Chief. He was anxious to give credit where credit was due. He knew Grace had come expecting criticism rather than praise.

"Then you're not looking for a container, you're looking for a blowpipe and another piece of stone like this, with the surface chipped." The Chief looked at Mahon, who said, "Yes, yes, sir."

"You'll have a strong case when you find it," said the Chief encouragingly, "And you have the thing narrowed down. I'd say there was only one person could have had the necessary knowledge. Mr. Grace, why aren't you satisfied?"

"Defense could pick holes in it," said Grace. "I thought at first, like you, sir, it had to be a man with a special knowledge of minerals, in other words, Mr. Sheed. But it needn't be. These bits of stone with labels on were lying about in boxes and on shelves all over the house. Anyone with a smattering of science would know how to work the trick."

"Who, for instance?"

"Mr. Gildea, for instance. Remember, he had a lot to do with those beehives. I always thought he could have slipped in the poisoned honeycomb. And then he started the idea of it being natural."

"You surely aren't going to try and pin it on Mr. Gildea," said Superintendent Menapia. "I've known the man all my life."

"That's where you might be prejudiced," said Colonel Tunney. "That's where the man on the spot is always handicapped. A stranger like Mr. Grace gets a better all-around view. Wait now, man, don't blow the roof off! We aren't going to arrest him on insufficient evidence. There's no motive for either him or Mr. Sheed, is there?"

"There's no material evidence either," said Grace. "It's all guesswork. The only reason to consider them at all is that the method tends to suggest one or other of them. The bees are Mr. Gildea's department and the mineral poison is Mr. Sheed's. You can't entirely neglect that kind of pointer. If we found either of them concealing a blowpipe we might begin to look round seriously for a motive."

"Mr. Sheed probably has a blowpipe for use in his work," said Menapia, who knew a little of mining, like most things to do with his district. "They can test for various kinds of ores that way, can't they?"

"They can, I believe. In his case we'd need something more. You know the trouble it is to pin a thing down with facts. But keep watching a man, and sooner or later he'll give himself away."

"But you still suspect Miss Prendergast?" said the Chief.

"I suspect her Number One," said Grace.

"What's your theory of the case?"

"I can't prove anything yet," said Grace, "but I shouldn't be surprised if Canavan was the villain of the piece. I believe he put her up to it. He'd be one of these deliberate wife murderers, the kind who meet a woman with money, make up to her, marry her, and bump her off, after making sure they come in for what she leaves. It's a good game if you don't weaken. In this case there was an extra murder to commit. That wouldn't stop him. But it was more convenient for her to do it than for him. He'd talk her round to it. And here's where the psychology of the criminal mind comes in." Grace warmed to his theme. "A criminal never likes to admit he's wrong. They're champions one and all at finding excuses for themselves. They've got to justify themselves in their own eyes. They blame society, or their upbringing, or the victim who provoked them, anything rather than say they did wrong. Canavan would most likely tell himself that he was only putting Phoebe Prendergast to the test. If she could be talked into committing a murder, that was her guilt, and she deserved to be the next. He'd make out his second crime was only a just retribution."

The Chief agreed with this analysis. He asked, "Which of them devised the method?"

"Both together. She had plenty of time to turn over these pieces of stone lying around the house and to wonder where the arsenic came in. She'd ask him, and if he didn't know, he'd the brains to find out."

"So you regard Canavan as accessory after the fact. You don't think he could have done the whole job?" Colonel Tunney did not look forward to arresting Phoebe Prendergast.

Grace said, "It isn't likely. Canavan was never in the house in the old man's time. He never got near the larder or the place where the things for the bees were kept. He's never kept bees or taken any interest in them, whereas Miss Prendergast helped to prepare the sections before they were put on the hive."

"It seems to me," said the Chief, "that the case isn't far from complete. If you could get the proof of how they obtained the arsenic—"

"There's one other possibility, though," said Grace. "I'd another suspect in mind from the beginning, and I haven't eliminated him yet, and that's Penrose."

"He was a miner himself," said Menapia, "and all his family."

"The motive in his case would be jealousy." Colonel Tunney showed he had a grasp of all the details and did not need reminding. "That wouldn't implicate the cook, I take it?"

"Only indirectly. She'd be chief witness against him."

Sergeant Rice felt the Chief's eye on him. He was the accepted specialist on Vera Byrne.

"Miss Byrne's a nice girl," he said. "Her trouble is she's too kindhearted. She means no harm. She's not speaking to him now. He's a tough if ever there was one."

"Does she think he did it?"

"She says not." Rice frowned. Penrose was certainly his favorite suspect. "She's the sort that wouldn't get anyone into trouble. Too kindhearted."

"She'd make a bad witness," said Grace.

There was a pause. All five policemen considered the two couples under suspicion: Phoebe, with Canavan behind her; Penrose, with Vera Byrne as the innocent occasion for the crime. They all felt they would prefer to arrest Penrose, but they were all trained to impartiality. The evidence was stronger against Phoebe.

Grace proposed to search Canavan's rooms. Penrose's rooms had been covered in the general search of the house and premises, with no result. Colonel Tunney asked if Grace meant to apply for a search warrant, but Grace's idea was first to call at the house, contrive to be left alone while Canavan was out, and see what he could find in a quick look round. District justices can be tiresome about search warrants; shortcuts have to be taken.

Last of all, they discussed the mine. They spread maps on the table; longitudinal plans and cross-sections revealed the complexity of the undertaking. There were miles of tunnels on different levels. There would be dangerous places: ladders might have rotted; shafts might be left without protective fencing round their open mouths; the roof might fall in. There was simply no possibility of searching thoroughly through all those underground chambers. Mahon was in despair, but Grace said it must be attempted.

He had also asked for a mineralogist to accompany the searchers. He explained that he was acting on a hunch.

"The search is necessary," he said. "It's also an excuse. You might find a blowpipe or an empty box that contained arsenic, and in that case we'd have to start to think again. But what I want most is a report on the state of the mine. Suppose it isn't as derelict as the family make out, that might throw a new light on the motive for the murder."

The Chief stipulated that all the searchers must wear miner's helmets. Grace said there were a number of them stored at the house, and others could be borrowed in the village. Everything was arranged for the work to begin next day.

Everything was well in hand. It was all a matter of time and patience.


## II


Arrived back at the barracks, Superintendent Menapia was told that Mr. Gildea had been asking for him and that he was still across in his office. Guessing that only something important would keep Edward Gildea in Drum-clash after office hours, the Superintendent went over to visit him. The clerk had gone home, but the door was on the latch. Menapia walked straight in and up. He found the solicitor sitting at his desk toying with something that looked very much like a blowpipe.

Edward explained, and Menapia felt better, but the policeman in him made a mental note to check the story with Hector Prendergast.

Meanwhile he pretended that this was all new to him.

"Don't you think it may help?" said Edward.

"It may help to make it more complicated."

"It's a grim thought," said Edward, "that this deadly stuff is lying about, though I suppose there are very few people who would know how to recognize it. I used to be all for teaching people to take an interest in nature and study natural objects. Now, I'm not so sure."

"Nature can be used or abused," said Menapia heavily, "and the spread of education and knowledge only makes life harder for us."

"But science is a weapon in your hands."

"Don't we need all the help we can get? Look at what we're up against. It's a miracle you can ever make a case against anybody."

"We must have judges' Rules of Evidence," said Edward, who knew what the Superintendent was getting at. "This is a democracy."

"It's money in your pockets, you solicitors," said Menapia. "Nine times out of ten we know who did a thing and you won't let us arrest him."

"Is that what's happening now?" asked Edward.

Menapia wore his poker face. "I wasn't talking about present circumstances."

"I suppose," said Edward, "that there are cases where you never know who did it?"

"A few, maybe."

"I do hope it won't be so this time. I don't like to think of that poor girl, Miss Prendergast, under a cloud for the rest of her life."

Menapia said, "I hear her engagement is broken off."

Edward explained that it was merely the official announcement that had been postponed. Menapia said, "Is that all?"

"What's the matter with you?" said Edward. "I never saw you so down in your boots. Is it the case going badly?"

Menapia made a visible effort to look cheerful. "Ah, not at all, Mr. Gildea. It's only the weather. It's been heavy all day, hasn't it? We've not done with the rain."

It was certainly stuffy in the office. The tide was out, and they were near enough to the coast to feel the drain of it and the deadness of the hour. The two men found nothing more to talk about and yet could hardly find the energy to take leave and part. As they sat there exchanging platitudes, they heard rapid steps outside. The steps stopped, then began again, and next minute they were on the stairs. The office door was flung open, and there stood Henry Sheed.

Edward and Menapia rose in amazement. They had thought he was fifty miles away, and he stood staring at them, hot and breathless with haste. They had never seen him so upset before.

"Superintendent, it's you I want," he said in a gasp. "You too, Gildea. I've bad news. Phoebe's disappeared."

## CHAPTER TWENTY

PHOEBE PRENDERGAST'S first action, after Humphry Madigan and the Claremorrises left, had been to write a letter to Michael Canavan. She was finishing it when Vera Byrne came with her tea. She gave it to Vera to give Canavan if he called that evening. She said she had a headache and did not want to see anyone. She would have a cup of tea and an aspirin and then go to bed. She did not want any supper and asked Vera not to disturb her till morning. Vera thought she looked white, "real puny," she said, describing it to the police. Vera was concerned. She suggested various remedies, but

Phoebe only said she would sleep it off. Vera heard her upstairs in her room undressing, then the house was quiet.

Two hours later, Henry Sheed arrived. Knowing that his room was always ready he had not troubled to send a telegram but took the household by surprise. Vera thought she should let her mistress know he was there. She went up and knocked at her bedroom door. There was no reply. She supposed Phoebe was asleep. She tried the door handle and found the door was locked. It was unusual, though natural perhaps if the invalid wanted to make sure of peace. Vera could hardly say why she became alarmed. Just then the police party returned from the conference. Inspector Grace learned the position of affairs. His mind was haunted by the fear of a suspect committing suicide.

Grace demanded a ladder. The window of the bedroom was one of those in the front of the house with a copper cockleshell over it. It was open a few inches at the top. The curtains inside were drawn.

The ladders were in the locked garage and Penrose was still off for his half day. They got in by unscrewing the staple that held the padlock. The longest ladder was brought to the window and Grace went up.

He knocked on the glass with no more result than Vera had got when she knocked at the door. He reached in and pulled the curtain back. The room was empty.

There was no rigid corpse on the bed or the floor. Instead, there were signs of someone departing in haste. Shoes and lingerie were scattered about; face powder had been spilled; a cupboard door swung open; a box of papers had been half unpacked and left with the lid off. Grace, kneeling on the windowsill methodically observing details, noted that the key was not in the door. It must have been locked from the outside.

He descended, looking grim. He reassured Sheed and Vera. Phoebe had apparently gone out herself of her own free will. How was it that nobody had seen her go?

Vera Byrne then remembered that her mistress had told her to bring in firewood. This meant carrying it all the way from a woodshed near the garage. D/O Lemon had helped her carry it. It had occupied them both for several minutes. And the wood was not needed. True, the stock in the house was low, but on these warm days the fire was never lighted. A blaze of a few sticks to start the kitchen range or heat up the oven for baking was all the wood they burned. It must have been an excuse to get the other two out of the way while Phoebe slipped out.

But why should she bother to give misleading instructions and creep away unobserved? Her movements were not shadowed. She was free to come and go as she liked, provided she did not leave the district without telling the Civic Guards.

She had gone, however, deliberately giving everyone the slip. There was that secret passage under the house, the ladders down into the mine, the tunnel ending in an outlet to the lane. The Inspector made for it, but the linoleum was in its place over the trapdoor, and the bolt was bolted.

The trapdoor in the garden was also fastened. In any case, it lay on the route from the woodshed to the house, so that Phoebe could hardly have used that way without being seen.

Mahon searched the garden for footprints. He found light depressions on the grass of the lawn, and following them across, he came on the print of wedge-heeled shoes on the path by the Bell Rock.

"Ah," said Grace, in the tone of one who saw it all, "it's to Canavan she's gone."

"But she left a letter for Mr. Canavan," said Vera Byrne.

Grace thought that might be a trick. He took charge of the letter and set off by car for the cottage at the foot of the Bell Rock.

He stopped the car in the lane and examined the door communicating with the underground passage through the mine to the house. The bushes round it had been broken down, but that had been done in the police investigation. The door was shut, but it yielded to a push; the bolt inside had not been driven home. Accident? Coincidence? Or could it have a bearing on Phoebe's flight? The Inspector bent to examine the ground. The dust was disturbed as if scuffled by many feet, which might have been those of yesterday's searchers, making it impossible to distinguish any clear print.

Grace went on down the hill. In the rose-covered cottage by the roadside the woman of the house said she had not seen Miss Prendergast. Canavan was in his room changing his clothes after work. He was startled by the Inspector's question. He tore open Phoebe's letter. It merely said that she had a headache and did not feel up to seeing anyone that evening. It ended, "Do come tomorrow."

Canavan's supper was ready. He refused to look at it, but insisted on returning with the Inspector to the house. He had to be given something to do. Grace asked him to drive to Mrs. Teely's and see if Phoebe were there. He also asked Henry Sheed to drive to the Gildeas' bungalow.

Sheed explained all this to the two in the office in Drumclash. He had Mollie Gildea with him, waiting up the street in his car. They all drove back with him to Coppermine House.

II

"What brought Sheed back all of a sudden?" Grace asked D/O Lemon, who did not know. Perhaps he had just happened to find he had a day to spare.

The Inspector took Vera Byrne up with him to Phoebe's bedroom. He wanted to know what clothes were missing. Phoebe had cast off the black linen frock she had worn all day, the slip that went under it, stockings and a pair of sandals. She had taken slacks, a sports shirt, and a pair of walking shoes. At first they thought she had gone hatless and coatless, but later Vera noticed that a hooded mackintosh cape had gone from the hall. She had taken no other clothes, no luggage. Her handbag had gone, but she had not touched the small reserve of cash which she kept in a locked drawer.

"Looks as if she didn't mean to be away long," said Grace. He thought of Canavan's letter with its "Do come tomorrow." Nevertheless he wrote out a description to be broadcast.

He went through the box of papers in the bedroom. They were letters, receipted bills, press cuttings, photographs, old theater programs, typescripts of acting parts. The presumption was that something had been taken, but there was no knowing what. Vera Byrne could not help.

Why had Phoebe Prendergast run away? Inspector Grace could think of several answers.

(a) She was guilty.

(b) She was innocent but afraid of being accused.

In either case she might have tried to disappear, but for that she would need money, unless she had some other way of getting it in some other place. Could she have had a reserve fund in that box of papers? And it was strange that she had taken nothing for the night. Could she mean to spend the night on the hills? It did not seem as if her escape could have been planned. She had seized the opportunity when the house was almost empty of police, acting probably on impulse. Inspector Grace frowned. He did not like the look of it. The girl had been under a nervous strain, now something had broken, and she had fled. He could not rid his mind of the idea of suicide.

But there were other possibilities.

(c) She had been decoyed away by the murderer.

Where was Penrose? He had not been seen since midday. Grace sent Sergeant Rice to Morna to find him.

(d) She had eloped with Humphry Madigan.

This fourth theory was produced by D/O Lemon, and he supported it with an account of Miss Prendergast's visitors of the afternoon.

"Soon as I saw that laddo getting out of the car," said D/O Lemon, "I said to myself, 'What brings you here?' The excuse they all made was something about Mrs. Claremorris's face. She needed treatment, God help her. But an excuse is all that was. I mean to say, she could have gone to a doctor. The way it looks to me, Miss Prendergast had told those Claremorrises she'd broken her engagement. She might have had some purpose in letting them know that. So what do they do but bring this other man along. Mr. and Mrs. Claremorris went into the house and lost themselves. I mean to say it was obvious they were leaving the other two together. And Mr. Madigan sat there arguing and persuading, and Miss Prendergast at first wouldn't listen to him, but in the end she weakened, and they talked a bit more, and then the Claremorrises came out, kind of scouting round, and Madigan called them over and they all looked delighted with themselves. And Madigan kissed Miss Prendergast good-bye. And if I know anything about women," said D/O Lemon with authority, "she meant to have him back all along."

"But how did she go?" said Grace. "Why didn't he take her then if he had a car?"

"She wouldn't go openly. She'd be in dread of Canavan. The minute he heard, he'd be out gunning for Madigan. What she wanted was to get a night's start of him."

Grace saw an innuendo in his assistant's suggestion. He did not care for it. "You're a great hand at a yarn, Mick Lemon," he said, "but you ought to know a lady like Miss Prendergast wouldn't elope without taking a nightdress."

### III

The lawn began to fill with people. Sheed's party arrived with other men from the barracks in Drumclash. The Inspector and the Superintendent proceeded to organize a search party. Sergeant Rice brought another man back with him from Morna. He reported that Penrose had been in a pub there early in the afternoon and had been joined by Hector Prendergast. After some conversation they drove off along the main road in Mrs. Teely's little car. Nothing had been seen of them since.

Canavan returned, bringing Mrs. Teely with him. The young man looked haggard. Mrs. Teely had not seen anything of Phoebe, nor could she give any information about the movements of Prendergast.

"I did not question him about his comings and goings," she said. "I did not like to seem inquisitive. I put my car completely at his disposal for the duration of his visit. It seemed to me the least I could do for the poor boy, after the way I'd misjudged him."

Mrs. Teely was carrying a small attaché case. The Inspector's first guess, that being a lady she had brought her night things, was mistaken. She had kept Canavan waiting while she packed a first-aid box.

"Just in case it might be needed," she explained. "I've brought bandages, dressings, splints, and disinfectant and brandy. Of course it may be too late when they find her, but I do believe in hoping for the best, don't you?" She collapsed in tears and Mollie Gildea took charge of her, removing her as far as possible from the neighborhood of Michael Canavan.

The Superintendent returned from Morna where he had been telephoning headquarters. They were getting out a cordon on all the roads. The Chief had said to him, "After this they'll have to allow us radio patrol cars."

Mahon had all this time been searching the hillside for tracks. He reported that the footprints continued down the path till they were lost in sandy gravel, the overflow of the slag heaps. Down by the road he had come on what might be a fragment of the same print, in loose dust on the edge of the tarmac. There were also marks of tires where a car had braked. Phoebe might have stopped it, or it might have been waiting to pick her up.

"See what I mean," said D/O Lemon.

"What do you mean?" asked Canavan. At the suggestion that Phoebe might have gone off with Humphry Madigan, he became violent. Two men had to hold him off of D/O Lemon.

Mahon said he could not be certain that the footprints were Phoebe's; they were large compared with shoes left behind in her room. But Vera Byrne, who knew all Phoebe's shoes from cleaning them, said those she had on were her stoutest pair.

Mahon resented the imputation that his men might have left the door to the tunnel unbolted. He and Grace went back down the lane to examine it. They found then what they had overlooked before, that the bolt could be reached from outside. There was a loose stone next to the wooden frame of the door, wedged in with grass and leaves. When it was dislodged it left a hole through which the bolt might be poked back with a stick. But Phoebe, by her own account, had not known of the tunnel's existence two days before. Would she have known how to get in by this trick?

Men moved to and fro over the hillside, searching round the base of the Bell Rock and in the chasm caused by the old landslide.

Henry Sheed and Edward Gildea paced up and down the garden. Restless as they were, they refrained from pestering the police with questions or suggestions. Sheed chain-smoked his cigars. They smelled luxurious and vaguely sinful. Edward asked what had brought him back so unexpectedly. Sheed said: "The hand of Providence."

A police whistle sounded over by the Rock. Everyone ran to the spot and crowded round a man kneeling with his ear to a crack in the ground. He had heard noises like the fall of stones. He thought there was someone down below.

Henry Sheed said noise underground was deceptive. It will be heard in one place, and not another nearer at hand. Through fissures in the rock a slight noise may travel hundreds of feet. He could not even guess where this came from.

Canavan cried, " She's in the mine. What are we standing here for?"

"Patience, Mr. Canavan," said Inspector Grace. "We're going in."

He meant himself and Mahon. Henry Sheed volunteered to guide them. Grace looked at Menapia. The Superintendent said, "There may be a murderer down there. He may be armed."

"Are you?" asked Sheed. "I can take a chance if you can." He advised them to put on helmets and gumboots, which he said were more essential than guns.

Canavan also insisted on coming, and Sergeant Rice was added to the party, mainly to keep an eye on the young tough. Detective Officer Lemon, to his disgust, was made responsible for his own theory and sent off to Seaport to interview Humphry Madigan.

Superintendent Menapia remained at the house. His place was at the center of organization, awaiting developments. The search continued over the hill, and the cordon was out on the roads.

The garden was suddenly quiet and deserted. The women had gone indoors. The light was fading and it was a little chilly. A few belated bees were still returning to Jason Prendergast's remaining hives, but none now went out.

Edward Gildea kept the Superintendent company. They sat on the garden seat or walked about when they felt cold; neither of them felt able to stay in the house. They watched the birds settle down over the woods, and a lone bat flying round, and rabbits on the Bell Rock. They compared observations of nature, and by tacit consent avoided talking about the case.

## CHAPTER 21

GRACE CHOSE to enter the mine by the door in the lane, since that was the way by which Phoebe was most likely to have gone. Mahon searched the first few yards of the tunnel for footprints and found all tracks there confused, as if something had been dragged over them. The searchers had left the marks of their own feet. In just one place was the mark of a woman's shoe. It might be fresh or left weeks ago by Vera Byrne. Sheed said that in old tunnels that had not been entered for a hundred years you might find the prints of feet and on the walls the marks of hands, looking as if they had been made that day. They did not stay to make a close examination of the ground. To reach the part of the mine where falling stones had been heard, they must press on into the bowels of the rock.

They walked in single file, stooping, protected from stunning themselves against projections by their helmets which were of bakelite lined with webbing, and which should have had carbide lamps fixed to the front. The lamps having suffered from disuse, each man had to carry a torch. They pointed them downwards like cinema usherettes. The going underfoot was thus made visible, but all the rest of the surroundings became one massive darkness except when Sheed, in front, swept the beam of his torch ahead. Then their eyes strained along the series of heavy timbers shoring up walls and roof, and the narrow gauge rails for trucks that ran along the floor. All these lines diminishing in perspective made the tunnel seem endless. In fact it was not more than two hundred yards, ending in a cross-tunnel at the spot where the ladders came down from the house.

The cross-tunnel brought them to a sizeable cavern, where the rock walls were hollowed out to house machinery at the head of a vertical shaft. The framework of a hoist remained. The shaft was fenced off by a rough wooden palisade; Sheed leaned on it and flashed his torch down. They saw ladders descending one below the other. Sheed jerked out scraps of information. The old Cornish, miners, who were also sailors and fishermen, measured by fathoms; their unit was six feet. In the older parts of the mine the distance between levels was ten fathoms; further down they were spaced at a hundred feet. Ladders were twelve feet between rests; there were five to go down here. Canavan muttered, "Stop talking and let's get on."

The lower tunnel was similar to those above. The men's eyes, becoming accustomed to the monotony of the rock, began to pick out small variations. Here a blue-green stain indicated copper, there a puddle was yellow with iron oxide. Stalactites made groups of dripping needle points. In one place all sounds were drowned in the rushing of water and they splashed for a few yards through an underground stream.

They came to a branch tunnel. Sheed went a little way along and listened. Then he calmly spun a coin. "Heads this way, tails the other." It fell tails. They followed him uncertainly. They began to realize what it implied to search the mine.

They went down another sixty feet and entered a tunnel in the middle. After they had followed it to the end in one direction Grace said, "Aren't we a good bit beyond the garden?"

"A good bit," said Sheed. "I tell you, there's no knowing to a hundred yards where those sounds came from. Anyway, whatever made them might not still be there."

He shone his torch upwards. They found themselves at the bottom of a chimney, that is, looking up another vertical shaft. Far, far above them shone what at first they took for small electric lights. It was daylight showing through chinks in a covering of planks.

"Light's not gone yet," said Sheed. He looked at his watch. It was then a little after nine.

"That's Middle Whim," said Sheed. "Place where they used to have a horse in the old days, walking round and round to turn a wheel to work a hoist."

"Let's try the other direction," said Grace. He licked a trickle of perspiration from the corner of his lip.

It was with an effort that they turned from the glimpse of sky back into total darkness. That brief reminder of the outside world had been reassuring, almost like a beatific vision in the dark night of the mine.

They retraced their steps. Again they came to a branch. Sheed went straight on without pausing to spin a coin. But as Grace, next in the file, was passing the fork of the tunnel, he suddenly stopped in his tracks and put out his torch. The others copied him. Sheed called back, "What's the matter?"

Grace gestured angrily for silence, and Sheed's torch too went out. From then on, Grace took the lead.

He had heard something. Not falling stones. Not footfalls. The clink of metal on rock.

He led them cautiously along the branch tunnel. At the far end a light was faintly glowing. It was round a corner, at a place where the tunnel widened.

The sounds grew more distinct, then stopped short. A powerful beam swung out and down the passage to meet them. Grace switched on his own torch, the beams crossed. Grace called out, blinking in the light.

"Who's there? This is the police."

"O.K., brother, don't shoot," said a transatlantic voice. "Looks like the Mounties get their man."

With all the torches on the cave was brightly illuminated. Two men stood there, dressed in shirts and trousers, armed with picks. At their feet was a sizeable heap of broken rock. Hector Prendergast, bareheaded and disreputable, grinned at them with a millionaire's grin of welcome. It took a moment longer to recognize the other man, who wore a miner's helmet with its lamp working. He was Penrose.

"What are you digging there?" asked Sheed harshly. "A grave?"

There was a gasp from Canavan. He plunged forward, but Grace stepped between.

Prendergast began talking. He ignored Sheed and concentrated on the Inspector. He was earnest, voluble, apologetic.

"Inspector, I know I'm acting out of turn. I just couldn't wait for your authorities to make up their minds to let me in. I've got my reservation on next Monday's B.O.A. plane—"

"Doesn't look as if you'll make it," said Sheed. "Inspector, aren't you going to arrest them for breaking and entering private property?"

Canavan broke out, "Don't waste time talking. Where's Phoebe?"

Prendergast lost the thread of his remarks and looked puzzled. He asked, "Is Phoebe missing?"

Everyone's nerves were on edge from weariness and confinement. Grace exchanged glances with his own men, Rice and Mahon. He felt the other two slipping out of his control.

"You have no business to be here, Mr. Prendergast" he said severely, "nor you neither, Penrose—"

"I only done what I was asked," said Penrose sullenly. "Mr. Prendergast said he'd square things up."

"Oh he did, did he?" muttered Sheed.

"Never mind that now," said the Inspector. "You can explain to the Superintendent later. We're looking for Miss Prendergast. When did either of you see her last?"

Hector Prendergast had not seen his cousin Phoebe since the party on Saturday night. Penrose had not seen her since morning, when he took his orders for the day.

"He's lying," said Sheed. "Inspector, you may be tied by judges' Rules, but we can't wait. This is all a put-up job. Penrose! The game's up. What have you done with her?"

Penrose's face was wooden. He said nothing.

Sheed pressed closer. "Talk, Penrose! You can't swing twice."

"What do you mean?" snarled Penrose.

"You murdered Jason Prendergast."

"It's a lie," yelled Penrose and struck out at Sheed. Canavan interposed, but in doing so knocked the torch out of Grace's hand. Prendergast stooped for it, blocking the way. Penrose's fist caught Canavan a glancing blow. There was a momentary rough and tumble. Then Penrose suddenly pulled himself clear and raced off down the tunnel that led on still farther than the cavern in which the two had been discovered, boring deeper and deeper into the rock.

The light on his helmet fled with him, lighting his way, but betraying him to his pursuers. Sheed, in spite of his years, was in front. He and Penrose had the same advantage, they knew the mine. They stooped and dodged instinctively, where the others banged their heads or tripped on the rail track along the floor. They drew away from the rest, and Grace's shouts, telling them to come back and not be fools, rang through the vaults till the echoes died in vain.

Prendergast was the first to give up. He saw no point in exerting himself. Grace told Mahon and Rice to stay behind with him, but he himself kept doggedly on, and Canavan, ahead of him, ran on stumbling but without a halt.

The tunnel went on two miles, as Grace learned afterwards by reference to the map. It was the main thoroughfare on that level, intersected by other borings. There were bends in it beyond which the fugitive was lost to view; he could have dodged sideways but he simply fled straight on. It was unreasoning panic rather than an intentional effort to escape.

Suddenly the rocks receded, the tunnel widened, and in the floor ahead a great hole gaped. It was a natural cavity underground, a place which the miners had used for tipping rubbish. The track continued on, though the rails ceased at the edge of the pit. Along one side was a ledge, a foot or more wide, made formidable by the sheer rock walls above and below, but not too difficult for a man with a good head. Penrose took it at full speed, with Sheed after him. Canavan hesitated at the edge. Grace reached his side and drew him back. They saw Sheed, halfway over, stagger. It was as if he had just realized where he was.

He grabbed wildly at the slippery rock wall above him, lost his balance and toppled over. Horrified, the two men behind saw him plunge down into the abyss.

He gave one cry. It went on echoing from rock to rock for seconds after his body had struck the bottom. At last there was silence.

Grace muttered a prayer. Canavan said, "Amen."

Penrose had vanished. It was useless to follow him. Not even Canavan wished to attempt the ledge after what they had just witnessed. Grace spoke of fetching ropes, recovering the body. They could see it, as their eyes got used to the darkness at the bottom. It lay without sound or stir.

"But Phoebe?" said Canavan.

"She's not here," said Grace. "We'd best get back." He led Canavan back to the rest.


## II


Prendergast convinced even Canavan that his presence in the mine with Penrose had no connection with Phoebe's flight.

Prendergast had only one idea in his mind, to vindicate his father's reputation. His father had impressed on him that the mine was valuable and that with modern machinery it could be made to pay big dividends. He had sold his son on the idea more thoroughly even than his former shareholders in the Vale.

Happening to hear from Edward Gildea that Penrose had worked in the mine, Prendergast had sought him out and persuaded him to act as guide and navvy. They had brought pickaxes and a sack for samples. They had gone in by the door in the lane. It had been Penrose's idea to drag the pickaxes along their trail, obscuring footprints. He had seen so much lately of police methods.

"It's too bad my cousin's missing," said Prendergast. "I'd have had good news to give her."

"What have you struck?" asked Inspector Grace. "Not gold, surely?"

"No sir, not gold, nor yet uranium. This isn't a fairy tale, it's sober fact."

Prendergast picked up a lump of the greyish rock at his feet and held it in the light of his torch.

"See that," he said. "See the bloom on it? That's cobalt. I ought to know. There's mountains of it back where I come from. The place is named from it."

"Cobalt? What paint's made of?" said Grace, surprised. "Is that valuable?"

"Sure. Also used for steel processing. It's in big demand now in industry. The armaments drive has sent the price up. There's a fortune there, waiting to be dug out."

"So that's it," said Grace. "And Mr. Sheed owned the mining rights. I suppose they revert to Miss Prendergast now."

"She has enough without them," said Canavan. "What's it matter? You've got to find her, Inspector. You and the rest have hounded her with your suspicions, you must get her back and tell her the case is clear now, and we know the murderer."

"It's early days to be telling her that," said Grace.

"Why, Inspector, are you telling us Penrose wasn't the murderer?" said Prendergast. "What did he run for then? Did he just lose his head?"

"I suppose poor Sheed knew what he was talking about," said Canavan.

"You can suppose what you like about Mr. Sheed, God rest him!" said Grace. "He's gone to a higher Court. His reasons for what he said are between himself and his Maker. All I know is that in this world we need more evidence than we have against Penrose before we'd get a jury to convict."


## CHAPTER TWENTY-TWO

PHOEBE was safe. The party from the mine was greeted with the news as soon as they reached the house.

Everyone indoors turned out to meet them. Once again the garden was peopled. Daylight by now had faded into moonlight. The new moon had reached its first quarter now, and the sky was clear and bright with its silver radiance. The men who had come from underground drew thankful breaths. But they had to exchange bad news for good. Inspector Grace drew the Superintendent aside and made his grave report. They began making arrangements to secure the body of Sheed.

Canavan collapsed on the garden seat. He had done a hard day's work before he joined in the search, and he had played his full part in that. The loss of Phoebe had roused him to superhuman exertions; now came the reaction.

Phoebe was in Seaport, with Humphry Madigan. D/O Lemon had found her. He had telephoned to the station at Morna. They were now on their way back.

Mrs. Teely laid a hand on Michael Canavan's shoulder.

"Try to forgive her, Mr. Canavan. You must be very, very understanding. Think of the strain she has undergone. Isn't it natural she should have turned to an old friend? A girl can't always help her feelings, and after all, the theater is in her bones."

"Whiskey and soda, Canavan?" interposed Edward Gildea, thus probably preventing a second murder. Mollie had thoughtfully suggested to Vera Byrne to have drinks and sandwiches ready for the search party when they returned.

There was a glare of headlights at the gate. Canavan stood up, squaring his shoulders.

Across the grass, proudly escorted by D/O Lemon, came Phoebe Prendergast, arm in arm with Humphry Madigan.

Phoebe in her hooded mackintosh looked like a wraith of the moonlight. Madigan, in his duffle coat, managed somehow to convey an impression of an early Christian martyr.

"Gracious heavens!" said Phoebe putting her hood back, "what a crowd of you! Whatever are you all doing out here? Why Mr. Gildea, are you here? And Mollie too? And Mrs. Teely? Are you all waiting for me?"

"You gave us a fright, Miss Prendergast," said the Superintendent.

"So I've been given to understand. I'm awfully sorry. I hoped I shouldn't be missed. I'm afraid," said Phoebe with a little laugh, "I underrated the Civic Guards."

Menapia shook his head at her. "You had no right to give us the slip like that, after promising not to leave the district."

"But I didn't leave the district. I was coming back, and here I am."

"After giving us all the trouble of finding you," said Menapia. "If you intended coming back, why did you slip out unbeknownst?"

"Look, Superintendent," said Madigan, "need you make such a thing of it? Since she's come back, need she be pestered with questions? Can't you fellows let anything pass?"

"What's this man doing here?" said Canavan. He had been looming all this time in the background. Phoebe cried, "Oh, Michael, there you are! Did you think I was never coming back?" She hurried to his side and put her hand in his. Canavan still remained rigid and scowling. Madigan said in a voice that sounded amused, "Calm yourself, dear fellow. I give you my word, you've no complaint."

Canavan dropped Phoebe's hand and stepped forward clenching his fists, but Phoebe kept hold of him.

"Don't be silly, Humphry," she said. "I'll have to tell them."

"Then throw the blame on me," said Madigan magnificently. "Tell them it was my fault."

"So it was, all your fault," said Phoebe. "I never ought to have listened to him for a moment," she told the Superintendent. "I'd forgotten what he's like when he starts talking. He'd inveigle the birds off the bushes. It's his magnetism."

"Nonsense, darling. I merely appealed to your better nature," said Madigan, preening himself nonetheless, and returning a withering look from Canavan with a bland smile.

"Well, now, what have you been up to?" asked the patient Superintendent.

"I should have thought you might have guessed," said Madigan. "She's been acting with us. Mrs. Claremorris was indisposed, and Miss Prendergast very kindly stepped into her part at a moment's notice."

To the anxious watchers and the tired men who had been seeking Phoebe in the depths of the earth this admission came as an anticlimax. There was a blank silence, then several people spoke at once. Canavan said, "You said you'd done with the theater." Inspector Grace and Superintendent Menapia asked both together, "Why all the secrecy?" But Mrs. Teely finally won the monopoly of the air.

"If no one else will protest, I shall. Somebody must uphold the standards of decency," said Mrs. Teely. "This will be the scandal of the neighborhood. It would have been bad enough in all conscience if you had run off with this—this mountebank"—Humphry Madigan made her a very deep bow— "but to fly in the face of your uncle's wishes, to appear on the stage as if nothing had happened, shameless girl! I give you up. I've stood by you in your troubles, shutting my eyes to your ambiguous conduct, sinking my feelings in the face of deliberate slights, but this is too much to endure. You have dragged the family name in the mud."

"Madam, you wrong her," said Humphry Madigan, unable to resist.

"Oh be quiet, Humphry!" said Phoebe on a note of exasperation. She turned to the Superintendent. "Now you can understand why I didn't want anyone to know."

"And there was no reason why they should," said Madigan. "Her name wasn't announced and she was well made up."

"I hardly ever go to Seaport," said Phoebe. "I didn't think I was likely to be recognized there, and I hoped nobody here would ever know I'd been away. I'm sorry I made such a mess of things. If I hadn't been rushed I might have thought better of it."

"It was just ill luck you didn't get away with it," said Madigan.

"But what need was there for you to go at all?" said the Superintendent, at last getting a word in edgeways. "What necessity was there for you to be acting, of all things?"

"Oh, Superintendent, I don't know how to make you understand. It was all for the sake of the Show. When you've lived in the theater, it's the first article of your creed that the Show must go on. Mrs. Claremorris couldn't appear because of a bee-sting on her face. She was so disfigured that no amount of makeup would make it possible for her to look the part of the heroine. She hadn't an understudy, because they'd taken a chance and cut down the numbers on tour. I'd played many of her parts. I was the obvious choice to take her place, and having me within reach really seemed providential. You see, it wasn't just one night's takings that were at stake, there was Mr. Bowman."

"Mr. Who?"

"Oh, you wouldn't have heard of him. He's from Hollywood, looking for talent. If he saw the show he might give somebody a big chance."

Mrs. Teely said, "If there was anything that would have disgusted your uncle more than your going on the stage, it would have been the idea of your becoming a film star."

"I didn't mean me," said Phoebe. "I was thinking of Humphry. You wouldn't have me stand in the way of his career?"

"Mr. Madigan's future does not interest me," said Mrs. Teely.

"It does me," said Humphry. "I'm eternally grateful, Phoebe, darling. Even if nothing comes of it, you did your best."

"I was bad, though," said Phoebe, suddenly turning to Madigan and forgetting everybody else.

"Oh, I wouldn't say that. You walked upstage on me twice in the first act, and you gagged a bit too much."

"I like that! When I had only an hour to get up the part."

"Which used to be one of your best."

"No, Humphry. I never was a good Kate Hardcastle, but tonight I was just wooden. I couldn't bring it to life."

"All this self-deprecation!" said Madigan. "You were under-rehearsed, that was all. I'll take you through it again tomorrow afternoon. Or is it this afternoon?"

"Neither, my dear. You'll have Grania back tomorrow, and I hope you appreciate her."

Michael Canavan's brow had not ceased to be thunderous as he listened to the foregoing conversation. He now enquired, coming in an octave lower with a menacing effect, "Did the Hollywood fellow turn up?"

"Indeed yes," said Madigan. "Charming chap."

"He saw Phoebe act?"

"He saw the whole show from the fourth row of the stalls. He was impressed, definitely impressed. He told me so afterwards, came round to have a chat, but we were interrupted." Madigan turned a suffering smile on the Superintendent. "I don't want to be difficult. I know you have your duty. But broad-minded as they are in the States, it really doesn't make the best impression when a plainclothes dick barges in and walks off with the leading lady after the final curtain."

"And I suppose you hope he'll make you an offer?" said Canavan to Phoebe.

"Nothing of the sort," said Phoebe. "The way I played tonight there's not the slightest fear of such a thing. If he did I wouldn't listen to him."

"So you say now."

"My dear Michael, why should I go fishing for contracts? I've got all the money I want."

"How false that rings," said Madigan. "As if anyone with imagination ever could have enough money!"

It looked as if the police would have to keep the peace between Canavan and Madigan. Phoebe looked distractedly from her angry, tough young man to her waspish debonair one. But Edward Gildea, who had not been paying much attention to this talk of Hollywood and careers, seized the first pause to bring back the conversation to something that did interest him. He asked, "Did you say Mrs. Claremorris had been stung?"

"And how," said Madigan.

"By a bee?"

"Yes, Mr. Gildea," said Phoebe. "By a nasty vicious bee. And nothing will convince me that bees are not dangerous. I look on them as one of the worst perils of country life."

"No, really, you're wrong," said Edward earnestly. "They never sting you unless you interfere with them."

"Oh, don't they? What about poor Mr. Sheed?"

A silence fell at Sheed's name. Phoebe did not yet know what had happened. She looked round in surprise. "What's the matter? Is something wrong?"

The Superintendent told her.

## II

Phoebe sat crying on the garden seat. Michael Canavan had his arm round her. Though she had not been particularly intimate with Henry Sheed, he had been her uncle's friend and their only regular visitor. The news of his death, sprung on her so suddenly, had been a great shock.

But the Inspector still had to ask questions. "Excuse me troubling you, Miss Prendergast," he said, "but it just might be important. What was that you said about Mr. Sheed getting stung?"

"Oh, that was weeks ago," said Phoebe indifferently.

"How did it happen?"

Seeing Phoebe was overwrought, Edward Gildea took it on himself to answer. "Miss Prendergast alleges that the bees set upon Mr. Sheed and stung him one day as he was walking in the garden by himself, when he was nowhere near the hives."

Vera Byrne corroborated this. "It's the truth, Mister. Mr. Sheed, God rest him, never did go anywhere near the hives, he didn't take any interest in them, but he was badly stung all the same, all over his hand."

"You say he was alone at the time?" said the inspector.

"He was, then. 'Twas of a Sunda' morning when he was here for the weekend. The master and Miss Phoebe were at church. Penrose had taken them and gone to Mass himself. I was cooking the dinner. He come in and asked me for ammonia, and I put some on for him, but his hand swelled all the same. It was a funny thing, he thought it was a horsefly bite."

"How d'you know it wasn't?" said Edward Gildea. "Much more likely."

Vera said calmly, "I seen two bee stings sticking in the cuff of his coat."

Inspector Grace looked at Superintendent Menapia.

"It made an unfortunate impression on Miss Prendergast," said Edward Gildea. "She's nervous of bees, and she tells this tale by way of justification. But I can hardly believe it. It wasn't as if Mr. Prendergast's bees were vicious. I've handled them myself without gloves."

"A penny for your thoughts, Inspector," said a flippant voice. Humphry Madigan was tired of standing in the wings.

But the Inspector ignored him. He was adding two and two together, but he was not ready yet to announce the total. And in any case there now occurred another diversion. Once again the beam of headlights drew all eyes to the gate.

The car was the Claremorrises'. They had a passenger. He was a little man, middle-aged, bald on top, but fresh as paint and jaunty as his own bow tie. He was hand in hand with Grania Claremorris, who was looking more herself, with the swelling going down. Lionel Claremorris as usual strolled benevolently behind. They all three looked prepared to make a night of it.

"Well, well, well, look who's here!" said Humphry Madigan, shaking the stranger's free hand. He turned to the rest with outstretched arm, "Gentlemen, meet Mr. Bowman!"

"Please, my dear fellow, no formality," said Mr. Bowman in a faultless

Oxford accent. Instead of looking at Humphry he searched round among the crowd. Humphry had to bid for attention. "Phoebe, darling," he said, "can we give Mr. Bowman a drink?"

"Bowman!" said Canavan. " I told you so."

"Hush, Michael! " said Phoebe. She had dried her eyes and pulled herself together. "What will Mr. Bowman have?"

"Have you got a Coca-cola?" asked Mr. Bowman hopefully. They hadn't and he said it did not matter.

Everybody, especially Madigan, Canavan and the police, waited expectantly to hear what Mr. Bowman was doing there. There was a pause during which Mr. Bowman's eyes continued to travel backwards and forwards, and everybody else's eyes were fixed on him. He said, in response to popular demand, "It's a funny business looking for talent. I work hard. I go to all the right places. I see everybody I'm asked to see. People think they've got what I want but I know they haven't. Can't always explain why not. I'm waiting for something." He tapped his chest. "A sensation here. It's physical. I always get it when I find what I'm looking for. Often I'm tempted to cut my corners, engage somebody the right height, weight and bust measurement, and take a holiday. Never pays. You waste more money trying to make do with the wrong type than looking for the right one. You have to have patience. Sometimes I'm in despair, but I don't give up. When they tell me I've been everywhere and seen everyone, I say, O.K., let's get off the beaten track. And sooner or later, just when I least expect it, sweet Jemima, there they are! And when that happens I don't let go. I don't listen to argument. I just keep following them around till I've signed them up."

Madigan was drinking whiskey which Mr. Bowman had refused. He raised his glass, "Success to your efforts!"

"Thanks," said Bowman. "Yes, it's happened. Found and lost in an evening, but I'm still hot on the track."

"And it's not who you think, Humphry," said Grania, her smile well spiced with malice.

People were now looking at Phoebe, and it was difficult for her not to look self-conscious. Her hand was on Canavan's arm, but it seemed to give him no consolation. For once he and Madigan were in sympathy; neither of them could bear the suspense. Canavan said, "If it's Miss Prendergast you've come for, sign her up for the love of Pete and let's all get off home to bed."

"Michael!" said Phoebe. "I've told you I've no intention of accepting any offer from any film company. I'm just not interested."

"Of course not," said Mr. Bowman suavely. "You have other plans, no doubt. In any case, no such offer has been made. Don't be depressed, my dear. I mean no reflection on either your personality or your performance. You know how these things are. Another time I might be only too glad to try you out. You've got looks, poise, and acting talent. Unfortunately, those don't happen to be the essential qualities for what I want at the moment."

"Now are you satisfied?" said Phoebe to Michael Canavan, and she would not have been human if she had not looked just a little vexed.

Superintendent Menapia had been in close conversation with Inspector Grace. They still had work to do. He turned to Phoebe.

"We'll be going now, Miss Prendergast. There's nothing to keep us here now, and I don't think you need feel alarmed. I'll be leaving Sergeant Rice with you overnight, and you may leave all arrangements in our hands about Mr. Sheed. I'll have someone here early in the morning."

Phoebe thanked him. Edward Gildea opened negotiations for a lift home (it seemed callous to take Sheed's car, and there was no Penrose to get out the saloon). As the group of policemen began to move away, Mr. Bowman gave a sudden yelp.

His roving eyes were focused at last. His left hand clutched his breast where he felt the pang. His right am came up to shoulder level. His right forefinger pointed straight at Detective Officer Lemon.

"There!" he said. "That's what I want. Just that combination of youthful good looks and unsophistication with an impression of sterling worth. Soon as I saw that man backstage at the theater I knew I had another 'Mr. Deeds.' I lost track of him behind the scene, but with this lady's assistance," he bowed to Grania, "I've succeeded in running him to earth. Perseverance rewarded! My dear sir, where can we talk?"

"Sorry, I'm on duty now," said D/O Lemon, and dived into the back of the nearest police car. Men were now crowding round the gate, and in the confusion of cars backing and turning Mr. Bowman was once again cheated of his prey. A procession set off down the lane, in which the Claremorrises' car was the last but one. Last of all came the baby Austin with Mrs. Teely driving. Hector Prendergast had been found fast asleep behind the big tree. He had had a hard afternoon and several whiskeys. Sergeant Rice and Michael Canavan carried him to the car.

When Vera had cleared away the glasses and Phoebe had finished saying good-night to Michael Canavan, there was nobody left in the garden but Sergeant Rice.

### III

The moon had gone down; the stars were keeping things up a bit longer; in the northern sky the Great Bear, like a great cat, arched its neck and stretched out one hind leg towards the Pole. Sergeant Rice was thinking of past and future, of various escapes he had had from matrimony, and of the comfort it would be to settle down, and also of how little even a sergeant's pay was to support a wife and children. Suddenly, in the midst of his meditations, he heard a slight click at the yard gate.

A man had slipped cautiously through the gate and was slinking across the yard to the garage. Rice went after him. At his steps the man turned and backed into the darkest corner. Rice told him to come out, speaking in his usual tone of a good-humored but hectoring Nanny. Before he could repeat the command the man went for him with his fists.

Rice could handle this. He was a boxer. He had, not long before, won the Heavyweight Belt presented to the District by the Chief Superintendent. The other man would not have been his equal in a fair fight, but of course he did not fight fair, and for the first ten minutes Rice had enough to do to protect himself, let alone attack. Science told in the end. Rice's opponent wore himself out, and left himself open at last to a hefty punch. He slumped down at Rice's feet like a sack of roots, and Rice, looking down at him, would hardly have recognized him, though by that time he knew who it was. Penrose had come home.

He was a miserable object, covered from head to foot with that particular clinging yellow mud, stained with iron oxide, that came from nowhere but the mine, and now dripping blood from his nose, and with a bruise darkening round one eye as well as numerous minor cuts and injuries.

His room was over the garage. When he had come round enough to struggle up the ladder to it Rice humanely helped him to bed, but took charge of the key. He said: "You're under arrest."

Penrose groaned out an oath. "I never killed him."

"Sure you half killed me," said Rice. "Isn't that enough for one evening? I'm arresting you for assaulting the police. You can tell the rest of it to the Superintendent. He'll be here in the morning."

## CHAPTER TWENTY-THREE

TO INSPECTOR GRACE in the end it was simple arithmetic. His sums till now had been coming out wrong; there was always some factor missing. Now he had everything: possession of arsenic, association with bees, plus a motive. It added up to the murderer of Jason Prendergast.

Detectives visited the house in Dublin which was Henry Sheed's headquarters. It could hardly be called his home; he had no family, cooked for himself and got the housework done by two sour sisters who used the top floor as a flat. They felt more indignant than grieved at the news of his death, which they felt would upset their routine. It was one of those bleak brown brick houses with granite steps between city and suburbs.

It contained boxes of geological specimens with labels on, a similar collection to that at Coppermine House except that there was no arsenical pyrites. They found that on the ash heap. The slow combustion stove had not altered its constituents.

This might not have been enough to make a case for the Criminal Court, but it was enough for Inspector Grace and Superintendent Menapia and Chief Superintendent Tunney, and also enough for the coroner and jury at the double inquest which was held in Drumclash. For the inquest on Henry Sheed was combined with the adjourned inquest on Jason Prendergast, and this was the last appearance of their names in partnership.

But this is going too fast. On the morning after the events of the last chapter, Edward Gildea drove over with Superintendent Menapia to Coppermine House. The Superintendent had been up till four, directing operations for the recovery of Sheed's body. A rescue party had reached it, had confirmed that he was quite dead, having broken his neck, and the task of getting out the corpse had been postponed till morning.

It was not surprising if the Superintendent looked more than his age in the callous sunlight of 10 a.m. Sergeant Rice, who should have gone off duty but had stayed to report, presented another harrowing picture. As they were taking him in, Hector Prendergast arrived bearing on him the marks of the morning after. Mrs. Teely, who accompanied him, was in better physical shape but in deeper mourning than ever, with a black-edged handkerchief very much in evidence. It was quite a comfort when the Chief Superintendent shortly after joined them to find the Colonel his usual genial self.

Phoebe herself looked fresh and charming. She had slept late and only began getting up when the first visitors arrived.

Mrs. Teely had come "to enquire," which was the exact word, for she was obviously bursting with curiosity. Hector Prendergast had come to apologize for trespassing and to discuss his findings in the mine. They had to wait while first the prisoner, Penrose, was haled forth, to the horror of the ladies and the grim satisfaction of Sergeant Rice. Perhaps it was a merciful dispensation of Providence towards Penrose that Vera Byrne, fed up with policemen and busy with household duties, never saw the figure he cut at this low ebb of his fortunes.

"What have you to say for yourself?" asked the Chief Superintendent.

"I never done it," said Penrose. "You can't make me swing for him. You can't make me swing for either of them."

"You aren't accused of murder," said Colonel Tunney. "You're accused of assaulting Sergeant Rice."

Penrose stared at the Chief Superintendent out of his good eye, and slowly his face lost its look of desperation. A revelation seemed to come to him. He said slowly, "It was Mr. Sheed killed the master. That's why he tried to pin it on to me."

"But why?" The question broke from Phoebe Prendergast. She looked bewildered and incredulous.

"I know why," said Hector Prendergast. "The mining rights. They passed to him on his partner's death, and he knew what they were worth. That's what I couldn't manage to figure out. I knew what my father told me about that mine. He said the stuff was there, all it needed to make it an economic proposition was up-to-date machinery and the current price. But there was Mr. Sheed on the spot, a mining engineer, and he just didn't seem to take any interest. Now I understand, he was holding out on his old friend and partner."

"He was not," said Penrose. "Mr. Prendergast knew as much as Mr. Sheed. I used to hear them talking in the car."

Hector Prendergast rounded on him. "My uncle knew? And you knew too? Say, what are you? A human clam? You never said a word to me."

"You never asked me," said Penrose. "All you wanted was for me to show you the way in and give a hand with the digging."

"But if they both knew—?"

"Mr. Sheed was always at the one talk with the master," said Penrose, "when would they start working again? But Mr. Prendergast was against doing anything. Once he came to live here he didn't want the mining going on all round, spoiling the country."

"Oh, yes," said Phoebe. "I remember my uncle saying once that after he died the mining would start again. He said I probably wouldn't want to live here afterwards. He just wanted to keep the place as it was for the rest of his life."

"Say, did everyone know then?" said Hector Prendergast. He looked deflated.

"I didn't," said Edward Gildea. "And I've entered that mine as derelict in the application for probate."

"If we'd had this information sooner—" began the Chief Superintendent.

"You never asked me," said Penrose again. He had recovered all his surly assurance.

Phoebe said, more apologetically, "I'm afraid it never occurred to me it could be important. You see, I never dreamed of suspecting Mr. Sheed."

"I had an instinct about him," said Mrs. Teely. "I didn't trust him. I don't wish to claim credit for superior insight, but at least I did prevent Phoebe's being left alone in the house with him."

"Would you have been able to make a case against him?" Edward Gildea asked the Superintendent.

"We might when we got on to the motive," said Menapia. "We'd have searched his house then, as Inspector Grace is doing now. If he finds arsenic there it ties everything up. Grace was going to have a mineralogist go down under pretense of searching in the mine."

"If you'd let me in on it," said Hector Prendergast, "I could have saved you the trouble."

"Unfortunately you wouldn't count as an unprejudiced witness, being one of the family. But you did speed up developments," said Menapia kindly. "It was you wanting to go down the mine that brought Mr. Sheed here in such a hurry yesterday. We found Mr. Gildea's wire in his pocket."

"What did he hope to gain by that?" asked the Chief Superintendent.

"He probably hadn't thought things out," said Menapia, "but according to Mr. Grace, he did his best to head the search party away from the lodes that contained valuable ore. Then when he was up against Mr. Prendergast, he did his best to create a diversion. He was improvising to the last. He was ready to chase Penrose to his death in the hope of inducing the police to accept him as the murderer. If he'd caught him up out of sight of the rest of us, he might have tried to throw him down a shaft, passing it off as suicide. Oh, he had a card or two to play when Fate caught up with him."

"Who owns the mining rights now?" asked the practical Canadian.

"I was wondering about that," said Edward Gildea. He turned to Phoebe. "I fancy your cousin may have some claim. They were vested not in Jason Prendergast individually but as survivor of that branch of the family."

"I won't dispute it," said Phoebe. "I'm more interested in forests."

"Maybe Mr. Canavan can supply us with pitprops," said Hector.

Edward brooded over the transformation of his beloved countryside. As long as a thousand years ago there had been the oak woods, bird haunted and changing with the seasons from green to gold. The woods had brought the metal workers. They had imported ores to smelt them where there was charcoal in abundance. Soon they found their materials nearer at hand, training began, and through the centuries the hills were turned inside out and slag and debris scattered over the fields. The oak woods dwindled, and the mountains inland took on the clean bare outlines that strangely satisfied the eye. Now they were being forested again, but instead of the changing green and brown and gold they all were one uniform smoky green all the year round and their edges saw-toothed with the pointed tops of fir trees. There would be fewer beasts and birds in these forests, but ceaseless human activity; foresters' bicycles were stacked in the clearings, the whir of circular saws, logs shooting down tracks on the hillsides, and lorries arriving to take away the loads. Meanwhile underground there was still more going on. The tunneling would go deeper and deeper as new demands sprang up for new ores to serve or destroy the human race.

The hills that stand as a symbol in hymns and psalms of the sure foundation of all things and the changeless order of creation appear in a different light as a challenge to ingenuity and commercial enterprise. "I hate waste," Henry Sheed had said, for he too had his vision. He had spoken with the earnestness of a fanatic. Edward suddenly understood, as clearly as if Sheed's spirit had communicated with him, that he had longed not so much for the profit he would make as for a part to play in the new conditions to be brought into being. But Jason Prendergast had not sympathized with his partner's religion and had settled down in Sheed's way like an Indian fakir meditating on a railway line.

In a way Jason, who had turned a deaf ear to all the representations of local inhabitants on the destruction of the amenities of the Vale, had died a martyr to the cause of their preservation. The Coroner said so at the inquest, and a subscription was got up to erect a monument, but it only raised enough for a tablet in the church.

The same *Irish Times* that carried an account of the inquest also published, in the "Social and Personal" column, the announcement of Phoebe Prendergast's engagement to Michael Canavan.

## CHAPTER TWENTY-FOUR

AT THE SMALL RECEPTION which was held after the wedding at Coppermine House, Mollie Gildea observed Mrs. Teely draw Vera Byrne aside. After a short conversation she edged away, and it struck Mollie her expression was somewhat discomfited. Mollie moved over to lend a sympathetic ear.

"A small plan of mine has come to nothing," said Mrs. Teely with a sigh. "It is only what one must expect to happen constantly throughout life. I'm sure I wish Vera every happiness in her marriage. They say it's where a woman ought rightly to find fulfillment, though I believe many are happier single, and it does seem a waste of a good cook."

"You don't mean to say she's marrying Penrose after all," said Mollie, with a nervous glance to make sure the chauffeur was not within earshot, for in spite of his not being a murderer she was still rather afraid of him and wondered how Vera could.

" Oh no, not Penrose," said Mrs. Teely. "Somebody quite different. Sergeant Rice. It's quite a romance."

Mollie thereupon said illogically, "Oh, poor Penrose!"

"Don't waste your pity, Mrs. Gildea," struck in Grania Claremorris. "Haven't you heard the news? Penrose is off to Hollywood. When Mr. Bowman couldn't get that young detective he consoled himself by signing up Penrose for gangster parts."

"What, do you mean to say Mr. Lemon wouldn't go?"

"Ah, he never gave it a thought," said Superintendent Menapia, who was also a guest, with his small, shy, smiling wife. He had brushed his uniform for the occasion. "The day after Mr. Bowman spoke to him, Mick Lemon had to go up to Dublin to help look for the evidence against Sheed, and when they got him back at the Branch he was put on another case. They kept him on the move for the next few weeks, and Mick says that what with international crooks coming over for the Horse Show, and the place full of English visitors, he thinks his country needs him."

Edward Gildea came in from the garden, oddly attired for a wedding guest in shirt and trousers and a bee veil. He had been examining the two remaining beehives, which Phoebe had given him as a parting present.

"Those are two fine, strong stocks with ample stores," he announced to his hostess. "Are you sure you want to part with them? Would you not think of taking up beekeeping, now you know bees are harmless?'"

"I don't know anything of the kind," said Phoebe.

"Why, it's the moral of the whole story," said Edward,.

"What does the Superintendent say to that?" asked Michael Canavan.

"It may not be true of bees," said the Superintendent, "but it is of beekeepers. I may tell you now, there was a time when some of us were inclined to suspect Mr. Gildea. The grounds of suspicion were that he had been the last person to tamper with the hive, and that it was he who started the theory of the honey being naturally poisoned. But I knew there was nothing in it, and so I told them. In my experience, anyone who takes up a hobby like that and gets so keen on it is just naturally innocent."

THE END

# Rue Morgue Press Titles as of April 2001

**Common or Garden Crime** by Sheila Pim. Lucy Bex preferred Jane Austen or Anthony Trollope to the detective stories her brother Linnaeus gulped down but when a neighbor is murdered with monkshood harvested from Lucy's own garden, she's the one who turns detective and spots the crucial clue that prevents the wrong person from going to the gallows. Set in 1943 in the small town of Clonmeen on the outskirts of Dublin, this delightful tale was written by an author who was called "the Irish Angel Thirkell." Published in Britain in 1945, this is the first appearance of this book in the United States. The war in Europe seems very distant in neutral Ireland, though it draws a little nearer when Lucy's nephew, an officer in the British army, comes home on leave. However, most of the residents are more interested in how their gardens grow than what's happening on the Eastern Front or in Africa. It's a death a little closer to home that finally grabs their interest. The Irish Guard is called in to investigate but this time it may take someone with a green thumb to catch the murderer. Pim's detective stories were greeted with great critical acclaim from contemporary reviewers: "Excellent characterization, considerable humour. . .do some more, Miss Pim."—*Sphere.* "Humour and shrewd observation of small town Irish life."—*Times Literary Supplement.* "Wit and gaiety, ease and charm. . .the kind of story I long to thrust into people's hands."—*Illustrated London News.* "Vivacious as a wall lizard."—*Observer.* "A truthful, humorous, and affectionate picture of life in an Irish country town."—*Daily Herald.*     **0-915230-36-4     $14.00**

**Black Paw** by Constance & Gwentyh Little. Thanks to some overly indulgent parents, Callie Drake was "brought up soft" and doesn't know the first thing about doing housework, which makes it a bit of a stretch for her to pretend to be a maid in the Barton household. She's there dressed in the skimpiest maid's outfit this side of Paris to snatch some compromising love letters written by her friend Selma, who's afraid that her brute of an estranged husband just might use these adulterous missives to lower her alimony. Altruism isn't a big part of Callie's makeup and she agrees to the scheme only after Selma offers to hand over the keys to her hot little roadster in exchange for this bit of petty larceny. But when murder erupts in the Barton mansion, the police think it's a little odd that the bodies started falling only hours after Callie's arrival. Even worse, Selma's soon-to-be-ex is on to Callie and seems to take perverse enjoyment in forcing this spoiled debutante to continue her domestic chores. In between long hot baths and countless cigarette breaks, Callie stumbles across mysterious pawprints in a house without animals and comes upon rocking chairs that move even when there's no one in the room. It's enough to make this golddigger start digging for clues in this 1941 charmer by the queens of the wacky cozy.     **0-915230-37-2     $14.00**

**Black Corridors** by Constance & Gwenyth Little. Some people go to the beach for their vacations, others go to the mountains. Jessie Warren's Aunt Isabel preferred checking herself into the hospital where she thoroughly enjoyed a spot of bad health although the doctors were at a loss to spot any cause. As usual, Jessie and her sister tossed to see who would accompany Aunt Isabel to the hospital—and, as usual, Jessie lost. Jessie's mother pointed out that pampering her rich aunt might do her some good in the future, even if it means that Jessie has to miss a date or two with some promising beaux. Aunt Isabel insists on staying in her favorite room, which means the current patient has to be dispossessed. And when that man's black wallet turns up missing, just about everyone joins in the hunt. That's about the time someone decided to start killing blondes. For the first time in her life Jessie's glad to have her bright red hair, even if a certain doctor—who doesn't have the money or the looks of her other beaux—enjoys making fun of those flaming locks. But after Jessie stumbles across a couple of bodies and starts snooping around, the murderer figures the time has come to switch from blondes to redheads. First published in 1940, *Black Corridors* is Constance & Gwenyth Little at their wackiest best.     **0-915230-33-X     $14.00**

**The Black Stocking** by Constance & Gwenyth Little. Irene Hastings, who can't decide which of her two fiancés she should marry, is looking forward to a nice vacation, and everything would have been just fine had not her mousy friend Ann asked to be dropped off at an insane asylum so she could visit her sister. When the sister escapes, just about everyone, including a handsome young doctor, mistakes Irene for the runaway loony, and she is put up at an isolated private hospital under house arrest, pending final identification. Only there's not a bed to be had in the hospital. One of the staff is already sleeping in a tent on the grounds, so it's decided that Irene is to share a bedroom with young Dr. Ross Munster, much to the consternation of both parties. On the other hand, Irene's much-married mother Elise, an Auntie Mame type who rushes to her rescue, figures the young doctor has son-in-law written all over him. She also figures there's plenty of room in that bedroom for herself as well. In the meantime, Irene runs into a headless nurse, a corpse that won't stay put, an empty coffin, a missing will, and a mysterious black stocking. As Elise would say, "Mong Dew!" First published in 1946.    **0-915230-30-5    $14.00**

**The Black-Headed Pins** by Constance & Gwenyth Little. "...a zany, fun-loving puzzler spun by the sisters Little—it's celluloid screwball comedy printed on paper. The charm of this book lies in the lively banter between characters and the breakneck pace of the story."—Diane Plumley, *Dastardly Deeds.* "For a strong example of their work, try (this) very funny and inventive 1938 novel of a dysfunctional family Christmas." Jon L. Breen, *Ellery Queen's Mystery Magazine.*    **0-915230-25-9    $14.00**

**The Black Gloves** by Constance & Gwenyth Little. "I'm relishing every madcap moment."—*Murder Most Cozy.* Welcome to the Vickers estate near East Orange, New Jersey, where the middle class is destroying the neighborhood, erecting their horrid little cottages, playing on the Vickers tennis court, and generally disrupting the comfortable life of Hammond Vickers no end. Why does there also have to be a corpse in the cellar? First published in 1939.    **0-915230-20-8    $14.00**

**The Black Honeymoon** by Constance & Gwenyth Little. Can you murder someone with feathers? If you don't believe feathers are lethal, then you probably haven't read a Little mystery. No, Uncle Richard wasn't tickled to death—though we can't make the same guarantee for readers—but the hyper-allergic rich man did manage to sneeze himself into the hereafter. First published in 1944.    **0-915230-21-6    $14.00**

**Great Black Kanba** by Constance & Gwenyth Little. "If you love train mysteries as much as I do, hop on the Trans-Australia Railway in *Great Black Kanba*, a fast and funny 1944 novel by the talented (Littles)."—Jon L. Breen, *Ellery Queen's Mystery Magazine.* "I have decided to add *Kanba* to my favorite mysteries of all time list!...a zany ride I'll definitely take again and again."—Diane Plumley in the Murder Ink newsletter. When a young American woman wakes up on an Australian train with a bump on her head and no memory, she suddenly finds out that she's engaged to two different men and the chief suspect in a murder case. It all adds up to some delightful mischief—call it Cornell Woolrich on laughing gas.    **0-915230-22-4    $14.00**

**The Grey Mist Murders** by Constance & Gwenyth Little. Who—or what—is the mysterious figure that emerges from the grey mist to strike down several passengers on the final leg of a round-the-world sea voyage? Is it the same shadowy entity that persists in leaving three matches outside Lady Marsh's cabin every morning? And why does one flimsy negligee seem to pop up at every turn? When Carla Bray first heard things go bump in the night, she hardly expected to find a corpse in the adjoining cabin. Nor did she expect to find herself the chief suspect in the murders. This 1938 effort was the Littles' first book.    **0-915230-26-7    $14.00**

**Brief Candles** by Manning Coles. From Topper to Aunt Dimity, mystery readers have embraced the cozy ghost story. Four of the best were written by Manning Coles, the creator of the witty Tommy Hambledon spy novels. First published in 1954, *Brief Candles* is likely to produce more laughs than chills as a young couple vacationing in France run into two gentlemen with decidedly old-world manners. What they don't know is that James and Charles Latimer are ancestors of theirs who shuffled off this mortal coil some 80 years earlier when, emboldened by strong drink and with only a pet monkey and an aged waiter as allies, the two made a valiant, foolish and quite fatal attempt to halt a German advance during the Franco-Prussian War of 1870. Now these two ectoplasmic gentlemen and their spectral pet monkey Ulysses have been summoned from their unmarked graves because their visiting relatives are in serious trouble. But before they can solve the younger Latimers' problems, the three benevolent spirits light brief candles of insanity for a tipsy policeman, a recalcitrant banker, a convocation of English ghostbusters, and a card-playing rogue who's wanted for murder. "As felicitously foolish as a collaboration of (P.G.) Wodehouse and Thorne Smith."—Anthony Boucher. "For those who like something out of the ordinary. Lighthearted, very funny."—*The Sunday Times*. "A gay, most readable story."—*The Daily Telegraph*         **0-915230-24-0     $14.00**

**Happy Returns** by Manning Coles. The ghostly Latimers and their pet spectral monkey Ulysses return from the grave when Uncle Quentin finds himself in need of their help—it seems the old boy is being pursued by an old flame who won't take no for an answer in her quest to get him to the altar. Along the way, our courteous and honest spooks thwart a couple of bank robbers, unleash a bevy of circus animals on an unsuspecting French town, help out the odd person or two and even "solve" a murder—with the help of the victim. The laughs start practically from the first page and don't stop until Ulysses slides down the bannister, glass of wine in hand, to drink a toast to returning old friends.
**0-915230-31-3     $14.00**

**Come and Go** by Manning Coles. The third and final book featuring the ghostly Latimers find our heroes saving an ancestor from marriage and murder in a plot straight out of P.G. Wodehouse.                              **0-915230-34-8     $14.00**

**The Far Traveller** by Manning Coles. The Herr Graf was a familiar sight to the residents of the Rhineland village of Grauhugel. After all, he'd been walking the halls of the local castle at night and occasionally nodding to the servants ever since he drowned some 86 years ago. No one was the least bit alarmed by the Graf's spectral walks. Indeed, the castle's major domo found it all quite comforting, as the young Graf had been quite popular while he was alive. When the actor hired to play the dead Graf in a movie is felled by an accident, the film's director is overjoyed to come across a talented replacement who seems to have been born to play the part, little realizing that the Graf and his faithful servant—who perished in the same accident—had only recently decided to materialize in public. The Graf isn't stagestruck. He's back among the living to correct an old wrong. Along the way, he adds a bit of realism to a cinematic duel, befuddles a black marketeer, breaks out of jail, and exposes a charlatan spiritualist. His amorous servant Franz is in the grip of an awkward dilemma himself. What if he's pursuing the granddaughters of village maidens he dallied with eight decades ago?         **0-915230-35-6     $14.00**

**The Chinese Chop** by Juanita Sheridan. The postwar housing crunch finds Janice Cameron, newly arrived in New York City from Hawaii, without a place to live until she answers an ad for a roommate. It turns out the advertiser is an acquaintance from Hawaii, Lily Wu, whom critic Anthony Boucher (for whom Bouchercon, the World Mystery Convention, is named) described as "the exquisitely blended product of Eastern and Western cultures" and the only female sleuth that he "was devotedly in love with," citing "that odd mixture of respect for her professional skills and delight in her personal charms." First published in 1949, this ground-breaking book was the first of four to feature Lily and be told by her Watson, Janice, a first-time novelist. No sooner do Lily and Janice move into a rooming house in Washington Square than a corpse is found in the basement. In Lily Wu, Sheridan created one of the most believable—and memorable—female sleuths of her day.                              **0-915230-32-1     $14.00**

**Death on Milestone Buttress** by Glyn Carr. Abercrombie ("Filthy") Lewker was looking forward to a fortnight of climbing in Wales after a grueling season touring England with his Shakespearean company. Young Hilary Bourne thought the holiday would be a pleasant change from her dreary job at the bank, as well as a chance to renew her acquaintance with a certain young scientist. Neither one expected this bucolic outing to turn deadly but when one of their party is killed during what should have been an easy climb on the Milestone Buttress, Filthy and Hilary turn detective. Nearly every member of the climbing party had reason to hate the victim but each one also had an alibi for the time of the murder. Filthy and Hilary retrace the route of the fatal climb before returning to their lodgings where, in the grand tradition of Nero Wolfe, Filthy confronts the suspects and points his finger at the only person who could have committed the crime. Filled with climbing details sure to appeal to both expert climbers and armchair mountaineers alike, *Death on Milestone Buttress* was published in England in 1951, the first of fifteen detective novels in which Lewker outwitted murderers on peaks scattered around the globe, from Wales to Switzerland to the Himalayas. **0-915230-29-1 $14.00**

**Murder is a Collector's Item** by Elizabeth Dean. "(It) froths over with the same effervescent humor as the best Hepburn-Grant films."—Sujata Massey. "Completely enjoyable."—*New York Times.* "Fast and funny."—*The New Yorker.* Twenty-six-year-old Emma Marsh isn't much at spelling or geography and perhaps she butchers the odd literary quotation or two, but she's a keen judge of character and more than able to hold her own when it comes to selling antiques or solving murders. Originally published in 1939, *Murder is a Collector's Item* was the first of three books featuring Emma. Smoothly written and sparkling with dry, sophisticated humor, this milestone combines an intriguing puzzle with an entertaining portrait of a self-possessed young woman on her own at the end of the Great Depression. **0-915230-19-4 $14.00**

**Murder is a Serious Business** by Elizabeth Dean. It's 1940 and the Thirsty Thirties are over but you couldn't tell it by the gang at J. Graham Antiques, where clerk Emma Marsh, her would-be criminologist boyfriend Hank, and boss Jeff Graham trade barbs in between shots of scotch when they aren't bothered by the rare customer. Trouble starts when Emma and crew head for a weekend at Amos Currier's country estate to inventory the man's antiques collection. It isn't long before the bodies start falling and once again Emma is forced to turn sleuth in order to prove that her boss isn't a killer. "Judging from (this book) it's too bad she didn't write a few more."—Mary Ann Steel, *I Love a Mystery.* **0-915230-28-3 $14.95**

**Murder, Chop Chop** by James Norman. "The book has the butter-wouldn't-melt-in-his-mouth cool of Rick in *Casablanca.*"—*The Rocky Mountain News.* "Amuses the reader no end."—*Mystery News.* "This long out-of-print masterpiece is intricately plotted, full of eccentric characters and very humorous indeed. Highly recommended."—*Mysteries by Mail.* Meet Gimiendo Hernandez Quinto, a gigantic Mexican who once rode with Pancho Villa and who now trains *guerrilleros* for the Nationalist Chinese government when he isn't solving murders. At his side is a beautiful Eurasian known as Mountain of Virtue, a woman as dangerous to men as she is irresistible. Together they look into the murder of Abe Harrow, an ambulance driver who appears to have died at three different times. There's also a cipher or two to crack, a train with a mind of its own, and Chiang Kai-shek's false teeth, which have gone mysteriously missing. First published in 1942. **0-915230-16-X $13.00**

**Death at The Dog** by Joanna Cannan. "Worthy of being discussed in the same breath with an Agatha Christie or Josephine Tey...anyone who enjoys Golden Age mysteries will surely enjoy this one."—Sally Fellows, *Mystery News.* "Skilled writing and brilliant characterization."—*Times of London.* "An excellent English rural tale."—Jacques Barzun & Wendell Hertig Taylor in *A Catalogue of Crime.* Set in late 1939 during the first anxious months of World War II, *Death at The Dog*, first published in 1941, is a wonderful example of the classic English detective novel that flourished between the two World Wars. Set in a picturesque village filled with thatched-roof cottages, eccentric villagers and genial pubs, it's as well-plotted as a Christie, with clues abundantly and fairly planted, and as deftly written as the best of Sayers or Marsh, filled with quotable lines and perceptive observations on the human condition. **0-915230-23-2 14.00**

**They Rang Up the Police** by Joanna Cannan. "Just delightful."—*Sleuth of Baker Street*

Pick-of-the-Month. "A brilliantly plotted mystery...splendid character study...don't miss this one, folks. It's a keeper."—Sally Fellows, *Mystery News*. When Delia Cathcart and Major Willoughby disappear from their quiet English village one morning in July 1937, it looks like a simple case of a frustrated spinster running off for a bit of fun with a straying husband. But as the hours turn into days, Inspector Guy Northeast begins to suspect that she may have been the victim of foul play. Never published in the United States, *They Rang Up the Police* appeared in England in 1939.     **0-1915230-27-5 $14.00**

**Cook Up a Crime** by Charlotte Murray Russell. "Perhaps the mother of today's 'cozy' mystery . . . amateur sleuth Jane has a personality guaranteed to entertain the most demanding reader."—Andy Plonka, *The Mystery Reader*. "Some wonderful old time recipes...highly recommended."—*Mysteries by Mail*. Meet Jane Amanda Edwards, a self-styled "full-fashioned" spinster who complains she hasn't looked at herself in a full-length mirror since Helen Hokinson started drawing for *The New Yorker*. But you can always count on Jane to look into other people's affairs, especially when there's a juicy murder case to investigate. In this 1951 title Jane goes searching for recipes (included between chapters) for a cookbook project and finds a body instead. And once again her lily-of-the-field brother Arthur goes looking for love, finds strong drink, and is eventually discovered clutching the murder weapon.     **0-915230-18-6   $13.00**

**The Man from Tibet** by Clyde B. Clason. Locked inside the Tibetan Room of his Chicago apartment, the rich antiquarian was overheard repeating a forbidden occult chant under the watchful eyes of Buddhist gods. When the doors were opened it appeared that he had succumbed to a heart attack. But the elderly Roman historian and sometime amateur sleuth Theocritus Lucius Westborough is convinced that Adam Merriweather's death was anything but natural and that the weapon was an eighth century Tibetan manuscript. If it's murder, who could have done it, and how? Suspects abound. There's Tsongpun Bonbo, the gentle Tibetan lama from whom the manuscript was originally stolen; Chang, Merriweather's scholarly Tibetan secretary who had fled a Himalayan monastery; Merriweather's son Vincent, who disliked his father and stood to inherit a fortune; Dr. Jed Merriweather, the dead man's brother, who came to Chicago to beg for funds to continue his archaeological digs in Asia; Dr. Walters, the dead man's physician, who guarded a secret; and Janice Shelton, his young ward, who found herself being pushed by Merriweather into marrying his son. How the murder was accomplished has earned praise from such impossible crime connoisseurs as Robert C.S. Adey, who cited Clason's "highly original and practical locked-room murder method."     **0-915230-17-8   $14.00**

**The Mirror** by Marlys Millhiser. "Completely enjoyable."—*Library Journal*. "A great deal of fun."—*Publishers Weekly*. How could you not be intrigued by a novel in which "you find the main character marrying her own grandfather and giving birth to her own mother?" Such is the situation in this classic novel, originally published in 1978, of two women who end up living each other's lives. Twenty-year-old Shay Garrett is not aware that she's pregnant and is having second thoughts about marrying Marek Weir when she's suddenly transported back 78 years in time into the body of Brandy McCabe, her own grandmother, who is unwillingly about to be married off to miner Corbin Strock. Shay's in shock but she still recognizes that the picture of her grandfather that hangs in the family home doesn't resemble her husband-to-be. But marry Corbin she does and off she goes to the high mining town of Nederland, where this thoroughly modern young woman has to learn to cope with such things as wood cooking stoves and—to her—old-fashioned attitudes about sex. In the meantime, Brandy McCabe is finding it even harder to cope with life in the Boulder, Colorado, of 1978.     **0-915230-15-1     $14.95**

## About The Rue Morgue Press

The Rue Morgue Press vintage mystery line is designed to bring back into print those books that were favorites of readers between the turn of the century and the 1960s. The editors welcome suggestions for reprints. To receive our catalog or make suggestions, write The Rue Morgue Press, P.O. Box 4119, Boulder, Colorado 80306. (1-800-699-6214).